Wolf's Brother

Megan Lindholm was born in California in 1952 and majored in Communications at Denver University, Colorado. She has been shortlisted for both the Hugo and Nebula Awards and wrote a number of successful fantasy novels, including *Cloven Hooves*, THE WINDSINGER TRILOGY and *Wizard of the Pigeons* before starting to write as Robin Hobb. *Assassin's Apprentice* was Robin Hobb's first novel, and was followed by the equally successful *Royal Assassin* and *Assassin's Quest*. Which together comprise THE FARSEER TRILOGY. Robin Hobb's second trilogy, THE LIVESHIP TRADERS (*Ship of Magic*, *The Mad Ship*, and *Ship of Destiny*) is set in the same world. She lives in Tacoma, Washington.

By Megan Lindholm

The Reindeer People
Wolf's Brother

THE KI AND VANDIEN QUARTET
Harpy's flight
The Windsingers
The Limbreth Gate
Luck of the Wheels

Wizard of the Pigeons
Cloven Hooves
Alien Earth

Writing as Robin Hobb

THE FARSEER TRILOGY
Assassin's Appprentice
Royal Assassin
Assassin's Quest

THE LIVESHIP TRADERS
Ship of Magic
The Mad Ship
Ship of Destiny

Voyager

MEGAN LINDHOLM

Wolf's Brother

HarperCollins*Publishers*

Voyager
An Imprint of HarperCollins*Publishers*
77–85 Fulham Palace Road,
Hammersmith, London W6 8JB

This paperback edition 2001
1 3 5 7 9 8 6 4 2

First published in Great Britain by
Unwin Paperbacks, an imprint of Unwin Hyman Ltd 1989

Copyright © Megan Lindholm Ogden 1988

The Author asserts the moral right
to be identified as the author of this work

ISBN 0 00 711434 6

Typeset in Goudy by Palimpsest Book Production Limited
Polmont, Stirlingshire

Printed and bound in Great Britain by
Clays Ltd, St Ives plc

☽ chapter
one

"THE THINGS I must do are not for the uninitiated to witness."

"But this is my hut!" Heckram protested in amazement. The assumptions of this scrawny old stranger amazed him.

"Out!" Carp repeated, and the big man went reluctantly, wondering why he obeyed at all. Carp remained standing until the door-hide had fallen into place behind him. But the instant he knew he was alone, he sank down to his haunches beside the hearth. Carefully he lowered himself the rest of the way to the earth, feeling the weariness that ate at his old bones, chewed at his strength like Beaver gnaws down a tree. But he would not fall yet. Not yet. He had a people to win.

The old shaman closed his eyes for a moment, tracked his mind back over the long trail he had followed since Tillu had run away with his apprentice. Tillu had not wanted her son to be a shaman, had not wanted to become the shaman's woman herself. How little she knew of the way the world was structured. The magic was strong in Kerlew, ran through the boy more redly than the blood in his body, was just as intrinsic to his life. She could not take the boy away from the magic. It was the magic that had called to Carp, guiding him down a hundred frozen paths, growing colder and then hotter, but always leading him on. And now he had found them, living very close to these reindeer herders, but not yet a part of their tribe. That was all to the good; it would make Carp's task easier.

Tonight he would impress these folk, would convince them that they must accept him as their new shaman. Once he had established that, it would be easy to take Kerlew from his mother's tent, to show her that the magic made the boy his. And if she still wanted her child? Carp laughed noisily through the gaps in his teeth. Then she must have Carp as well. Women. So little did they understand of how the world was put together. Tillu was already his, just as surely as if she were a reindeer and he a herder, notching his mark into her ear. It would be good to warm his old flesh against a woman again, sweet to sleep with his face pillowed on her hair. He nodded to himself sagely, rubbing his chilled thighs with his gnarled hands.

But first he must bring it to pass. His back protested as he reached to seize the strap of his small pack and drag it closer. He studied the knots in the fine sinew that tied it shut. They were his, marked with the signs of his magic. No one had tampered with it. And after tonight, no one would dare. He untied it carefully, the sinew snagging on the rough skin of his hands. His knuckles and wrists ached. Wet snow coming. He rubbed his hands briefly, sighing at the pain the weather brought him. Then he nodded, accepting what the spirit world sent him. He would use it, as he used everything his magic brought him. Every scrap of rumor, every guilty start, every anguished dream-starved stare became the fuel for his magic. He reviewed what he already knew of this people, every gleaning from the few days he had spent among them.

They had been long without a shaman. A najd, they called a spirit bridger, and feared their magic men as much as they revered them. It was time for them to have a najd again, to renew their ties with the spirit world. He would take that place within them and make it secure. And when he was too old to hold them with fear and magics, there would be his apprentice, strange young Kerlew, to take over. Kerlew of the staring eyes and halting speech, Kerlew with his slightly misshapen appearance and the spirits hovering palpably all around him. Then Kerlew would rule as najd, and Carp's final years would be easy ones. They were a wealthy folk, these herders. They could afford to treat their najd very, very well. He would see that they learned that right away.

The pack was finally open. He sighed as he tugged its mouth wider, reached within. He must choose his garments carefully; they must see him as a najd, not a ragged old man who had been close to starving for half the winter. He drew out the soft leather sacks that held his beads and rattles, chose carefully among the smaller pouches that held the herbs and roots of his magics. There was one small pouch, lighter than the others. He hefted it carefully; it was close to empty, and who knew when he would find more? But he would need the strength it would give him tonight. Better to use it now and win a people to himself than to be chary of it and lose all. He upended the sack over the small fire and drew close to it.

The blue smoke that billowed had an oily cast to it. He leaned forward to immerse his face in it, opened his gray-clouded eyes to it. The vision that was fading in this world saw all the more clearly in the spirit world. Breath after breath he drew of it, feeling the sudden vigor that washed through his body. The pieces of gossip he had painstakingly gathered danced in his head, began to fall into a pattern beneath the clever fingers of his spirit guides. There had been a woman who had died recently, some said by man's violence, some said by a demon's touch. Elsa. Yes, this would serve him well. And Kerlew. Already he made the herdfolk uneasy with his pale brown eyes and strange ways. And the reindeer soon to calve, and the snow in the air, the migration soon to begin, and the big man, Joboam, who wished himself already the Herdlord, and the Herdlord's son, too arrogant and fearful to ever lead this people. Yes and yes and yes. The pieces moved, shifting and tumbling through his mind, fitted together a dozen different ways, broke apart, and formed new patterns. There would be one to suit Carp's purpose. His vision would find it for him.

The herdlord's son, Rolke? Kerlew had spoken of him. The youth was a bully, and as such Carp well knew he was the ideal target for intimidation. His arrogance covered his own fears. But he had not the heart of the people. What was the use of ruling a man if the man himself controlled nothing? No. Not Rolke. Joboam. Perhaps. He was big, bigger even than Heckram, who stood almost as a giant among these folk. And he was wealthy and admired. If Carp could find a fitting handle, the man would be a sharp tool indeed. It was a pity that Kerlew disliked him so; but the boy would have to learn to use those he disliked, not cast them aside and destroy them. And Joboam would have to learn to leave the boy alone, not abuse him every chance he got. But Carp could teach him that. Once he found the proper reins to hold Joboam in, the big man would leave his apprentice in peace, yes, and avoid the woman that Carp had marked as his own. He would learn. All Carp had to find was the proper grip upon the big man. He knew the spirits would show it to him, perhaps even tonight.

He inhaled the smoke again, feeling its blueness clear his head and open his fogged eyes to unseen vistas. Capiam the herdlord. Carp must go to him tonight, must present himself and claim his spot as najd for the herdfolk. Carp exhaled slowly through his mouth. Capiam. There was little power to the name, and he sensed no spirits guarding the man. He was alone, nothing at all to be concerned about. The threads that held his people to his command were thin ones. Carp would gather those threads to himself, and then consider if the man himself were worth keeping.

The smoke filled the sod hut, settling densely to the ground instead of rising to find the smoke hole. Carp moved within its blueness, breathing in its strength and vision as he drew his shaman's garments on over his wracked old body. Heckram. Yes, there was Heckram to consider. This was his hut. Yes, and it was a well-made and large one, with a warm fire and food beside the hearth. Heckram had made him comfortable here, had treated him well. Yet Heckram was not all that useful a man. His ambitions bent in the wrong direction. He dreamed of seeing far places and owning many reindeer. Better to find a man who dreamed of leading, of having power in his hands. Such a one was almost always more useful to a shaman. Besides, had not that Elsa, the killed woman, had not she been Heckram's? What had he had to do with her death? Carp wondered, and the spirit guides swirled around the thought, seeking handles on it. Heckram was a problem in another way as well. He liked Tillu too well, yes, he did, and he did not fear Kerlew as the other men did. His eyes were keener than he knew, and he saw the worth and power in the boy. No. Heckram was too dangerous a tool to be cast aside. He must be blunted first, must be taught that Tillu and her strange son were not for him. He frowned to himself. He sensed the Wolf in Heckram, lurking about the man, waiting to claim him. Wolf spirit liked him as he had never liked Carp. All to the worse was it that Wolf also showed an affinity for Kerlew. Better that the boy were given to Bear, as he was, or to Wolverine, who did not fear to wield power. Wolf must be kept from bringing the two together. For a moment the old shaman knew doubt. It was one thing to manipulate the world of men; to challenge the spirits and seek to impose his will on them—this was a difficult thing, and far more dangerous.

Carp grinned hard, his narrow lips writhing back from his bad teeth. Difficult and dangerous, but he was not alone. Could not Bear break Wolf's back with a swipe of his great paw? Carp drew closer to the fire once more, settled himself on a soft reindeer hide that was cushioned from the cold earth by a layer of birch twigs. He reached his bare hand into the flames, poked bravely at the glowing coals to stir yet another billow of the strengthening smoke. It wafted away the fears that had sought to weaken him. "Bear!" he called softly, and drew his drum closer. The smoke enveloped him as he took up the tiny beartooth hammer and began the beat. His chant flowed out into the smoke and mingled with it as it filled the hut.

> chapter
> two

THE YEAR AFTER Capiam became herdlord, he had torn down his old hut and put up a larger one. It was done, he said, so that his folk might gather comfortably in his hut and tell him the things they were thinking. Bror had snickered that it was actually to accommodate his wife's growing girth. Remembering Ketla's outrage and Bror's bruises, Heckram grinned briefly. He lifted the doorskin from the low door. Carp preceded him.

Earlier Carp had dismissed Heckram from his own hut, saying that he must prepare for his meeting with Capiam, with rituals the uninitiated could not watch. Disgruntled, he had taken refuge with Ibb and Bror, and spent the early evening helping Bror deliver a calf. The calving had gone well, and Heckram had returned feeling optimistic.

He had washed the blood and clinging membranes from his hands and wrists, trying to ignore the smell of scorched hair and burnt herbs that had permeated his hut. Carp had been sitting cross-legged before his hearth, once more clad in his garments of snowy white fox furs. Strings of rattles made of leather and bone draped his wrists and ankles. He wore a necklace of thin black ermine tails alternated with bear teeth. He had not spoken a word to Heckram, but had risen with soft rattlings when he suggested that they go to the herdlord.

And now he entered the herdlord's hut just as wordlessly as he had left Heckram's. Heckram stepped in behind him and let the door-hide fall. He set his back teeth at the sight that greeted him. He had requested time with the herdlord, not a hearing of the elders. Yet, in addition to Capiam and his family, there were Pirtsi, Acor, Ristor, and of course, Joboam. Men richer in reindeer than in wisdom, Heckram told himself. But Carp detected nothing wrong. He advanced without waiting to be greeted, and seated himself at the arran without an invitation. Once ensconced, he let his filmed eyes rove over the gathered folk.

"It is good that you have gathered to hear me." Carp began without preamble. Capiam shifted in surprise at this assumption of control, and Joboam scowled. Carp took no notice. "The herdfolk of Capiam are a people in sore need of a shaman. A najd, I believe you say. I have walked today through your camp. The spirits of the earth cry out in outrage at your carelessness toward them." He let his eyes move over them accusingly. His gnarled hand caught up the rattles that dangled from his wrist, and he began to shake them rhythmically as he spoke. The fine seeds whispered angrily within the pouches of stiff leather.

"Huts are raised with no regard to the earth spirits. Children are born and no one offers gifts or begs protection. Wolves are hunted, and no offering given to Wolf himself. Bear mutters in his den of your disrespect and Reindeer grows coldly angry. A great evil hovers over your folk, and you are blind to it. But I have come. I will help you."

There was a white movement in the still room as Kari, the herdlord's daughter, fluttered from her corner. She flitted closer to the najd and the fire that moved before him. Heckram caught the flash of her bird-bright eyes as she settled again. Avidity filled the gaze she fixed on Carp. No one else seemed to notice her interest.

"Spirits of water and tree are complaining that you use them and make no sign of respect. Reindeer himself has been most generous to you, but you ignore him. How long have you taken his gifts, and made no thanks to him?"

Carp's rattles sizzled as he turned his gaze from one person to the next. Ketla was white-faced, Kari rapt, Acor and Ristor uneasy. Pirtsi picked at his ear, while Joboam looked sullenly angry. Rolke was bored. Capiam alone looked thoughtful, as if weighing Carp's words.

"The herdfolk do not turn the najd away," he said carefully. "But—" The sharp word caught everyone's attention. "Neither do we cower in fear. You say the spirits are angry with us. We see no sign of this. Our reindeer are healthy, our children prosper. It has been long since we had a najd, but we keep our fathers' customs. You are not herdfolk, nor a najd of the herdfolk. How can you say what pleases the spirits of our world?"

Acor nodded slowly with Capiam's words, while Joboam stood with a satisfied smile. He crossed his arms on his chest, his gaze on Heckram. He nodded slowly at him. It had gone his way. But Carp was nodding, too, and smiling his gap-toothed smile.

"I see, I see." The rattles hissed as he warmed his hands over the fire. Abruptly he stopped shaking them. The cessation of the monotonous noise was startling. He rubbed his knobby hands over the flames, nodding as he warmed them. "You are a happy folk; you have no need of a shaman. You think to yourselves, what need have we of Carp? What will he do? Why, only shake his rattles and burn his offerings and stare into the fire. He will eat our best meat, ask for a share of our huntings and weavings and workings." Carp leaned forward to peer deep into the fire as he spoke. "Like a dog too old to hunt, he will lie in the sun and grow fat. Let him find another folk to serve. We are content. We do not wish to know . . . to know. . . ."

His voice fell softer and softer as he spoke. The flames of the fire suddenly shot up in a roar of green and blue sparks. Ketla screamed. The men leaped to their feet and retreated from the blaze. It startled everyone in the tent, except Carp, who moved not at all. The fountaining of sparks singed his hair and eyebrows. The stench of burning hair filled the hut. Thin spirals of smoke rose from his clothes as sparks burned their way down through the fur. He swayed slightly, still staring into the reaching flames. "Elsa?" he asked, his voice high and strange. Everyone gasped. Heckram stopped breathing. "Elsa-sa-sa-sa!" The najd's voice went higher with every syllable. "The calves are still! The mothers cry for them to rise and follow, but their long legs are folded, the muzzles clogged with their birth sacs. Elsa-saa-saa-saa-saa-saa-saa!"

His voice went on and on, his rattles echoing the sibilant cry. As suddenly as the flames had leaped up they fell, and returned to burning with their familiar cracklings. The najd's head drooped onto his chest in a silence as sudden as death.

"Elsa! He saw Elsa!" Kari's shrill cry cracked the silence. Acor and Ristor leaned to mutter at Capiam. Ketla sank slowly to the floor, the back of her hand blocking her gaping mouth. Every hair on Heckram's body was a-prickle with dread. He swallowed bitterness in a throat gone dry and felt an icy chill up his back. It took him a moment to realize it had an earthly source. The unfastened door-hide flapped in a new wind from the north. Heckram pegged it down. Straightening, he noticed another interesting thing. Joboam was missing.

"Najd! What did you see in the flames?" Capiam demanded.

Carp lifted his head smoothly. "See? Why, nothing. Nothing at all. A happy and contented folk like yours, what do they care what an old man sees in a fire? Just smoke and ash, wood and flame, that's all a fire is. Heckram, I am weary. Will you grant this old beggar a place in your tent for one night?"

His answer was drowned by Capiam's raised voice. "The herdlord gladly offers you shelter this night, Carp. But certainly it will be for more than just one night?"

"No, no. Just for a night or two, for an old man to rest from his travels. Then I shall take my apprentice and move on. I will stay at Heckram's hut. It's a very large hut, for one man alone. A shame he has no wife to share it. Have you never thought of taking a woman, Heckram?" The old man asked innocently.

"Not since Elsa died!" Kari shrilled out. She flitted over to Carp, her loose garments flapping as she moved.

She crouched beside him, her dark eyes enormous. "What did you see in the flames?" she asked in a husky whisper.

"Kari!" her father rebuked her, but she did not heed him. She peered into Carp's clouded eyes, her head cocked and her lips pursed. For a long moment their gaze held. Then she gave a giggle that had no humor in it and leaped to her feet. She turned to fix her eyes on Pirtsi. Her face was strange, unreadable. Even Pirtsi, immune to subtlety, shifted his feet and scratched the nape of his neck uneasily.

"Heckram and I will leave now!" Carp announced, rising abruptly. He took a staggering step, then gripped the young man's shoulder and pulled himself up straight.

"But I wished to speak to Capiam, about Kerlew," Heckram reminded him softly.

Carp's eyes were icy and cold as gray slush. "Kerlew is my apprentice. His well-being is in my care. He is not for you to worry about. Do you doubt it?"

Heckram met his gaze, then shook his head slowly.

"Good night, Capiam." Carp's farewell was bland. "Sleep well and contentedly, as should a leader of a contented folk. Take me to our hut, Heckram. This foolish old man is weary."

A north wind was slicing through the talvsit. Icy flakes of crystalline snow rode it, cutting into Heckram's face. It was more like the teeth of winter than the balmy breath of spring. Heckram bowed his head and guided the staggering najd toward his hut. The talvsit dogs were curled in round huddles before their owners' doors. Snow coated their fur and rimed their muzzles. Heckram shivered in the late storm and narrowed his eyes against the wind's blast. In a lull of the wind came the lowing cry of a vaja calling her calf. A shiver ran up Heckram's spine, not at the vaja's cry, but at the low chuckle from the najd that followed it.

It took two days for the storm to blow itself out. There came a morning finally when the sun emerged in a flawlessly blue sky and the warmth of the day rose with it. The storm's snow melted and ran off in rivulets down the pathways of the talvsit, carrying the remainder of the old snow with it. Icicles on the thatching of the huts dripped away. Earth and moss and the rotting leaves of last autumn were bared by the retreating snow. As the day grew older, and the herdfolk sought out their reindeer in the shelter of the trees, the retreating snow bared the small still forms of hapless calves born during the late storm. Vajor with swollen udders nudged at little bodies, nuzzled and licked questioningly at the small ears and cold muzzles.

Silent folk moved in the forest, leading vajor away to be milked, leaving the dead calves to the relentless beetles that already crept over them. During the storm, the tale of the najd's words had crept from hut to hut until all the talvsit knew. Carp sat outside Heckram's door, stretching his limbs to the warmth of the sun as he fondled something small and brown in his knuckly hands. Those who passed looked aside in fear and wonder, and some felt a hidden anger. Heckram was one of them. What demon had guided this old man to him, and what foolishness had ever prompted him to bring Carp back to the talvsit?

"I lost two calves," he said coldly, standing over the old man. "And my best vaja, who sometimes bore twins, cannot be found at all. I think wolves got her as she gave birth."

"A terrible piece of luck," Carp observed demurely.

"One of Ristin's vajor died giving birth."

Carp nodded. "A terrible storm." He tilted his filmed eyes up to Heckram. "I will be leaving in a few moments. I wish to spend the day with my apprentice."

Heckram was silent, conflicting urges stirring in him. "I can't take you today," he said at last. "The bodies of the calves must be collected, skinned, and the meat burned. It is already spoiled. Otherwise the stench of it will draw wolves and foxes and ravens to prey on the new-born ones as well."

Carp looked at him coldly. "I do not need you to take me. That is not what I said. As for you, you have no reason to see Tillu. Your face is healed. You have tasks to do. To visit the healer would be a waste of your time." His tone forbade Heckram.

"The healer and her son are my friends," Heckram

countered. "And sometimes a man goes visiting for no more reason than that."

"Not when he has work. You have calves to skin and bury. Don't waste your time visiting Tillu."

Capiam approached as they were speaking. Acor and Ristor hung at his heels like well-trained dogs. Heckram glanced at them in annoyance, wondering where Joboam was. Carp showed them his remaining teeth in a grin, and went on speaking to Heckram.

"Hides from just-born calves make a soft leather. Very fine and soft, wonderful for shirts. It has been a long time since I had a shirt of fine soft leather. But such luxuries are not for a wandering najd." He moved his head in a slow sweep over the gathered men. Then, with elaborate casualness, he opened his hand. One finger stroked the carved figure of a reindeer calf curled in sleep. Or death. Acor retreated a step.

"You might have a shirt of calf leather, and leggings as well," Capiam said in a falsely bright voice. "My folk have urged me to invite you to join us on our migration. We will provide for your needs."

"I myself will give you three calf hides this very day!" Acor proclaimed nervously.

Carp closed his hand over the figurine. "A kind man. A kind man," he observed, to no one in particular. "An old man should be grateful. But it would be a waste of hides. My teeth are worn, my eyes are dim, my hands ache when the winds blow chill. An old man like me cannot work hides into shirts."

"There are folk willing to turn the hides into shirts for you. And your other needs will be seen to as well."

"Kind. Kind, generous men. Well, we shall see. I must go to visit my apprentice today. Kerlew, the healer's son. I am sure you know of him. He has told me he might not be happy among your folk. Some might be unkind to him. I would not stay among folk who mistreat my apprentice."

A puzzled Capiam conferred with Acor and Ristor, but both looked as mystified as he did. He turned back to Carp. "If anyone offers harm to your apprentice, you have only to tell me about it. I will see that the ill-doer pays a penalty.''

"Um." Carp sat nodding to himself for a long moment. Then, "We will see," he said, and got creakily to his feet. "And you, Heckram. Do not waste your time today. Get your work done, and be ready to travel. The journey begins the day after tomorrow."

The men looked to Capiam in confusion. "We do not go that soon," Capiam corrected him gently. "In four or five days, perhaps, when . . ."

"No? Well, no doubt you know more of such things than I. I had thought that a wise man would leave by the day after tomorrow. But I suppose I am wrong again. What an old man sees in his dreams has little to do with day-to-day life. I must be going, now."

Carp set off at a shambling walk, leaving Capiam and his men muttering in a knot. Heckram called after him, "Be sure to tell Tillu that I will come to see her soon." The old man gave no sign of hearing. With deep annoyance, Heckram knew that his message would not be delivered.

"Here he comes! I told you he would come as soon as the storm died!" Without waiting for an answer, Kerlew raced out to meet Carp.

"*I* told *you* that he would come as soon as the storm was over." Tillu offered the truth to the empty air. Kerlew had been frantic when Carp had not returned. He had spent a miserable two days. Kerlew had paced and worried, nagged her for her opinion as to why Carp hadn't returned, and ignored it when she told him. So now the old shaman was here, and her son would stop pestering her. Instead of relief, her tension tightened. She stood in the door, watched her son run away from her.

She watched the old man greet the boy, their affection obvious. In an instant, they were in deep conversation, the boy's long hands fluttered wildly in description. They turned and walked into the woods. Tillu sighed.

Then she glimpsed another figure moving down the path

through the trees. Despite her resolve, her belly tightened in anticipation. The long chill days of the storm had given her time to cool her ardor and reflect upon what had nearly happened the last time she had seen Heckram. It would have been a grave mistake. She was glad it had not happened, glad she had not made herself so vulnerable to Heckram. The trees alternately hid and revealed the figure coming down the path. He was wearing a new coat. She dreaded his coming, she told herself. That was what sent her heart hammering into her throat. She would not become involved with a man whose woman had been beaten, and then slipped into death by too large a dosage of pain tea. She would not become close to a man that large, so large he made her feel like a helpless child. She would be calm when he arrived. She would treat his face, if that was what he came for. And if it was not, she would . . . do something. Something to make it clear she would not have him.

He paused at the edge of the clearing, shifting nervously from foot to foot. It wasn't him. Recognition of the fact sank her stomach and left her trembling. He hadn't come. Why hadn't he come? Had he had second thoughts about a woman who had birthed a strange child like Kerlew? Kerlew, with his deep-set pale eyes and prognathous jaw, Kerlew, who dreamed with his eyes wide open. But Heckram had seemed to like her son, had responded to him as no other adult male ever had. So if it was not Kerlew that had kept Heckram from coming to see her, it was something else. Something that was wrong with her.

Whoever it was who had come hesitated at the edge of the clearing. Tillu watched as her visitor rocked back and forth in an agony of indecision. Then suddenly the figure lifted its arms wide, and rushed toward her hut in a swooping run. The girl's black hair lifted as she ran, catching blue glints of light like a raven's spread wings. The wind of her passage pressed her garments against her thin body.

A few feet from the hut, she skittered to a halt. She dropped her arms abruptly and folded her thin hands in front of her high breasts. Her fluttering garments of loose white furs settled around her. She stood perfectly still and silent, regarding Tillu with brightly curious eyes. She did not make any greeting sign, not even a nod. She waited.

"Hello there," Tillu said at last. She found herself speaking as to a very shy child. The same calm voice and lack of aggressive movements. It seemed to Tillu that if she put out a hand, the girl would take flight. "Have you come to see me? Tillu the Healer?"

The girl bobbed a quick agreement and came two short steps closer. She looked at Tillu as if she had never seen a human before, with a flat, wide curiosity, taking in not the details of Tillu's face and garments, but the general shape of the woman. It was the way Kerlew looked at strangers, and Tillu felt a sudden uneasiness. "What's your name?" she asked carefully. "What do you need from me?"

The girl froze. Tillu expected her next motion to carry her away. But instead she said in a whisper-light voice, "Kari. My name is Kari." She bobbed a step closer and craned her neck to peer into the tent. "You're alone." She swiveled her head about quickly to see if there were anyone about. Tillu didn't move. The girl leaned closer, reached out a thin hand but didn't quite touch her. "I want you to mark me."

"What?"

"Listen!" The girl seemed impatient. "I want you to mark me. My face and breasts, I think that should be enough. Maybe my hands. If it isn't, I'll come back and have you take out an eye. But this first time, I think if you cut off part of one nostril, and perhaps notched my ears. Yes. Notch my ears, with my own reindeer mark. To show that I belong to myself."

Tillu felt strangely calm. She was talking to a mad woman. The last snow was melting, leaf buds were swelling on twigs, and the trunks of birches and willows were flushed pink with sap. And this girl wanted Tillu to cut off pieces of her face.

"And there is a mark I want you to make on each of my

breasts. We will have to cut it deep enough to scar. Look
Here it is. Can you tell what I meant it to be?''

From within her fluttering garments, the girl produced a
small scrap of bleached hide. She unrolled it carefully,
glanced warily about, and then thrust it into Tillu's face.
She was breathing quickly, panting in her excitement.

Tillu looked at the scrap of hide, making no movement
to take it. A black mark had been made with soot in the
center of the hide. Four lines meeting at a junction. ''It
looks like the tracks shore birds leave in the mud,'' Tillu
observed carefully.

''Yes!'' Kari's voice hissed with satisfaction. ''Almost.
Only it's the mark of an Owl. A great white owl with
golden eyes. I want you to put one on each of my breasts,
above the nipples. Mark me as the Owl's. Then Pirtsi will
know I am not for him. My ears will show me as mine,
my breasts will show me as Owl's. Must it hurt very
much?''

The pang of fear in the last question wrung Tillu's heart.
It was a child's voice, not questioning that it must be
done, but only how much it would hurt.

''Yes.'' Tillu spoke simply and truthfully. ''Such a
thing would hurt a great deal. Your ears, not so much after
it was done. But your nose would hurt a great deal, every
time you moved your face to speak or smile or frown. The
nose is very sensitive. As would your breasts be. There
would be a great deal of blood and pain.''

She peered deeply into the girl's eyes as she spoke,
hoping to see some wavering in her determination. There
was none. Tillu felt a tightening within her belly. This girl
would do this maiming, with her help or without it. She
must find a way to deter her. Slowly she gestured toward
her tent. ''Would you care to come inside? I made a tea
this morning, of sorrel and raspberry roots, with a little
alder bark. As a tonic for the spring, but also because it
tastes good. Will you try some?''

Kari opened and closed her arms several times rapidly,
making her white garments flap around her. Tillu thought
she had lost her, that the girl would flee back into the

woods. But suddenly she swooped into the tent. She fluttered about, looking at everything, and then alighted on a roll of hides near the hearth. She cocked her head to peer into the earthenware pot of tea steeping on the coals. "I'd like some," she said decisively.

Tillu moved slowly past her, to reach for carved wooden cups. "What made you decide to mark your body?" she asked casually.

Kari didn't speak. Tillu sat on the other side of the hearth, facing her. She dipped up two cups of the tea, and offered one dripping mug to Kari. She took it, looked into it, sniffed it, sipped it, and then looked up at Tillu and spoke. "The night the najd came to my father's tent and spoke, I felt the truth of his words. And more. He spoke of how many of us had no spirit guardian to protect us. I had heard my grandmother speak of such guardians, a long time ago, before she died. Her spirit beast was Hare. He does not seem like much of a guardian, does he? But he was good to my grandmother.

"So that night, I stared into the fire as the najd had and opened myself and went looking for a spirit beast. But I saw nothing in the flames, though I watched until long after all the others slept. So, I gave up and went to my skins and slept. And in the night I felt cold, heavy claws sink into my beast."

She lifted her thin hands, her narrow fingers curved like talons, and pressed them against her breasts. Then she looked up at Tillu. The girl's eyes were a wide blackness. She smiled at Tillu, a strange and wondering smile. Tillu held her breath. "The weight of his claws pressed me down, crushing my chest until I could not breathe. The sharp cold claws sank into me. I struggled but could not escape. It grew dark. But when I was too tired to fight anymore, the darkness gave way to a soft gray light. I felt moss beneath my back, and the night wind of the forest blew across my naked body. And atop my chest, near tall as a man, was Owl, perched with his claws sunk into my breasts!"

Her nostrils flared as she breathed, and Tillu could see

the whites all around her eyes. The hands that held the wooden mug trembled as she raised it to her lips. Tillu was silent, waiting. Kari drank. When she took the mug from her mouth, her eyes were calm. She smiled at Tillu, a tight-lipped smile without the showing of teeth. "Then I knew," she said softly.

Tillu leaned forward. "Knew what?"

"That I belonged to Owl. That I didn't have to let Pirtsi join with me by the Cataclysm this summer. I am Owl's. When I awoke, I told my dream to my mother, and asked her to explain to my father why I cannot be joined to Pirtsi. It was always his idea, never mine. I never wanted to be joined to any man at all, let alone a man with dog's eyes. But my mother grew angry, and said that a man was what I needed to be settled, for nothing else had worked. So I have come to you. Mark my face and body, so all will know to whom I belong. Pirtsi will not take me if I am scarred. He would not take me at all, except that he thinks Capiam's daughter is a way to Capiam's favor."

Tillu sipped at her tea, watching Kari over her mug. The girl was determined. In her mind, it was already done. She spoke carefully. "Kari, I am a healer, not one who damages bodies."

"Damage? No, this would not be damage. Only a marking, like a notch in a calf's ear, or a woman's mark carved into her pulkor. Not damage."

Tillu chewed at her lower lip. "I do not think we should do this thing," she said softly, and as anger flared on Kari's face she added, "If Owl had wanted you so marked on your flesh, he would have marked you himself. Is this not so?"

For an instant, Kari looked uncertain. Tillu pressed on, glad for once that Kerlew had nattered on so much about Carp's teaching. She wanted her words to sound convincing.

"Owl has marked your spirit as his. That is all he requires. You need not mark your face to deny Pirtsi. Or so I understood during the time I spent with the herdfolk, when Elsa . . ."

"Elsa died." Kari finished in an awed whisper.

"I understood then that the women of your folk can choose their mates. You have a reindeer of your own, do you not? Are not the things you make yours to keep or trade as you wish?" At each of the girl's nods, Tillu's spirits lifted. "Then say that Pirtsi isn't what you want. Cannot you do that?"

Kari had begun to writhe. Her fingers clawed at her arms as she hugged herself. "I should be able to do that. But no one listens. I say I won't have him. They pay no attention. Everyone is so certain that we will be joined at the Cataclysm. It is as if I cried out that the sun would shine at night. They would think it some childish game. They cannot understand that I do not want him; that I cannot let him touch me."

"Why?" Tillu spoke very, very softly.

Kari's eyes grew larger and larger in her face. She touched the tip of her tongue to the center of her upper lip. She trembled on the edge of speaking. Then, the tension left her abruptly, her shoulders slumped, and she said, "Because I belong to Owl now, and he tells me not to. Why won't you mark me?"

"Because I do not believe Owl wants me to," Tillu excused herself smoothly. "Who am I to make Owl's mark for him? If he wishes you marked, he will do it himself."

Kari once more lifted her hands, sank taloned fingers against her breasts. "And if I do it myself?" she asked.

"Then I would try to see that you did not become infected. A healer is what I am, Kari. I cannot change that. Let me offer you another idea. Wait. There is much time between spring and high summer. Tell everyone that you will not have Pirtsi. Say it again and again. They will come to believe you. Tell Pirtsi himself. Tell him you will not be a good wife to him."

"And if they do not believe me, when the day comes, I will show them that I am Owl's. By the Cataclysm."

Tillu sighed. "If you must."

The girl sipped at her tea, suddenly calmed. "I will wait." Her eyes roved about the tent interior. "You should be spreading your hides and bedding in the sun to air, before you pack it for the trip. Where are your pack saddles?''

Tillu shrugged. ''I have never traveled with an animal to carry my things. I have always dragged my possessions behind me. This migration will be a new experience for Kerlew and me.'' Tillu spoke the words carefully, tried to sound sure that her son would travel with her. The old shaman had said he would take Kerlew from her. Kerlew himself had said that he was near a man now, and had chosen to go with Carp. But perhaps he would change his mind. Perhaps he would stay with his mother and be her son a while yet, would not slip into the strange ways of the peculiar old man and his nasty magics. With an effort she dragged her attention back to what Kari was saying.

''You know nothing of reindeer then? You do not know how to harness and load them?''

Tillu shrugged her shoulders, looked closely at the girl who now spoke so maturely and asked such practical questions. ''There are two animals hobbled behind my tent. The herdlord provided them for me. I suppose he will send Joboam to help me when the time comes.'' Tillu could not keep the dismay from her voice.

''That one?'' Kari gave a hard laugh. ''I was glad when he wouldn't have me. I knew why. He made many fines excuses to my father, saying I was so young, so small yet. As if that . . .'' She paused and stared into her mug for a breath or two. ''I didn't know my father would find Pirtsi instead,'' she finished suddenly. She cocked her head, gave Tillu a shrewd look. ''I could show you. Now, today. Then, when the time came, you wouldn't need help. You could send a message that you didn't need Joboam.'' Kari smiled a small smile. ''And I could tell my father that I had already taught you, that he need not spare so important a man as Joboam for such a simple task.'' There was frank pleasure in the girl's voice as she spoke of spiting Joboam's plans.

Tillu lifted her eyes from her own slow appraisal of the flames. She was beginning to have suspicions of Joboam that made her dislike him even more. She was also beginning to have a different opinion of Kari. The girl was shrewd. As oddly as she might behave, she had wits. And how old was she? Sixteen? "When I was her age, I had Kerlew in my arms," Tillu thought to herself. "And I thought my life belonged to him as surely as Kari believes hers belongs to Owl. We are not so different." Kari smiled her tight-lipped smile again, a smile of conspiracy that Tillu returned.

> chapter
three

REINDEER. THE HERD came first, flowing through the trees like water flowing through a bed of reeds. The males led, most with antlers missing or stubby in velvet. Their shedding coats were patchy but they stepped proudly, eyes alert, moving down the hillside and past her with slow grace. At first the sheer number of the animals cresting the hill and pouring down into her little valley had frightened Tillu. It was her first glimpse of the wealth of the herdfolk. Up until now, she had lived apart from them in her own dell, tending to their hurts but not sharing their lives. Now she was to be swept into it as surely as the moving herd of beasts swept past her. She trembled at their numbers. But the flood of beasts paid her and Kerlew and the two laden harkar no mind.

She gripped the damp rein tighter. Either one of the laden animals could have dragged her off her feet. The second beast was tethered to the first one's harness, as Kari had taught her. If they decided to follow the herd, there would be nothing she could do about it. She glanced at them, felt sweat break out anew. They carried the new tent Capiam had sent, and all her supplies. If they bolted, she would lose all her herbs and household implements, everything. But the two animals stood placidly, regarding the passing reindeer with calm brown eyes.

She had spent the last two days packing her possessions and learning to manage the animals. Kari had been a good teacher, matter-of-fact and tolerant of Tillu's nervousness.

But Tillu was still not comfortable. It was one thing to watch wild reindeer from a distance, or crouch over a dead one to butcher. It was another thing entirely to stand close to a living animal, to hold a strap fastened to it. The harke whose lead she held shifted its weight. Its large, deeply cloven hooves spread atop the ground. It sneezed, spraying her with warm drops and then shook its head to free the long whiskers on its muzzle from the clinging moisture. Tillu forced herself to stand still as the new antlers, encased in pulpy velvet, swept close to her. When they were grown they would be solid hard brown bone. A brow antler would extend forward and downward over its muzzle to protect the animal's face; the rest of the antlers would be swept back. She had already known that both females and males grew and shed antlers. But Kari had given her the casual knowledge of one whose life had always interlocked with the herd.

The vajor were coming now, mistrustful of everything as they shepherded their gangly calves along. The calves were an unlikely assembly of knobby joints and long bones, of pinkish muzzles and wide, awe-stricken eyes. One calf halted, to regard Tillu with amazement. "Stand still, Kerlew," she breathed to her son as the mother watched them with hard eyes. She snorted to her calf, and then nudged it along. They merged back into the flow of grayish-brown animals and Tillu breathed again. She glanced up at the crest of the hill, and felt her trepidation rise. Why did she feel more threatened by the people than she did by the passing animals?

"See, Kerlew, there is Capiam the herdlord, leading the others. Soon we shall join them." Kari had delivered her message that she needed no help to prepare for the journey. Tillu wondered if it had caused any upset in the village. She had seen nothing of Joboam or Heckram since Carp's arrival.

"If Capiam is the leader," Kerlew asked, his piping voice carrying clearly, "why didn't he come first, leading that big reindeer? A different man is leading the herd."

"Hush. There is more than one kind of leading. The

first man was leading the guide animal. Capiam is leading the people.''

Kerlew fixed her with an unreadable look. ''I would rather be lord of the herd than herdlord,'' he said. ''And someday I shall.'' There was no doubt in his voice nor sense in his words. Tillu sighed. She put her arm across his shoulders, but he bucked free of her irritably. She sighed again.

Capiam's shirt was bright red wool and his cap was gay with tassels. His reindeer wore harness bedecked with colors and metal. He led a string of seven harkar, each heavily burdened. He waved a greeting and gestured to her to join them. She nodded her agreement but stood still, watching the parade of people and laden animals. Behind Capiam came a stout woman, leading a string of five harkar. Behind her came Rolke with a string of seven harkar, and then Kari leading two. Kari waved gaily and called something to her. The reindeer made their own sounds of passage; the clicking of their hooves, the creak and slap of branches as they pushed through the woods, their coughing grunts as they called to their fellows.

Next came men and women Tillu didn't know, their wealth apparent in their woolen garments and bronze ornaments. Each person led a string of animals, usually six or seven to the adults, and two or three for each child. Tillu smiled at a fat babe atop a lurching harke. The infant's cheeks were very red, her face grave as she held to the wooden pack frame and rode tall. Tillu's smile faded as her eyes met the next walker.

Joboam led a string of nine harkar. He met her eyes deliberately, and veered out of the caravan line. Tillu kept her face impassive, but her heartbeat quickened. Kerlew took a quick breath and stepped behind her. Joboam gave no greeting until he was a few steps away. His dark eyes flicked from Tillu to Kerlew.

''Here, boy. Hold the lead while I check those pack animals. The loads look uneven to me. And don't startle them.''

Kerlew didn't move. Joboam's eyes narrowed and his

color came up slowly. "Boy. . . ," he began in a savagely low voice.

"I'll hold your animals if you must check my work. But Kari showed me how to lead, and was satisfied I could do it."

"Kari!" The word was full of contempt. He glared at Kerlew. Then, he jerked the harke's head around and slapped the rein into Tillu's outstretched hand. The animal shied from Joboam's sudden movement, nearly dragging Tillu off her feet, but she kept hold of the rein.

"Don't let him jerk you around," Joboam commanded her as he moved to her laden animals. He tugged and pushed at the bags and bundles tied to the pack frame, tightening the ties, and once moving a bag from one animal to the other. His competence could not be denied; somehow that annoyed Tillu even more. He was talking, voice and words hard as he readjusted the harnesses. "A harke has to know that you're in charge. You can't let it doubt it for one moment. If you're going to insist on doing something you know nothing about, at least know that. Keep a tight grip and make it obey you." He shot a venomous glance at Kerlew. "If you can make anything obey you." Kerlew was trying to smile at Joboam placatingly, but fear distorted the smile until it looked like a sneer. Joboam stared at him, his eyes going blacker.

"I can manage them," Tillu said, surprised at how calm her voice sounded.

"Can you?" He glared at her. "And that boy? Can you make him obey you, keep him from being a burden to all of us?" She could hear the checked fury in his voice. He'd been saving his anger for days. At the least excuse, he'd show it. She looked at his big hands, the thick muscles in his neck, and felt cold fear. But only the chill was in her voice when she spoke.

"Kerlew is my responsibility. I am sure that if Capiam thought he would be a problem, he would have spoken of it to me."

"And you are my responsibility! I have told Capiam that I will see to it that you . . ."

"I am no one's responsibility!" Tillu's voice flared out of control. Passing herdfolk were staring at them curiously.

"That is not how the herdlord has ordered it," he reminded her, an odd note of triumph in his voice. "I am to see that you lack for nothing, that you travel easily with us." He finished tugging at a final strap. Rising, he pulled the harke forward, to put its rein back into Tillu's hand and take his own animals. He looked down at her. "I am in charge of you and your boy. To be sure that no one harms the najd's little apprentice. Now you will follow me. And if . . ."

"Heckram! And Carp!" Kerlew's voice split Joboam's words. The boy dashed past her, running headlong toward the line of folk and beasts. Tillu's breath caught as she watched, expecting the animals to startle and run. But the harkar only looked up curiously at the boy pelting toward them. A few perked their ears foolishly, but there was no stampede. Heckram saw the boy coming, and pulled his animals from the cavalcade and waited. The folk behind him moved past.

Morning surrounded the man and framed him. He wore summer clothes, a tunic of thin leather stretched over his chest and shoulders, rough trousers of leather and leather boots that tied at the knee. A hat of knotted blue wool could not confine his hair; the breeze lifted bronze glints from it. She dared not believe in the wide smile that welcomed her son. The lead harke nudged Heckram for assurance, and he rested a hand on its shaggy neck, waiting. Kerlew halted inches from Heckram, to tilt back his head and grin up at him. It squeezed her heart to see her strange son so confident of a welcome. Heckram reached out a hand. She saw him tousle the boy's wild hair, then clasp his thin shoulder in a man's welcome. Carp's sharp voice parted them, imperiously summoning the boy to his side.

Heckram led a string of four harkar, with Carp perched atop the first one. Up until now, Tillu had seen only the very young and the very old riding the pack animals. Carp's legs were sound under him. She wondered why he chose to ride. He leaned down to speak to Kerlew, gesturing to the boy to walk beside the animal, and then to Heckram to move on. Heckram looked a question at her. She lifted a hand in a greeting that was an acknowledgment but not an answer to anything. Behind her Joboam made a sound without syllables, a rasping like a beast's growl. She was shaken by the black fury in his eyes. His hatred was bottomless; she wondered which of the three was its target.

"Follow!" he snapped and jerked his string of harkar to an ungainly trot. She pulled her unwilling animals to match his pace and ran to keep up. He threaded a trail through the widely spaced trees, paralleling the path of the herdfolk. She had no breath for questions, but could only follow in grudging obedience.

She took deep breaths of the scents of early spring. The aroma rose from the humus and early tufts of sprouting grasses and moss in an almost visible mist. Small yellow leaves and shriveled berries still clung to some of the brambly wild roses, beside the swelling leaf nodes that would soon unfurl into foliage. She saw a circle of new mushrooms but could not stop to investigate them. Joboam swung his animals back toward the cavalcade, motioning to Pirtsi to make a space. She followed him, glad to slow to a walk again.

"Keep up," was the only thing he said. She fell in behind him. His animals separated them, making talk thankfully impossible. She glanced back at Pirtsi but he seemed immersed in simply walking. She set her eyes forward and followed his example, letting the day fall into easy monotony.

Before her the haunches of Joboam's last harke swayed, its ridiculous white tail flicking. She glanced at the animal she led, surprised at how easy it was. She held the rein, but her beast simply followed the one in front of them. The strap between them was slack. The reindeer's head bobbed, its moist breath warming the air by Tillu's shoulder. Its eyes were huge, dark and liquid beneath the brow ridges. They reminded Tillu of a small child's frank stare.

Boldly she put her free hand out to touch the animal's shaggy neck. She was pleased with the contented rumble the animal made at her touch. She scratched it gently as she had seen Heckram do, and it leaned into her touch.

There was a strange giddiness to striding along on a spring day, unencumbered by any burden. She remembered her staggering flight from Benu's folk, the weight of everything she owned heavy on her shoulders as she fled from Carp and his influence over her son. This was better. The animals carried their packs easily, and Tillu matched their pace with a swinging stride. Stranger still was that Kerlew was not at her heels. She was not calling him back from investigating things far off the trail, wasn't scolding him for dawdling, nor answering his pestering questions. Her life had been so intertwined with her son's since his birth that she could not become accustomed to surrendering him to Carp. At the thought of the old man, her stomach knotted and she glanced back. But Kerlew and the shaman were far down the line. And Heckram was with them. She thought of the smile he had given her boy today. As if he didn't resent his presence. His tolerance couldn't last forever, might well be gone by the end of this day. But let Kerlew enjoy what acceptance he could. Soon enough he would know rejection again; soon he would walk at Tillu's heels again, asking her the same question ten times and never remembering her answer. She forced herself to believe it would be so.

She gave herself up to the forest around her. Once she heard squirrels chattering overhead, and then the hoarse cries of a raven. The forest of the morning was pine and spruce, with a scattering of birch. By midday they were crossing rivulets, swift and noisy with the melt of winter snow. The first few were narrow streams, easily jumped by the humans as the reindeer stoically waded through the icy waters. Then came a wider one, and Tillu found herself stepping from rock to slippery rock. By now it seemed natural to put a hand on the reindeer's shoulder to steady herself, and the animal evinced no surprise at her touch. On the far bank she paused to stroke its neck once, pleased with the feel of its living warmth seeping up through the stiff hair of its coat. Behind her, Bror was swinging his young grandson up to a temporary perch on a pack animal for the crossing.

Then they were walking on again. Tillu began to feel the complaints of muscles unused to long walking at such a steady pace. The day had warmed, and her heavy tunic was a burden. She halted to drag it off and sling it across the harke's other burdens. The cool breeze touched her bare arms. Her sleeveless tunic of thin rabbit leather felt so light she had a sensation of nakedness. She stretched her arms and rolled her shoulders in the pleasant sun. Then Joboam angrily called to her to keep up. She pulled her harke back into motion.

Gradually the forest changed. The cavalcade of reindeer and folk wound through valleys and across streams, leaving the steep hillsides behind and emerging onto soft slopes of Lapp heather, with twisting willow ossier now covered with fuzzy catkins and alders with cracked gray bark. The plant life was lusher here, the hillsides open to the blue sky and the softly pushing wind. She thought that the reindeer would lag and graze, but they moved on with a single-mindedness that made her legs ache.

Great gray rocks pushed up randomly on the hillsides through the yellowed grasses of last summer. The earliest of spring's flowers opened blooms in their shelter and stored warmth. She saw plants she could not name, and familiar plants shorter than she remembered them. She itched to touch and smell. Had she been alone, she would have gathered willow and alder barks for tonics and medicines, and the tips of the emerging fireweed for a delectable green. She glimpsed a violet's leaves, but could not leave her animals to investigate. She had to pass a patch of stink-lily with its nourishing starchy roots, for when she knelt to dig her fingers into the turfy soil, Joboam yelled to her to hurry. She hissed in frustration. There were drawbacks to having an animal carry one's belongings and being part of such a great moving group. She took dried fish from her pocket and nibbled it as she walked. And walked, while the sun slipped slowly across the blue sky and toward its craggy resting place.

She heard and smelled the river long before she saw it. The reindeer picked up the pace as they scented the water. Her hips and lower back complained as she stretched her stride, and her buttocks ached as if she had been kicked. The sinking sun glinted off the wide swatch of moving water, rainbowing over its rocky rapids. Tillu saw the line ahead of her pause and drink, but then rise and follow the noisy river and its trimming of trees. Her heart sank. Surely, they must stop soon! She paused at the river to let her beasts drink and take a long draught of the icy water herself. The cold made her teeth hum. Wiping her mouth, she rose to follow Joboam and his string of harkar. They wended through trees, naked birches and willows and oak hazed with green buds, following the river. Shadows lengthened and the day began to cool as the earth gave up its harvested heat to the naked skies. And then, far down the line of animals and men, she glimpsed a sheen of silver through the screening trees.

Abruptly they emerged on the shore of the lake. With relief Tillu saw the red glow and rising smoke of fires. Hasty shelters went up, a mushroom village sprang up from the warm earth. Unladen animals grazed on the open hillside above the lake. Gray boulders, rounded and bearded with lichen, poked their shaggy heads out of the deep grass of the slope. Children raced and shrieked among them or splashed and threw stones along the water's edge, enlivened rather than wearied by the day's travel. Dogs barked and bounded with them. Tillu envied them their energy. She would have liked nothing better than to sink down and rest. She watched Joboam glance about the scene, and then move surely into it, his campsite already selected. A child and a dog playing tug with a leather strap scrabbled hastily from his path. Tillu hesitated, wishing she could settle in a less central area of this hive of activity. But she couldn't risk offending some custom of theirs. She would camp where Joboam told her. She began to lead her harkar after him.

From the shadow of a boulder, Kari rose, startling Tillu and spooking even the stolid harkar. But as it jerked the rein from Tillu's hand, Kari caught it and turned to Tillu with her narrow smile. "Come!" she said, and put up a swift hand to cover a giggle. Her eyes were bright. Without another word, she led them off up the hill.

One boulder, larger than a sod hut, jutted from the earth halfway up the hillside. To this Kari led her, and then around and above it. On the high side of the boulder, facing away from the camp by the lake, was a shelter of pegged and propped hides. A small fire already burned and a pot of water was warming. A jumble of hides was spread inside the shelter, and Kari's harkar grazed outside it. Kari grinned at Tillu. "In the talvsit, I live in my father's and mother's hut. But here, in the arrotak, I have my own shelter, and invite my own guests. You will stay with me? You and Kerlew," she added hastily when Tillu hesitated.

Tillu did not relish the idea of company this weary night. But the fire was bright, the sky already darkening, the shelter welcoming and Kari so pleased with herself that Tillu could not refuse. She nodded. With a glad cry Kari sprang to unloading the harkar. Tillu moved to assist her, her weary fingers fumbling at the unfamiliar harness. Kari's experience showed as she capably stripped one animal, led it to grass, and hobbled it before Tillu could unload the other. Soon both beasts were grazing. Kari stepped into the shelter, sat down on the hides, and patted the place next to her invitingly. Tillu sank down beside her with a sigh. The new aches of sitting down were a relief from the old ones of walking. Tillu slowly pulled off her boots, pressed her weary feet into the cool new grass.

"I should find Kerlew," she reminded herself reluctantly. "Heckram must be sick of him by now."

"He will be here soon," Kari assured her. She leaned back on the hides and rolled onto her side to watch the hillside above her as the night stole its colors.

"It is kind of you to invite me to stay with you," Tillu observed belatedly, but Kari only shrugged.

"You are someone to talk to, and as you have shared

your tent and tea with me, I would do the same for you. Besides, if you are here it will be less problems."

The last remark puzzled her until Lasse rounded the boulder and dropped an armload of firewood. "I told you I'd find plenty," he said, and ducked into the shelter with a pleased smile. It faded abruptly, to be replaced with an abashed grin as he found himself face to face with Tillu. She guessed instantly that he had hoped to find Kari alone. She glanced at Kari, but the girl seemed immune to Lasse's disappointment.

"I wouldn't call it plenty, but it's enough," Kari observed heartlessly. "Lasse, go and find Tillu's son now, please. He was walking with Heckram. They should be at the lake by now. Bring them here. We may as well all eat together." When Lasse hesitated, Tillu saw Kari tip her head back and, after a cool silence, suddenly smile at him with such melting warmth that the boy all but staggered with the impact. He nodded quickly, and left, face flushed, to obey her. As soon as he was gone, Kari's smile faded, to be replaced with her usual pensive frown. "I want to show you something," she said suddenly. She swiftly unlaced the leather jerkin she wore. She tugged it open and turned to Tillu, a smile of anticipation on her face.

Tillu recoiled. Kari had a long, lovely neck, and proud young breasts jutted high on her chest. But incised into the soft rise of each breast were Kari's four-stroked symbols, as if indeed an owl with fiery talons had rested upon them. "Carp told me about the soot," Kari said proudly. "Now the cuts may heal, but the mark will remain." She looked up from her handiwork to Tillu's averted eyes and sickened expression. The girl's smile vanished. "What's the matter with you? I thought you'd be happy to see that they didn't get infected!"

"Carp." Tillu said the word with loathing. "Yes, he'd be glad to tell you how to scar yourself." And she had left Kerlew with the old man for the whole day. What had she been thinking of? If this was what Kari had learned from him, what grisly marvels was he teaching Kerlew?

"Yes, Carp. Last night he ate at my father's hut. He

spoke of the people he used to live among. At birth, the baby's spirit guide is found, and the mark of it is sliced into the baby's thigh, and soot rubbed in. It binds the guardian to the child. Now Owl is bound to me as I am to him.''

"Yes. All will know now." Tillu's voice was flat. It was done, there was no sense in rebukes, in making her miserable over what could not be undone.

"Yes!" The hard pride in Kari's voice challenged Tillu's regret. Tillu chose silence, letting the challenge pass in the darkening evening. After a moment, Kari laced up her jerkin again. Tillu watched her covertly, marvelled at the intensity of her features. Life roared in the girl, like a torrent of water in a narrow chasm. She was never at peace, for even when she sat still, as now, with her eyes fixed on some distant place and her lips parted over her white teeth, she seemed to be moving. One sensed her mind traveled far and swift while her forgotten body poised here. Tillu could understand how her impassivity would distance many folk. Yes, and intrigue a young man like Lasse.

"It was kind of Lasse to bring firewood all the way up here," she ventured.

Animation snapped back to Kari's face. "He is a kind person," she said softly, and then, with more vehemence, "with most peculiar ideas." She sat up straight, then crawled out of the shelter. "I am going to cook for us," she announced, and went to the packs and began to dig through them.

Tillu rose, feeling uncomfortable watching someone work. "I wish I'd had more time to myself today. I could have gathered fresh greens for us, and replenished some of my healing supplies."

"I suppose you look for your healing herbs in far and strange places?" Kari's voice had a strange, sly note.

"No. Most of them grow in the meadows and woods among the ordinary plants. Today I saw stink lily, and I think violets. And of course . . ."

"Violets?" Kari's voice was incredulous.

"Yes. Picked and dried, they are good against skin rash. They can be used against illnesses of the lungs, also."

Kari looked at her in wonder. "Why do you tell me this?"

"You seemed interested." Tillu stopped, confused.

"And you do not mind telling me?"

"Why should I?" In the dying evening, a cuckoo called and was silent.

"The old midwife Kila was our last healer. She would never say what herbs were in her mixes, or where she got them. She learned from her mother, and said it was her wealth, and not to be shared. So when she left, only the commonest healing was known. I thought all healers would be jealous of their secrets."

"Selfish, if you ask me." Tillu was appalled.

"Then, if I wanted to learn the herbs of healing, would you teach me?"

"Of course. When we have time, I will be happy to show you how to gather herbs and how to use them."

"Tomorrow?" she pressed.

"Don't we move on tomorrow? We'll both be leading animals tomorrow. We'll have no time to stop and gather herbs and talk."

Kari grinned knowingly, looking girlish and less strange. "Oh, we may. One never knows." Taking wood from the pile Lasse had brought, she built up her fire, and began preparing food. The savory smell as the meat simmered in the pot made Tillu aware of her hunger. She came out of the shelter, stretched, and suddenly felt every pang of the day's long hike.

"Here we are!" Lasse strode into the firelight, pleased at having accomplished his task.

"You were long in coming," Kari observed coolly.

"They had stopped on the riverbank, to fish!" Lasse's voice was between annoyance that they had been hard to find and wonder that they would do such a thing.

"See what we caught! Carp said they'd be there, under the bank behind the roots! And they were. See, Tillu."

The char shone silver in Kerlew's hands, fat and slippery. They flopped from his grasp onto the grass. Kari eyed them with approval.

"Gut and spit them, Lasse, and we'll grill them over the coals," she ordered calmly, never doubting that fish and boy were hers to command. Lasse moved meekly to her directions. Tillu and Heckram both stared after him as he took the fish to one side. When they lifted their eyes, their gazes met, sharing amusement and sympathy for the boy. Then Heckram's eyes warmed to something else. Tillu turned from him hastily, to watch Kerlew wiping his slimy hands on the grass.

"Did you behave today?" she asked him automatically.

"Yes." He didn't seem to feel any need to enlarge on his answer. His deep eyes were guileless as they stared up into hers. She wanted to ask how his day had been, if he had missed her, what Carp had taught him. But she could not in front of all these people. She had been stupid not to put up her own shelter. She would have no time alone with her son tonight, or tomorrow. Deep frustration edged with loneliness overtook her. She was severed from Kerlew, blocked by the layers of people around her. And to have Heckram so near strained her resolution. Every time he caught her eyes, her skin tightened. She had not found a way to let him know that she had changed her mind. He was looking at her again, his brows lifted slightly. The fuzzy beginnings of a beard softened his jawline. She stared at it, wondering if he had known she would find it attractive. Then she asked herself why she imagined he would even think about such things. Did she fancy she was the only woman he might consider bedding? Did she imagine he slept alone each night as she did? The thoughts stung her. She turned aside, avoiding him. Kari was directing Lasse as he cleaned the fish. His eyes were bright with her attention, and neither seemed to mind Kerlew crouching nearby and sorting curiously through the entrails. Tillu dropped to one knee, to crawl into the shelter and rest until the food was ready. Perhaps it would ease her aching muscles.

But Carp was already there, lying on the skins as if he were lord of all. His mouth hung ajar and the light from the fire revealed an occasional tooth behind his slack lips. It reflected off his grayed eyes like a sunset in a scummy pond. He nodded at her, his mouth widening. His hand gestured her in. Tillu drew back, stood again. Until she had met the herdfolk, she had never known how to describe Carp's smell. But now she knew he smelled just like a wet dog. It did not make him any dearer to her.

The evening was cooling the land; moisture was settling to the ground. The cooking food gave off a marvelous aroma, making her dizzy with hunger. She put one hand against the rough side of the boulder that backed the shelter, and then, without thinking, began to walk around the boulder, away from the firelight and the murmur of Lasse and Kari. The soft lichen on the stone was warm with the day's heat, like a man's rough beard against her skin. She leaned back against it, looking out over the lake and wide valley below her.

The small fires of the herdfolk blossomed like white wildflowers on the shore. Their tents were an unevenness in the dark. The people and dogs were moving shadows that passed before the fires. Beyond them, the lake was a shining blackness, and in the deepest part the moon and stars shone. Tillu felt dizzy looking at the sky at her feet. She lifted her eyes and looked beyond it, and realized for the first time how far they had come in one day. Kari had said they would travel for ten days. Where would they be then?

Far behind her were the mountains that were the winter grounds of the herdfolk. Before her was the wide lake that tomorrow the herd would skirt. And beyond it, beyond the last dwarfed trees and bushes, rolled the tundra. It was featureless in the darkness, and it was hard to tell where the lake left off and the tundra began. She had heard of the tundra, in legends of Benu's tribe, but she had never walked upon its wide flat face. A nameless dread of such a barren place rose in her, followed by a more pragmatic fear. In such a place, where would she gather willow and alder barks, birch cones to burn for a congested head, birch roots to boil down for cough syrup, willow roots for colic medicine, and a thousand other remedies that came from the tall trees of the hills and mountain valleys? A feeling akin to panic rose in her, to be replaced by resolve. Tomorrow she must be free to gather as the herd moved along the forested edge of the lake. She must have her supplies before they left it for the barren vast lands to the north.

She felt more than heard the step of the man who approached her from the darkness. Had Heckram followed her, mistaking her leaving the fire for an invitation? Dread of the confrontation rose in her, even as her body betrayed her with a tingle of excitement. She turned to him in the darkness, taking a deep breath to speak. She gasped in surprise instead as hard hands gripped her shoulders and shook her.

"Where have you been?" he demanded gruffly. She pushed away from him, but he seized her wrist in a grip that numbed her hand. Joboam shoved his face close to hers.

"Capiam tells me to watch over you and see that you are cared for. When I tell you to follow, you wander off, so when he comes to my fire to speak to you, I must say I do not know where you are. I lose his confidence. The healer, the najd, and her idiot boy, all are vanished. Capiam thinks you have changed your mind and left us, that the herd will face another summer without a healer. He asks me if I have offended you. Me! And I must leave my fire and my food and come seeking you, going from tent to tent, fire to fire, like a fool, asking if any have seen you!"

Fury tightened his relentless grip on her wrist, and when she pulled at his fingers with her free hand, he captured it, holding both her hands in one of his as he spoke. He made the differences in their sizes obvious by drawing her hands up high. She stood on tiptoe trying to ease the pull, feeling she couldn't breathe, made speechless by fear as much as by pain. Joboam's eyes glittered in the dark. Her aching muscles screamed with the stress of being stretched up.

"Kari . . . invited me . . . to stay with her. . . ," she gasped the words. The man was huge. She stifled the fury that rose in her, the desire to kick and scream and fight. As well take on a bear. If this was all he was going to do, she could stand it. She had endured worse from men just like him and survived. But if she screamed and Kerlew came, if he turned his anger on him—

"Kari?" There was puzzlement in his voice, and a sudden easing in the strain on her arms. Tillu took a gasp of air.

"Yes. Kari. She . . ."

"Get the boy and your things. And the two harkar. Thank Kari, but say you must join me now, so that her father will know I am doing my duty. Do it now." His voice was an odd mixture of emotions. There was the anger still, and the hard pleasure he took in domination, but a discordant note of uneasiness as well.

He released her wrists abruptly and Tillu almost cried aloud at the relief. She could not keep from rubbing at them, even though she knew he took satisfaction in it. Which was more dangerous for her, to go with him as he commanded, submit to his control, or to defy him and stay with Kari, keep herself and Kerlew out of his reach? She wished she knew. The night was full dark around her, and all choices equally black.

She turned away from him and headed for Kari's fire. Her heart pounded still, and the night seemed to tilt around her as the uneven turf rose to trip her. She put out a hand to catch herself. But big hands caught her and set her on her feet. She found herself gripping the front of Heckram's tunic. He didn't make a sound. He stared at Joboam over her head. She felt the tension in his wide chest, the catch in his breath, smelled the anger that rose in him. This time she would not be able to stop them from fighting.

Kari swooped past them in the darkness, flying into Joboam's path. He recoiled from her and when she spread her arms wide, he retreated a step. She hung before him like a hide stretched to dry, her garments as black as the night, her face more pale than the moon's. A light wind stirred her flapping garments, ruffled her black hair. Even Tillu found herself swallowing dryly at the sight. Heckram's hands on her shoulders tightened. He moved to step forward, and she found herself clutching at his chest, holding him back. A killing energy coursed through him.

For a long succession of moments, Kari swayed before Joboam. He stood his ground, his fists knotted, his gaze fastened on her face in unnamable dread. With a hissing sigh, she finally lowered her arms. It seemed impossible for her to be so suddenly small. But Joboam made no move to push her aside or step around her. She transfixed him.

"Tell my father," she said, her voice ringing in the night, "that Tillu the healer takes her meal with me. That I have extended the hospitality of his family. And that Tillu shall be with me all day tomorrow as well, for I am to help her gather herbs for healing. Tell him you found her comfortable and well, and did not wish to disturb her. Do you understand?"

There was a subtle lash to her words. She threatened him just as surely as he had threatened Tillu a moment ago. But Kari did not use physical dominance to cow him. There was something else she wielded, something more than her fey appearance and strangely powerful presence. Tillu wondered what it was, and how long it would be before the girl overplayed it and lost. For though Joboam backed wordlessly away from her, he did not hide the hatred in his eyes. He lifted the look as he moved, and before he turned it included Heckram and Tillu. Tillu shivered in its impact and Heckram pulled her closer. The gesture was the final infuriation for Joboam. He made a sound of hate and determination and vanished into the darkness.

For a long moment no one spoke. Then Kari drifted past them, letting her fingers trail lightly across Tillu's back. "The fish is done," she said, and left them.

Tillu felt suddenly the ache of her fingers clenched in

the leather of Heckram's tunic. She loosened her fingers, but he still held her close against him. The smell of him, sweat and leather and the reindeer, filled her nostrils. The maleness of it weakened her knees. His tunic was only loosely laced; the thongs pressed against her cheek, and she felt the prickle of the hair on his chest. His big hands moved slowly down her back, pressing her to him and easing the ache of her muscles with their warm touch. She felt numbed to everything but his touch and the sudden safety it meant. She felt her breasts respond to his body warmth and pressure, the nipples tightening with a pleasurable ache. His breath was warm against the top of her head; his lips pressed her hair as his hands gently kneaded the flesh of her back. A moment more, she told herself, and then I shall have to push him away, have to tell him I do not want this. But as she formed the lie he sighed heavily and gently eased away from her. "The others are waiting for us," he said, his soft voice like far thunder in his chest. "And you must be hungry and tired."

She found she could not move. She knew that if he pushed her down onto the earth and took her, she would not resist him. She almost wished he would, that he would master and mount her and take his pleasure of her, so that she could break free of his fascination. He was a man, like any other. This brief play of gentleness was a sham, a trick of human males to lure women closer, like the bright plumage of a male bird. It meant nothing. It lasted but a moment, a prelude to the rut. And afterward, he would either avoid her because of her strange son, or take her as casually as he warmed himself at her fire. She waited, knowing what would happen. She would be glad when he betrayed himself, when she could see him clearly again and know him as the man who had sent Elsa into the death-sleep.

"Tillu," he said slowly. She felt his breath on her hair. "You're shaking. But you don't have to be afraid. He doesn't dare hurt you. Come. You need food and rest." And then he carefully stepped away from her, to take her hand and lead her back to Kari's fire.

*   *   *

He had only meant to help her to her feet, but her touch
and nearness had made him want her with a fierce heat.
His hands had been on her and her musky fragrance had
drowned his senses. He had wanted to smooth Joboam's
rough touch from her body. This woman was strong as a
good bow was strong, with resilience and stamina. In an
instinctive reaction to her silent courage, he had wanted to
mate her. A woman like her would not be a responsibility,
but a partner. He had gathered her close, forgetting that
she might not feel as he did. Then he had felt her stiffen,
become aware of her stillness in his arms. Now, as he
groped his way around the boulder, he cursed himself for a
blundering fool, and worse. What was wrong with him?
Couldn't he be around this woman for a moment without
behaving like a sarva in rut? Her hand was quiet in his, she
had leaned against him like a wooden thing. He knew he
had frightened her just as badly as Joboam had, and in
much the same way. Twice now, this gentle healer had
seen him on the edge of violence. Twice he had caressed
her, with lust, without her invitation. No wonder then, that
she shook when he touched her. She still knew little of the
herdfolk. His behavior would make her think the men little
more than savages.

He glanced back at her as they approached the fire. She
looked away, and his heart smote him again. He tried to
find a way through his tangled emotions. He should be
mourning Elsa still, not feeling wild lust for this woman.
Yet it was not just lust. Lust would have been simpler to
face, easier to handle than what this woman stirred in him.
Since that day in her tent, he had awakened to her. He still
suspected she had eased Elsa into death. How else would
the stricken woman have reached the sleeping tea and
drunk too much of it? Who besides Tillu and he had known
of the tea and its potency? But he could not fit that thought
with his other feelings about her. Something about her,
and Kerlew, made him want to protect them, to give them
shelter and food and an easier life. He did not understand
the feeling, had never experienced it before. When he had

seen Joboam's rough hands on her tonight, he had wanted to kill the man. To kill like an animal, to rend him like a wolf fighting for its mate. But he was not an animal, and Tillu was not his.

And now she would not even look at him. He released her hand, felt her whisk it from his grasp as his fingers loosened. Well, and how did he expect her to react? A herdwoman would have struck him for his crude advances. A resolve hardened in him as she walked past him to the fire. He would find a way to prove himself to her. He would show her that herdmen were not savages, but knew how to be patient and await a woman's attention. The resolve settled solidly in his mind. He took a deep breath. His life, which had seemed so still within him since Elsa's death, suddenly warmed his veins.

chapter four

TILLU AWOKE WITH her mind still filled with last night's events. They had all eaten, consuming the flaky hunks of juicy fish and the soup that Kari had made earlier. Lasse had reluctantly departed for his own shelter, after Kari had instructed him to return in the morning to take charge of her harkar and the ones carrying the healer's belongings. The others had slept sprawled in careless proximity on the hides within the skin shelter. Kerlew had curled up between Carp and Heckram. Tillu had slept beside the boulder's flank at the shelter's back, easing her aching body with its stored warmth. She had been aware of Heckram, scarce an arm's length away, and glad when Kerlew engaged him in a sleepy conversation for it kept his face turned away from her. Kari had been sitting by the fire, humming softly to herself, when Tillu dozed off. And she had risen first to put on tea and stir the remainder of the fish into a soup. Tillu had opened her heavy eyes to find Kari crouched before her, offering her a hot mug of tea.

The others slept on. In his sleep, Heckram had turned toward her. His cheek was cradled on the crook of his arm and a tousle of hair hung over his forehead. His lips were parted as he slept, and his brow was smooth. At rest his face was youthful, the lines of his smile deeper than the lines that crossed his brow. Tillu tried to look at him impassively. She wondered if any woman could remain impervious to a man who cared for her child.

The solitude of the early morning drew her. She rose,

whispering thanks to Kari, who nodded mutely. She sipped
the tea as she crouched by the reawakened fire, then rose
and left the camp. She needed a few moments alone. She
walked, pushing her aching legs to carry her up the hill.
The twiggy blueberry bushes scratched her legs and soaked
her feet with dew. She paused in a mossy area to look
down at the lake. Streamers and tendrils of mist rose from
it. The grass and moss sparkled with dew. Tillu ran her
hands over the sward and then wiped the chill moisture
over her stiff face. It dispelled the last of her sleepiness,
and she turned back. The awakening sounds of the camp
below reached her ears. She heard a single laugh, and
children calling merrily to one another. She sighed. She
still ached from yesterday's walking, and today's would be
just as wearying. She forced herself to hurry.

Lasse had already arrived. His face was scrubbed, his
eyes as bright as a squirrel's. Tillu stood uphill of the
camp, watching, as Kari poured a mug of tea for him. He
took it from her awkwardly, managing to catch one of her
hands between the mug and his hand. For a long moment
Kari stood very still, looking only at the mug and their two
hands. Lasse stood breathlessly silent, too shy to smile,
looking down on the dark head bent before him. But just
as Tillu believed that a girl's heart beat beneath the owl
claws on her breasts, Kari jerked her hand free, careless of
the scalding tea that sloshed them both. Kari moved away
swiftly, stooping to stir the fish stew. Lasse shifted the
mug to his free hand and shook the hot tea from his
fingers. Neither one of them had made a sound, and now
he gazed after her, looking neither puzzled nor rebuffed,
but pleased.

"Like trying to tame a wild bird," Heckram said softly
behind her. "He has to be content with his small victories,
for now."

Tillu had started at the deep rumble of his voice so
close behind her. Now she stared up at him, embarrassed
to be caught spying on the two and more embarrassed at
confronting him by daylight. His beard was more than
stubble now, the hair growing in more bronze than that on

his head. She wanted to stroke it, to see if it were rough or
soft. She was staring. She tried to keep her voice steady,
her comment casual. "It must demand a great deal of
patience. I suspect that if he tried to move too fast, she'd
reject him completely."

"Probably," Heckram agreed blandly. He lifted a slow
hand to her face. Just as she moved to avoid his touch, he
plucked a strand of dried grass from her hair. He flicked it
away and stood looking down on her. "Herdmen learn
patience at an early age." He looked out over the lake as
he held out a hand toward her. For a long moment it
hovered empty in the air between them. Then Tillu put
hers into it, watched her small fingers wrapped and covered by his large ones. He lifted his other hand to point.
"There's our herd, already moving. Look at the way
patches of white flicker through it and then all is grayish-
brown again. All the little white tails flashing. And beyond
it, like a brown shadow moving over the earth? That's the
wild herd. They'll be far ahead of us before this day's out.
We may not catch sight of them again until we reach the
Cataclysm."

His hand was dry and warm. His voice was deep, and
he spoke so softly she had to strain to hear. He moved his
eyes to look at her. On the hillside behind them, a bird
called, its note high and clear in the morning air. She
wanted to smile at him, but could not. She looked down,
feeling foolish.

"We'd better go down and eat, or there won't be anything left. And there's a long walk ahead of us today."

She nodded silently. He closed his fingers on hers,
holding them firmly a moment before releasing her. They
walked down the hill to the camp, not touching, but
together.

All the others were stirring now. Kerlew had taken food
for himself and Carp into the shelter. He crouched by the
shaman, eating and nodding to Carp. He did not look up as
Tillu returned. She wanted to call him to her side, to make
him talk to her, but could think of no excuse for it. She
greeted Lasse and thanked Kari when she scooped out a

serving of fish stew for her. It tasted too strong in the light air of morning, but she ate it anyway. She looked up once from her food, her eyes seeking Heckram, but he sat, bowl in hand, staring into the shelter. His brows were drawn together and his eyes were grave as he watched Kerlew rocking with laughter at something Carp had said. An emotion very like envy washed across his face. In an instant it was gone, and he dipped his head to sip from his bowl again.

The time for rest was suddenly over. Pots were scrubbed out with a wad of grass and packed again onto the patient harkar. The shelter hides were rolled and tied. The harkar were led off down the hillside to be added to Lasse's string.

"I'd best go see to my beasts," Heckram admitted with a suddenly guilty look. "I left them with Ristin last night. She'll have words for me, for having to unload and picket them for me." He addressed the words to all, but Tillu had the foolish notion that he spoke to her. He looked at Kerlew and asked carefully, "Are you going with me today, Kerlew, or with your mother?"

"Where's Carp going to be?" Kerlew asked immediately.

To Carp, there was no question. "Come, apprentice, and carry our things. I will ride with Heckram, and you will walk alongside." The old man stood slowly, and Tillu saw his stiffness. She could make a salve for it; the dampness of the spring nights probably made mornings a torment for him. But . . .

She wavered in ambivalence. The najd was good to the boy, kind and attentive to him. But he was stealing her son from her, putting his feet on a narrow, dangerous path. Tillu watched them walk away down the hillside, taking comfort that Heckram at least would be close to Kerlew today. But as she noticed three other boys of Kerlew's age peering from some bushes at them, her heart sank. What did the other children think of this boy who walked always beside the najd, who did not run and play with them, but talked dreamy-eyed to an old man who rode a harke like a baby?

She was startled from her dark mood by Kari's hand on her arm. "And now you will teach me?" she asked. Her eyes were bright. She had a basket on her arm, and she offered a shoulder pouch to Tillu. Good thing one of them had remembered such necessities. Tillu touched the knife at her belt, and Kari held up hers to show she was prepared. "First, we need to make digging sticks," Tillu told her, and was rewarded with a joyous smile. Her heart lifted inspite of herself.

The day reminded Tillu of the days when she and her aunt had gathered herbs and roots together. But this time it was Tillu who pointed and explained, and Kari who rubbed the roots clean on the grass and stowed them in her basket. Yet Tillu did not feel like a mother or aunt, but more girlish than she had felt in her childhood. She tried to worry about Kerlew, but found herself remembering that he was safe with Heckram. Then her mind would wander to the way the early sunlight glinted on Heckram's new beard, and his smile slowly dawned on his solemn face. A curious anticipation touched all her thoughts of him. Spring, she told herself firmly. Sap was running in the trees, and her blood was racing through her veins. A good tonic would take these imaginings away. But she gave no thought to concocting one.

Instead, they gathered the bark and roots of the birch for cough syrup and acne medicine. Strips of willow bark peeled easily from the trees leaving the slick white cambrium exposed. "Later, we will gather the leaves," Tillu instructed Kari. "Bound on a bleeding wound as a poultice, they stop the flow of blood. But for now we will take the bark, to make a tea for fever, or pound to a poultice for sores. Get a bit of root, too. I'll show you how to make a colic medicine from it."

Kari knelt on the forest debris to dig for the root. Tillu continued to peel bark from the branches in long ragged strips. Beyond a thin fringe of trees, the wide blue surface of the lake glinted. Behind them, they could hear the reindeer and folk on the traditional path. The folk did not hurry today. No one minded if a harke paused to nip new buds from a tree, or snatch up a mouthful of moss. Tolerance and good fellowship warmed the air with the spring sun. The adults had stripped back to sleeveless jerkins of light leather and short trousers or skirts. The children were all but naked, their skins soaking up the sun's warmth. Tillu folded her long strips of bark into a bundle and stuffed them into the shoulder pouch. Already it bulged gratifyingly. They would have to hurry ahead to Lasse and change this pouch for an empty one.

Kari shook the clinging soil from the network of roots. Willow roots were tough, and she had had to use her knife to get this chunk loose. She wadded up the tangle of roots and stuffed it into her basket. She smiled up at Tillu. Dirt smudged the side of her nose and the look of distance and mystery had left her eyes. Her face was shining as she said, "You meant it, then. I thought perhaps you only needed me to help with the gathering. But you will really teach me the healing herbs." She reached into the hole and dragged up another hank of willow root.

"Of course I will." A reckless enjoyment of companionship settled on Tillu. "If Carp is to have an apprentice, I see no reason why I shouldn't."

Kari dropped the root she was cleaning, and reached up to seize Tillu's hands in a pinching grip. Startled, Tillu tried to pull free, but Kari did not release her. Her black eyes were wide and shining. "This is true? You are not making a joke of me? You would take me as your apprentice?"

"If it is what you wish," Tillu replied, confused by her intensity. The young woman let go of Tillu's hands and sank slowly back on her heels.

"Ah!" she sighed slowly with quiet satisfaction. "We shall see what my father can say to me about marriage when I tell him this. We shall see." Then, suddenly grabbing at Tillu's sleeve again, she added urgently, "But not yet! We shall not tell him until we are closer to the Cataclysm. Not until after you have begun to teach me."

Tillu did not understand Kari's fierceness. "Yes. All right, I shall not tell anyone that you are my apprentice, until you wish to tell them. But as for teaching you, well, we have begun that already." Stooping, Tillu took up the cleaned root and put it back into her apprentice's hands.

Kari looked down on it. When she spoke again, her voice was thoughtful. "It is what you know, Tillu, that lets you be as free as you are. A woman with no man to bind her, no one to fill her with children and weight down her days." She glanced up suddenly, her bird-bright eyes pinning Tillu's. "Was that why you became a healer? To be rid of men?"

"No." The question puzzled Tillu. "I became a healer because it was what the women of my family knew and did. Just as my father tended animals and crops." She sighed softly. "I never, as a child, imagined I would live so often alone."

"Then take a man." Kari's voice was as careless as if Tillu had spoken of fashioning a new garment for herself. "Heckram would have you, if you let him."

"Heckram . . ." Tillu hesitated. "I know so little of him, Kari. And I wonder so many things. . . ."

"He is a good hunter," Kari told her, as if that were all of a man's worth. "And a generous man. Even with Elsa, for whom he felt only friendship. When she asked his protection, he gave it to her, and the gifts of joining as well."

Tillu was silent, staring at her, praying she would go on. Kari smiled slowly. "I hear many things, when folk come to gossip with the herdlord and his wife. And Elsa, too, was not shy of speaking to me. She was as close to a friend as I have ever had . . . and we shared at least one thing. We both wished to be rid of Joboam."

Kari rose slowly and began to drift after the moving line of reindeer and folk. Her voice was soft, and Tillu hurried behind her, almost ashamed to be so anxious to hear her words.

"Some have said that Heckram only took Elsa to wife because Joboam wanted her. It is not secret that those two hate one another. So many have said in the herdlord's tent, saying it was a shame Elsa was given to one who loved her with friendship but not with passion. Some say Joboam would have cared more for her, kept her within and safe. . . ."

"And what do you say?" Tillu prodded gently.

Kari turned bottomless eyes back to her, stared through her as the girl continued walking. "I say that Elsa knew more happiness in her short months with Heckram than Joboam would have given her in a lifetime. Heckram showed no lack of concern. Elsa but went to the spring at night, to draw water, such as any herdswoman might do. It is not Heckram's shame that she was not safe there. Whatever attacked and killed her within her own talvsit is the shame of all the herdfolk!"

Her words were suddenly fierce. She rounded on Tillu, madness in her eyes, coming so close to her as she spoke that her breath was hot on Tillu's face. "It is not right that any herdfolk should fear to walk by night. The world, both day and night, is given to all of us. Why should one exist who can say, 'Beware, Elsa, the night is death'?"

"No. It isn't right." Tillu put calming hands on Kari's shoulders. The girl steadied under her touch. The wild shaking passed. "What did you see?" Tillu asked gently, sure of her suspicion.

"I?" Kari gave a shaky laugh. "I saw nothing. I was within that night, inside my father's tent. But Owl saw, and he knows, and what he knows, I know." She pulled suddenly free of Tillu's hands. "Take Heckram, Tillu. You could heal him, could purge him of the worm that gnaws at his soul. He looks to you to save him."

It was Tillu's turn to pull back. She shied from the idea, throwing out words to turn Kari's mind from the thought. "And you, Kari? Have you never seen how Lasse looks at you?"

"Lasse?" Kari's voice set suddenly, her face going hard. "Lasse is a child. He has no idea what he wants, but I do. And soon I will tell him. He wants a girl who plays yet in front of her mother's tent, a pretty little thing with wide eyes and easy laughter. A girl who will come to him like a calf sipping clear water for the first time, with wonder and surprise at the goodness of it. That is what he wants . . . what he deserves. . . .'' Her voice had gone softer and softer as she spoke. Now she suddenly lifted her head. ''Foolish talk! We had best hurry, Tillu, if we are to exchange our full baskets for empty ones.'' She turned suddenly and began to hurry up the line.

> chapter
five

THE DAYS FELL into a pattern both restful and ennervating. Tillu awoke with interest to each dawn, and lay down at night in weary peace. Animals and folk left the lakeside and its brushy banks and emerged onto the wide flats of the tundra. She and Kari gathered herbs and roots by day, and Kari learned the uses for each. Then came the sweet evenings when the folk halted and campfires were kindled and sleeping skins spread on the ground. Heckram's shelter was never far away. Kerlew migrated in happy circles from the fire Carp shared with Heckram to the one Kari shared with his mother.

Yet she saw less of her son than ever before in their lives. She felt her guilt as an uneasiness, a sense of a task uncompleted. Hidden from herself was the relief she felt at being freed from his constant presence. Tillu began to live a separate life of her own. If Kerlew felt neglected or missed her, he did not show it. The boy was more confident than she had ever seen him. But for his dragging speech, and the strange topics he chose, he might have been a normal boy. His circle of tolerant adults was larger than it had ever been, and his status as Carp's apprentice gained him a small measure of acceptance by the other children. They did not play with him, but they did not taunt or beat him either. Another boy might have felt his isolation as loneliness. Kerlew only felt relief. He moved through the camp without fear of thrown stones and blows. He seemed unaware of the children who ceased their noisy games to watch his passage with widened eyes.

There was an interlude Tillu was to long remember. She was returning from one of the tundra's myriad ponds with water for the evening's cooking. Carp must have been napping somewhere, for she spotted Kerlew alone, atop one of the worn gray boulders that dotted the tundra. He was stretched out on his back on the hard warm surface. Over his face his slack wristed hand held a ranunculus. He was twirling it by its stem, watching the bright petals spiral. His lips smiled foolishly and from his throat came a sound like the happy grunting of a suckling babe.

A few strides away three boys crouched behind a screen of brush and watched him. The grins on their mocking faces were hard and sharp as knives. Their giggling was muffled behind dirty brown hands. Two years ago, Tillu thought to herself, I would have rushed forward, jerked Kerlew to his feet and scolded him. I would have chased the other boys off to their mothers. She blinked her eyes, wondering what had changed, her boy or the way she regarded him. She walked on, water spilling in bright drops from the clay-and-moss-calked wooden buckets she carried.

In the evenings folk came to Tillu, for a salve for a blistered heel or a rub for a wrenched knee. Her healings were seldom more complicated than that. The herdfolk were a stout and healthy people, given to little worry about minor ailments. The runny noses of the bright-eyed children were ignored, as accepted as their ruddy wind-chafed cheeks and the bumps and scratches from their tumbling play. The work did not tire Tillu; she took pleasure in the chance to better know the folk she had joined. Of Capiam she saw nothing. He seemed content to trust her to perform her own tasks, or perhaps he was too busy to be bothered with her. Several times Joboam brought meat to her, the portion allotted to Tillu by the herdlord. He spoke little but the few words he said sounded both superior and threatening. The tension Tillu felt in his presence did not abate; it was like a slowly swelling abcess that must eventually be lanced or burst of its own pressure.

At those times she took comfort from Heckram's nearness. Whenever Joboam came to Kari's fire, Heckram, too, appeared. His errand was always an innocent one; to borrow some grease for a harness strap, or to ask the loan of a larger cook pot. He did not confront Joboam, but his very presence seemed to restrain the other man. But as soon as Joboam left, Heckram did also. He smiled at her, he was courteous, but he never lingered for a word with her, nor tried to be alone with her. Tillu could not understand the man. At first she tried to believe that it was the public nature of the caravan. The clustered tents and flat tundra offered no quiet rendezvous, even if the two could have eluded Carp, Kerlew, and Kari. But she noticed other couples left the arrotak, to "fetch water" or "hunt eggs." Yet Heckram never invited her on such an errand. If he had decided to reject her because of her son, why did he still offer Kerlew shelter and food? Because of Carp? She did not understand, but as the days marched past she persuaded herself she did not care. He was a man, like any other man. Her body had wanted a man, that was all that was between them. But that did not explain why she could not interest herself in the other men in the caravan, nor why it was his image that lingered in her mind in the twilight.

The one variance in their lives was the changing land they crossed. It became increasingly unfamiliar to Tillu, but the others accepted the wide emptiness of the sky as natural. The foothills dwindled behind them, leaving the world a flat and daunting place. The horizon moved away to an unattainable distance. The sun's warmth thawed the top few inches of the tundra, but couldn't reach the permanently frozen soil beneath it. Water did not soak into the earth, but stretched in wide flat ponds and pools, or flowed lazily across the near flat surfaces. The thawing earth and running water brought burgeoning life. Birds appeared, ones Tillu had never seen before, and in an abundance she had never imagined. They settled in the wildly sprouting grasses, and mated and fought and made hasty nests on the earth. Their muttered conversations filled the dusky evenings, and their cries of challenge and courtship filled the days. Eggs were added to the herdfolk's diet.

Plant life sprouted in a bewildering array, familiar plants in dauntingly unfamiliar shapes. But willow ossier, Tillu found, for all its dwarfed and twisted shape, had the same properties as willow. And fireweed greens were as tender whether they stood tall and slender, or writhed flat across the earth.

Not in weeks, but in days the colors of the tundra ripened and deepened, here brown and gold, there purple and mauve, there a green of unbelievable intensity. Even the coldest stone was coated with lichen of white or yellow or dun, while the mosses bloomed frantically in their haste to rise, live and reproduce before winter returned. Heather vied with butterwort, the bells of linnaea rang in contrast to the daisies of arnica. Tiny blue forget-me-nots were trodden underfoot, while cloudberry and tangles of arctic raspberry promised later bounty. Everywhere there were new plants to be crushed and sniffed and tested against the tip of her tongue for healing virtues.

Kari proved an able assistant, and was full of questions. She did not yet help Tillu with the healing, but her bright black eyes took in every detail of mixing and application. After the salved or bandaged folk were gone, Kari would question her: why this herb and not that one? Why a salve and not a tonic? Why had she lanced that abcess, but put a poultice on the one she had seen two days ago? The girl's mind was quick and retentive, her questions betraying an intellect seldom used. But the wildness never faded completely from her eyes, nor the strangeness from her movements. Her interest could shy suddenly from a pragmatic discussion of bandaging material to her latest dream of Owl. She was so like, and yet unlike, Kerlew.

Kerlew she watched from afar. He was changing in ways she could not understand or control. He was learning and growing, and, she grudgingly admitted, discovering himself as a person apart from her. She watched his relationship with Heckram, and finally accepted that Heckram's affection for Kerlew was not feigned. He always had time for the boy. Tillu watched from Kari's fire as Kerlew shifted between Carp and Heckram, testing the reality of one man against that of the other. He shadowed Heckram at the evening chores, eventually carrying one of the water scoops, and even helping prepare the meals, despite Carp's scornful derision of men doing "women's work." He ate at Carp's side, receiving whispered instruction about the spirit world. An hour later he would be at Heckram's elbow, watching him mend worn harness or holding the ends as Heckram braided a new leadrope from long, thin slices of leather. She sensed the struggle in him. She longed to help him but during those rare moments when he sought her out, she refrained from advice. Pushed, Kerlew would resist. She hoped he would eventually find Heckram's attraction the more powerful one.

Yesterday Kerlew had come to her, bringing his shirt to be mended. He had torn out both shoulder seams. She had measured the worn garment against him, and found that the fault was not in her sewing, but in the boy's sudden growth. She had given it back to him, minus the sleeves, to wear while she pieced out a new shirt for him. For a quiet time he had crouched beside her, watching her select leather for the shirt. She decided to make it from the calf-hide, now scraped and supple ivory-colored leather. Drawing her knife, she cut out the needed pieces quickly. She styled it after the herdfolk's way, a collarless, loose-fitting garment that could be belted at the waist and worn alone, or over leggings. She had held the leather against him, swiftly marking the length of tunic and sleeves he would need. He moved docilely to her commands, holding out his arms obediently as she checked the cut pieces against him. Then Kerlew had crouched beside her, watching intently as his new shirt took form. With a sigh he leaned against her, and the heavy warmth of his small body was so poignantly familiar that Tillu's throat closed. She turned her eyes away from her stitching, to watch the light of the fire make hollows and curves of his face. He was losing the rounded chin of a little boy, his cheeks narrowing and flattening as he grew. The firelight gave his skin a sallow cast, and suddenly she saw the faces of the race that had fathered him, the black-haired, hard-eyed men that had killed her mother and carried her away from her home. Fierceness washed through her, and she cried out aloud as her bone needle plowed a long gash in one of her fingers. She jerked the needle free of her flesh, and the blood followed it, rushing from the gouge and staining her work.

Dropping the needle, she thrust her injured finger into her mouth. This was what came of not keeping her mind on her work. Kerlew never flinched at her cry; his dark eyes fixed on her face. She looked at him questioningly. He put a fingertip to the wet blood on his new shirt, and then casually raised it to his mouth to lick it away. "Spilled blood," he said softly. The shadows of ghosts danced over his features. "The stain never comes out entirely. Somewhere it shows." Then he had risen, without another word, to seek Heckram's fire and Carp's company. The words had chilled her.

The next night she sat again by Kari's fire, scraping at the stain with a scrubbing stone. Bits of leather rolled away before her efforts, but the blood had soaked through. It would not be taken out by anything Tillu might do. With a sigh she gave it up, and set to work on the final seam. From time to time, she glanced up from her sewing, wondering where Kerlew was. This was the first time Heckram's shelter was not near Kari's, and she wondered at that as well.

Kari crouched on the other side of the fire. Her eyes were half-lidded, and Tillu could not tell if she drowsed or stared. The day had been a long one and the whole camp was unusually quiet. When Lasse stepped into the circle of their firelight, Tillu started, but Kari only raised her eyes slowly. "What do you want?" Kari asked with heartless disdain. But Lasse had not come courting her and he did not flinch. His eyes jumped from Kari to Tillu and back again.

"Heckram just came into camp," he said slowly.

Tillu glanced up, and anxiety ran cold through her belly. "What kept him?" she demanded. She wadded up the shirt and set it aside as she reached for her healer's supplies. Her mind leapt to her own conclusion. "Who's hurt?"

Lasse looked straight at her, and then past her, to peer into the darkened shelter. He cleared his throat. "Not Heckram. Only a harke. It started to stagger earlier today, and Heckram had to put its load on the other harkar, so Carp had to walk. It slowed Heckram's whole rajd and angered the najd. Carp sent Kerlew forward to find you, to ask you to come and purge the sick reindeer. He thought that would cure the beast." The youth raised his eyes to meet Tillu's and asked, "Is Kerlew here?"

Tillu couldn't answer. Her hand gripped her herb pouch too tightly, bending her nails against its leather. The night grew darker and closer, pressing against the small fire. She realized how little she could see beyond the fire's circle. The moon was a sliver of light in the far sky. The warmth of the day was already fleeing the earth, seeping away into the empty sky. The night would be cold, and black. Alone, in the darkness, in this wide flat place, this tundra, where every stretch of land looked like every other piece, where the horizon didn't change and every pool they passed looked just like the last one. Kerlew.

Emotions raged through her: Anger with Carp for sending the boy to find her, and with Heckram for letting him go. Fury with herself, for trusting the boy to strangers. Kerlew was her son, she should have kept him by her, she should have killed the old shaman before letting her son become so attached to him. How had she let herself forget that she was a mother before all other things, before healer or friend or woman? Where was her son now? Walking blindly in the dark, stumbling on, calling for her? Or was he crouched somewhere, huddled against the night's chill, stubbornly waiting to be found? Had he been distracted from his errand by a shining flow of water, by a leaf spinning in a spider's web as the wind blew past? Did he even know he was lost or was he wondering why Carp had sent him on such a long walk?

Kari broke into her thoughts. "He's probably some-where in the camp, playing with the other children. No doubt he forgot his errand entirely, and won't remember it until he get hungry. Lasse, go and ask until you find him."

But this time her imperious command didn't move him. Lasse met her eyes steadily as he slowly said, "I already have. I knew Kerlew wasn't with you when I brought your harkar to you earlier this evening. So, before I came, I went to every family that has children his age. Some saw him pass, on his way to find Tillu, but no one spoke to him, or saw him leave the caravan. I was hoping that somehow he had reached the camp and found you since last I was here." Lasse's voice was husky. He folded his arms against his chest and hugged himself against the night's chill.

Tillu was empty. "He's gone," sang a small mocking voice in her mind. "You'll never see him again. He'll never lean against you, never need your protection, never annoy you again. You're free. No one will call you Mother, no one will shame you with this strangeness, no one, no one, nothing. He's gone, you'll never even find his body. The wolves that follow the reindeer will have him, or the cold will take him, or both. And haven't you always wondered what it was like to be alone this way, haven't you always secretly wished he'd die and leave you to live your own life? Didn't you wish him dead, isn't this all your fault, didn't you kill him when you entrusted him to strangers, didn't you always know this would happen if Carp had his way? Haven't you killed him just as surely as Heckram killed Elsa?

Over the maddening voice she heard her own voice, calm and grave, saying, "I have to go back and look for him."

"You'd never find him in the dark. You don't even know where to begin looking." Heckram's voice, coming from the darkness behind the fire. She hated him in that instant, hated his steady, reasonable words, hated the deep, resonating voice that uttered them. Then he stepped into the light and looked at her in dumb agony, and her hate died. She had no need to accuse him of the loss of her son. Heckram already accused himself.

"My father would never allow it anyway," Kari added morosely. "Twelve years ago, two families were separated from the herd. One of the women had a hard birth, and they decided to rest a few days. There were seven of them, it seemed there could be no danger. But they never caught up with us, nor reached the Cataclysm. No trace was ever found. Some say wicked spirits carried them away. No, Capiam never lets anyone stray from the herd once the migration is begun. It is his duty."

Tillu was scarcely aware of the girl's words. Her eyes searched Heckram's face. "How?" she faltered, and then, "Where?"

He looked away from her, moved forward to crouch by the fire. The soft light of the flames touched the hard angles of his face and body, turning him to a figure carved of stone and misery. "This morning. We hadn't traveled far . . . do you recall the big boulder with the red and yellow lichen over it, near the thicket of ossier? Not far from the third stream we crossed?"

He didn't look up to see Tillu's tense nod. Kari and Lasse had moved in closer, drawn by the low voice. Kari gripped one of Lasse's hands in both of hers, but seemed unaware of him. "It was there, by the boulder. One of the harke must have eaten something; it began to bloat, and then to stagger. It's not so unusual a thing to happen. If I had more harkar, it would have made no difference. But it was my largest reindeer, and carrying the heaviest load. I had to unload it. So, Carp had to walk, so that the other harkar wouldn't be overburdened. He began to mutter and complain. And we had to go slowly, for the sake of the sick beast. Carp seemed upset as the other folk passed us. He said we should send Kerlew to find you, and you could come and tend the sick animal. He thought you could purge it. Kerlew was anxious to go, and I didn't see anything wrong with the idea.''

His eyes pleaded with Tillu. "I didn't think he could get lost. All he had to do was follow the line of folk to where you were. He was so pleased to run ahead.''

She nodded slowly. She could imagine Kerlew, impatient with the slow pace, and perhaps grown a little bored of Carp's lectures. Had he wanted to show off for Heckram? Probably.

Kari broke silence. "But if he came forward, along the line of people, how could he get lost? Why didn't he find us?''

Heckram shook his head, and anger crept into his bafflement. "That's what I can't understand. If he was following the line of people, what could have happened to him?''

"Kerlew happens to himself," Tillu said softly. "Anything might have led him away from the caravan. He might have sat down to watch a bird and fallen asleep in the warm sun. Something as simple as that.''

"Where's Carp?'' Kari demanded suddenly. Irritation tinged her voice, as if there were questions she wanted answered.

Heckram's own voice was tinged with disgust. "He's by my mother's fire. Chanting. When I wanted to find Kerlew before we did anything else, he got angry. He said the boy had allies I could not imagine, and that only a fool would worry about him. That Kerlew was walking on paths I could not follow. Then he went to Ristin and demanded food and a place by her fire. He got it, but more from her graciousness than from his demanding. Now that he has eaten, he sits by the fire and chants to a rabbit.''

"A rabbit?'' Tillu was baffled.

"Earlier today he saw one of Kelr's boys playing with a rabbit he had caught. He called the boy and traded him a hunting charm for the rabbit. He wrapped the rabbit in a skin, like a baby. Now it's dead, but he keeps it. He laughed at me when I told him the meat would spoil. He said the sweetness of the meat would bring Kerlew back to him, and keep him safe ever after.''

Disgust filled Tillu's face. Lasse and Heckram looked uneasy and Kari seemed to retreat within herself. "We cannot hope to understand the way of the najd," she said softly. "We can only watch him and learn."

"I'd rather be out looking for Kerlew than watching him chant to a rabbit," Heckram said sourly.

A sudden slow throbbing sounded in the night. The sound of a drum carried far on the still air, reaching beyond the call of a voice. Tillu saw Heckram and Lasse exchange slow glances, and then look away as if fearful of sharing too much. No one spoke. The drum sounded on and on, beating with a raw monotony that scraped determinedly at Tillu's frayed control. She rose abruptly. "I'm going to see the herdlord," she announced. The others looked at her, and Kari nodded slowly.

The herdlord's tent was no mere stretching of hide over a pole or two. It was domed like a hut, and made of hides sewn together in a pattern. Even the earth outside it was coated with soft hides of black wolf, tanned with the lush fur on. The tents surrounding it were large but Capiam's was twice the size of the others. It squatted beneath the tundra's wide sky as if it had always been there. Smoke rose from its vent flap, and with it the smell of roasted meat and burned fat. A muttering of voices seeped from its snug walls, and then laughter. Tillu did not notice the sound, nor the lushness of the furs her dirty bare feet trod. She lifted the door flap and peered into the tent.

It boasted no less than four travel chests, each carved and painted with bright figures. One was decorated with bits of bronze and amber set into the polished wood. Brightly woven baskets were stacked about the interior walls; cheeses and tools hung from the pole-supports. The shelter smelled of reindeer and dog, smoke and sweat and heat. After the cool night air, it was stifling. Tillu stepped in.

The circle of men about the fire did not notice her at first. Capiam was turned away from her, listening to some low-voiced suggestion from Pirtsi. The boy hadn't been to Kari's fire since the migration began. So Kari's intended

husband courted her father, not her. Tillu wondered if
Capiam knew how little interest Pirtsi had in Kari. Or if he
cared. To Capiam's left were Acor and Ristor, one dozing
in the fire's heat, the other sucking on a marrow bone. A
woman's broad back was turned to Tillu, the framework of
her bones mantled by fat. Her black-haired head was bent
over some work in her lap, while beside her Rolke picked
chunks of flesh from a fish's bones and stuffed them into
his mouth. And beyond Rolke, closing Capiam's circle,
was Joboam. A smile widened his mouth but didn't extend
to the darkness of his eyes. And his eyes went darker still
when he lifted them to Tillu. He did not speak. It was
Rolke who followed his gaze, and spoke around a mouthful of fish.

"Father, it's the healer, come at last! I would think she
would have come sooner to make her courtesies!"

Pirtsi started to nod his agreement, then stopped when
Capiam's black eyes shot an arrow of reproach at his son.
But the herdlord smiled as he rose to greet her. "Come,
Healer, we are glad whenever you can find time to share
with us. I do not fault one who does not visit, not when
many have told me of her healing skill. I trust Kari has
been of some aid to you?"

Tillu found her courtesy. "Kari is a great help to me,
and could be a fine healer herself someday. But that is not
why I have come to you tonight."

The headman's smile had grown stiff as she spoke, and
then faded entirely at the grave tone of Tillu's voice.
"Well?" he prompted her.

"My son is missing. He left Heckram and Carp to come
and find me, and somehow strayed from the folk." Ketla
had turned to Tillu as she spoke. Her wide round face was
a mirror of concern as she tilted it up to Tillu. Her black
eyes were set deep in a face swollen with fat, but there
was no mistaking the genuine sympathy and concern that
shone in them. "The poor little lad! Alone, in the great
dark like that!" She turned to her husband. "Capiam,
surely we can send men back with torches. The little one
will see them and come to them. Send them out now!"

"Little one!" Joboam snorted before Capiam could speak. "You have a kind heart, Ketla, but the boy is ten or so, is he not, Tillu? Not some toddler. Leave him alone and he'll come into camp on his own. The trail is plain enough after our passage. No doubt he's but enjoying a little time on his own, as boys that age do. Has he a little sweetheart, perhaps?"

Tillu's voice was softly cold. "I am sure you are aware that he has no friends of any kind, Joboam. Nor is he as capable as one might expect a boy of ten to be."

Capiam's face was serious. "You don't think he would follow the trail? Or come to a torch?"

Tillu shrugged helplessly, at a loss to explain that no one could know what her son might or might not do. "If he crossed the trail, he might follow it. But he might follow it the wrong way just as easily. And if he saw a torch, he might come if the one carrying it were calling his name. But when he is frightened, he does unpredictable things." Her voice caved in on itself. "He might even hide. I don't know." She fought for steadiness in her voice, tried to banish the tears that threatened her. They must not think her a hysterical woman who worried for nothing. They must see her as calm, in control.

Ketla didn't. She rose, lifting her bulk with remarkable agility, to enfold Tillu in a smothering embrace. "Now, now, don't you worry. How I used to fret over Kari when she was that age! But children are always smarter than one gives them credit for. When you have a second one, you'll find out! Ten years old? Of course he'll be fine. He's struck his own little fire by now, and is enjoying a night on his own. And in the morning he'll come in as hungry as a spring bear, you see if he doesn't."

"Kerlew isn't . . . Kerlew won't . . ." The words choked Tillu and she found herself taking a ragged breath. "He's different." She squirmed free of Ketla's hug, only to have the big woman put her arm across her shoulders.

"Now don't worry. Capiam, I know you'll think it silly, but just send Joboam back down the trail with a torch, won't you, to call for the boy? Remember how frantic I used to get when Kari would go off and hide from us when she was that age. Joboam will find him. Though he may not be happy to be found. Kari used to kick and scream and cry when Joboam would drag her home.''

Tillu could imagine that she might. As Kerlew would, too, no doubt, if Joboam managed to find him by accident. She could not believe he would actually search for the boy. But it seemed the best she could hope for.

"I'll go, too, with a torch of my own. He may be more prone to come to my voice."

"Nonsense," Capiam cut in firmly. "Joboam can handle it. No sense in putting the whole camp in an uproar. Get some sleep, Healer. Joboam will bring you your boy before morning."

"And if he doesn't?" Tillu asked.

"He will, he will. If the boy can be found, Joboam will find him. Stop worrying."

"If he doesn't," Tillu pressed relentlessly, "I'll have to go back and search for him. And catch up with the herd later."

Capiam shook his head in slow regret. "I can't allow it, Tillu. One person alone with burdened reindeer is a gift to the wolves. Let's not fool ourselves. If Joboam does not find the boy tonight, he won't be found. It doesn't happen often, but children do stray and perish. Sending the mother to die also is not a solution. The herdfolk must remain together. But all this is foolishness anyway. Joboam will have him to you by morning."

Joboam gave his leader a smile as unctuous as last season's fish. "Of course. Though if the Healer and her son had traveled under my protection, none of this would have happened. Someone should speak to Heckram about this, Capiam. This is the second time that someone trusted to him has perished."

"Oh, don't say perish, don't!" Ketla wailed before Tillu could respond. "Surely the boy hasn't perished. But Capiam is right. There's no point to your going back down the trail tonight. None at all. You'd only come back too weary to keep up tomorrow, and cause all sorts of problems. Now you listen to me and go back to your fire and rest. Joboam will bring you your boy. Is Kari feeding you well? We were so glad to hear that you were sharing her fire. Though she was rather rude to Joboam to take you over like that.''

"Oh, please don't blame Kari for that. If there was any rudeness, it was mine. I felt more comfortable with her companionship. And she has helped me to understand your ways.'' Tillu filled in her courtesies while her mind raced. She had been ordered to return to her fire and stay there. What would the herdlord do if she disobeyed? Abandon her and her son on the tundra? Beat her? Other than Elsa, she had seen few incidents of violence among the herdfolk. But that was not to say she wouldn't be beaten if she disobeyed. She had never met a people who were tolerant of independent women. The herdfolk seemed so, and yet . . . She bid them good night and thanked Capiam for sending Joboam to search for Kerlew. She backed from the tent, scarcely hearing Ketla's murmured reassurances. Her heart sank deep in her body, beating raggedly with a rhythm that vibrated through her flesh and matched Carp's insane drumming. She had to go back to look for him.

She stumbled past sleeping dogs and hobbled reindeer and fires banked for the night. Twice folk called out to ask her if Kerlew had been found yet. When she replied, she felt their sympathy, but also their condescension. What a fool they must think her, worrying over a boy ten years old. Any son of theirs would have followed the trail through the darkness, or built himself a shelter of bushes to weather out the night. Any son of theirs would not have wandered away or would have been able to find his way back.

Kari had pitched her shelter away from the other tents. Tillu set out across the empty space, her small fire a beacon in the night. Overhead the stars were myriad and tiny, the moon a discarded paring of cheese rind. Hummocks of grass dotted the ground and Tillu stumbled. Tears were very close and even more useless. Think, think. If she took a torch and went back down the trail,

Joboam would find her. She didn't want to imagine what would happen next. If she didn't, the boy would never be found. And if she tried to go in darkness, circling around Joboam, hoping to strike the trail ahead of him? The night was too dark, the tundra too foreign a place to her. She would be as lost as Kerlew. "Kerlew," she whispered.

A dark shape rose between her and the camp fire. Heckram's arms enfolded her, holding her closely. The coarse leather of his shirt was rough against her cheek, but comforting. His voice rumbled in his chest and she felt the vibrations of it through her hands pressed flat against him. "Go to Kari's, and get some sleep. I'm going back to look for Kerlew. I'll find him."

"Capiam won't allow it."

"I'm not asking Capiam." His quiet words suddenly conveyed to her the depth of the rift between him and his people. It shook her.

"I can't ask this of you, Heckram. I think it will anger him greatly and . . ."

He sounded almost amused. "I didn't hear you ask me. I'm doing it for myself, and for Kerlew. That boy. I have no claim on him, but I couldn't bear for harm to come to him."

"It wasn't your fault," she said uselessly. When he did not reply, she added, "Watch out for Joboam. Capiam has sent him back along the trail to find Kerlew. If he found you instead . . ."

This time there was no mistaking the bronze-edged humor in Heckram's voice. "Perhaps I shall find him first. Did you never think of that?"

Kerlew:
The Seite

IT WAS GETTING dark. He glanced about anxiously, his lower lip sagging away from his bottom teeth and brows puckered as he scanned the empty plain. He still didn't see Tillu or Kari. He didn't see anyone. He had walked and walked and walked, and still she wasn't here. He sniffled angrily. He was tired and hungry, and getting cold. Tillu should have been where he could find her. Why was she being so mean to him? And Carp and Heckram, too. They were all mean to him today.

He sat down abruptly and began to cry. Softly at first, and then, when that brought no results, louder, until his angry cries filled his ears. No one came. But Tillu almost always came when he cried. Where was she? His crying became frustrated screams, screams that tore his throat with their force. Still, no one came. He stopped suddenly, and opened his eyes to look around him. He snuffled miserably, and then lifted the front of his shirt to wipe his face. He tried to think what to do next.

What was he supposed to be doing? He thought back carefully. But his memories were tangled. Carp had spoken to him early that morning about the necessity for a shaman to seek his own vision. He had spoken of long fasts and journeys and sacred smoke. Then Heckram . . . or was it Carp? . . . had told him to run and find Tillu when the reindeer got sick. And something else? His mind plunged about erratically, and then suddenly brought up an image of Joboam. Joboam had smiled at him, and pointed the way to Tillu. He rubbed at his eyes again, and then slapped angrily at a mosquito on his wrist. It popped redly and left a smear of blood on his skin. For a moment he played with it, seeing how far his finger could spread the smear.

When he looked up, he couldn't see anyone. Where had they all gone? Instinctively he stood up to see farther. "Tillu?" he called questioningly. "Carp?" No one answered. He shivered and hugged his arms around himself. It was going to be night soon. They shouldn't have gone on. They should be pitching their tents and lighting warm fires and cooking food. His belly roiled at the thought of food. He sniffed hungrily, but smelled no smoke, no scent of bubbling stew or roasting meat. He swallowed the saliva that had welled up in his mouth at the thought of food.

Once more he looked around himself. In the distance, he picked out a shape that might be a great gray rock. He squinted his eyes. Were there scrubby trees growing at the base of it? Then that was where they were. Kari liked to pitch her tent against a stone for the warmth that it kept. And Tillu complained that the dung-fires stung her eyes. Tillu would like a fire of wood from the trees. Pleased with himself for figuring it all out, Kerlew set out for the shape in the distance.

Dark caught up with him as he walked. Gnats and mosquitoes sang shrilly in his ears, and stung him until he ran from the cloud of insects around him. He ran until he was out of breath and then walked again, until the stinging insects once more gathered around him and forced him to run. Always he kept the gray rock before him. In the uncertain light of the stars, it was no more than a lighter patch against the black horizon, a lump that rose above the blackness. Slowly it grew in his sight, until it was a thing that reared up taller than a man, taller than two men. And then he stood before it, panting with the effort of his last run.

He stared at the immense stone jutting up from the tundra. It was huge, bigger than three tents put together, and taller than one tent atop another. The stone itself was white and gray and black. Its planes of color changed as Kerlew walked slowly around it. What was a black hollow became a facet of glistening white mottled with silver when viewed from another vantage place. Lichen clung to it, softening some of its harsher facets, fuzzing its edges with life. The grass grew taller and lusher around its base, and small bushes crouched in its shelter. The warmth the dead stone gathered by day and released by night made its shelter a refuge for many forms of life.

Other things clung to it, too. Scraps of fur had been fixed to its rough surface with resin. An old offering of meat showed as a scatter of rib-bones on the tundra's sward. Here was a small circle of amber pellets left beside the great stone. Symbols were painted on the flat surfaces of the stone in red and white and black pigment. Stark outlines of reindeer and men and other paintings more difficult to interpret decorated it. Here were the painted tracks of a rabbit, there a man's handprint, and beneath it in red the toe-pad tracks of a wolf. Kerlew shivered and hugged himself tightly. He tried to remember why he was here, but all he could recall was running toward the stone. He thought Carp might have sent him.

He walked around the stone, watching it change as he moved. Power. Power radiated from it like heat from a fire. It attracted Kerlew and filled him with fear at the same time. He dared not go close enough to touch the stone, even though he longed to feel the warmth of its rough surface, to trace with his fingers the power signs that decorated its sides. He contented himself with stooping by the circle of amber pellets. Around the circle he dotted his forefinger, touching each pellet in turn. One called him, and he plucked it from its bed, held it close to his eyes to examine it. He felt its sleek sides, knew that in light it would be full of yellowness. He hesitated only a moment, then pulled his shaman's pouch out of his shirt and slipped the pellet inside. It might hold some of the power of this place. He hoped it was the right thing to

choose. He wished Carp were here to tell him what to do.
Carp.

He closed his mouth firmly, pressing his lips together.
Maybe Carp had sent him here. A shaman had to seek his
own vision. No one else could do it for him. And Carp had
told him that sometimes shamans went for long periods
without food or rest or warmth to find a vision. Had Carp
told him to seek this place? He slapped a mosquito on the
back of his neck, then suddenly battered angrily at the
shrilling swarm that hung about his face and ears. He ran
to escape them, then stopped again to stare at the great,
gray stone. Would he find his vision here? Would he find
his spirit brother and be a true shaman?

He chewed his lips, worrying at the idea. He knew it
distressed Carp that he had no spirit guardian. Lately the
old man talked of nothing else. He nagged almost as much
as Tillu, telling him over and over again that he must have
a spirit brother before he could be a full shaman. Was that
why he had sent Kerlew into the night and the cold? To
find this place?

He shivered, and wished suddenly for fire. But he didn't
know how to make fire in the open. He only knew how to
make fire inside the tent with Tillu's fire bow, and how to
keep fire burning once it was started. He wished that Tillu
were here to make a fire. Or Heckram. Heckram was
nicer. He didn't nag the way Tillu did when Kerlew
couldn't do something. Usually Heckram just did it himself and let Kerlew do something else that he could do. He
didn't scream at him for letting the fire go out, or nag him
to go out and find a spirit brother. "Heckram?" he called
plaintively to the night. But even he didn't answer.

Kerlew's eyes had adjusted to the waning light so gradually that he was scarcely aware that it was full night now.
He noticed only the increasing cold that made him shiver
in his thin summer shirt, and the swarms of mosquitoes
that were attracted to his body heat and blood. Every few
moments he would dash a few steps to escape the humming insects, and then pause to once more ponder his

situation. But he never went far from the rock. He orbited the great gray stone as the night grew deeper and colder.

Details faded from the world with the passing of the light. There was the vast blackness of the tundra, the great arch of star-sparked sky overhead, and the looming grayness of the stone. That was all. The humming of the mosquitoes filled his ears. Kerlew muttered angrily at them and at the unfairness of the world in general, and circled the stone. He was cold. He was hungry. He was sleepy. And he was alone, and beginning to be a bit frightened of the empty darkness and the ominous power-stone.

And then he was not alone.

He became aware of a brush of sound, of darker moving shadows in the surrounding dark, and then the sudden flash of a glistening eye. He stopped batting at the gnats that screamed so incessantly in his ears and froze. The shapes gathered and drew closer, but stayed beyond the reach of his eyes. He backed closer to the rock, forgetting his awe of it in his new fear. Its harsh cheek rasped suddenly against his back, and he felt his body steal warmth from the stone. His arms fell to his sides and he pressed his palms back against the stone's rough surface as he faced the night creatures that ringed him.

He heard their breathing, their curious snuffling of his scent, and sensed how they shifted positions as they studied him. For long moments he could not think or move, could only stand at bay. He clamped his jaws shut against his own hoarse panting. He took a deep, shuddering breath through his nostrils and became aware of their scent. Less rank than a dog's smell, hotter and sharper somehow, so that in his awareness it stung the back of his throat.

Wolves.

The mosquitoes still sang in his ears, and beneath their high whine was a deeper thundering. He was no longer cold, but his legs shook beneath him. What to do, what to do? The question rattled in his head. If they were bears, he would have dropped everything and run, run back to Tillu.

No. Tillu was lost. Climb a tree, some vague instinct whispered. No. The trees here were no taller than he.

Go toward them. Touch one between the eyes and claim Wolf as his spirit brother. Kerlew closed his eyes in sudden sickening terror. He swallowed. But behind his closed eyelids, he could see Carp's image, hear his insistent voice. "A shaman must have a spirit brother. The most powerful shamans have many guardian spirits in the shadow world. But most important is your spirit brother, the one first to choose and be chosen by the shaman. He is the shaman's strength. If he forsakes the shaman, the shaman dies. Without a spirit brother, you cannot be a shaman. Without a spirit brother, you are barely a man at all."

And here was Wolf, come to claim him. And here he was, sent out to seek a vision by his master. All he had to do was step forward and boldly set a hand between the eyes of the Wolf and claim him. "Show no fear," Carp had warned him. "If you flee or show fear, you will be torn to pieces." He opened his eyes.

They had drawn closer. He could see them now, or parts of them. Sharp ears, lolling tongues, gray coats with edgings of black, black sleeker than the night, glistening. He saw eyes that watched him intently, and some that took little notice of him at all. One bitch with sagging teats lay down suddenly and began licking at the dark blotches that spotted her light forepaws. A young male stood, neck and tail stretched out flat as he stared at the boy. He took a cautious step forward, but an old male with a hairless scar down the side of his muzzle growled a warning. The younger wolf froze, and then lowered his head and slunk abashedly back amongst the pack. The scarred male sat down, and curled his tail neatly around his forefeet. Kerlew looked at him carefully.

"Are you come to be my spirit brother?" the boy asked softly. The sharp ears pricked at his words, but the wolf gave no other sign. Kerlew lifted a hand free from the stone, slowly extended it toward the Wolf. "I come to touch you," he announced hoarsely. As the boy's hand moved, several of the wolves bounded into the shadows, but the scarred male only stared. He lifted his writhing black lips in a silent snarl. "I must not be afraid," Kerlew told himself. But he could not remember how to take the two steps that would put him within reach of the Wolf.

Then, from some incredible distance beyond the stars, the lone howl of a wolf rose. The scarred wolf swiveled his head sharply, stared off into the night. The howl rose and fell, paused breathlessly, and began again, to climb higher still. Tension suddenly tightened among the wolves that circled Kerlew. They moved in small anxious movements, glancing from one to another as the howl filled the night. The boy was forgotten. The young wolf lifted his voice in a whining plea, but when the old bitch leaped at him, snarling, he broke off with a yelp and rolled on his back before her. She stood over him, teeth bared, and once more the howl paused. This time it was taken up by other distant voices, wildness blending into a single tongue.

The scarred wolf bayed once, briefly, a short sound as unlike a dog's bark as a man's voice might be. Almost, Kerlew understood him. The other wolves did, for when he wheeled away from the boy and trotted off purposefully, they followed in twos and threes. The old bitch gave him a last baleful glare, and then trotted off after the leader. Even the young wolf rolled to his feet, and, tail tickling his belly, hastened after them.

Kerlew remained flattened against the rock, watching the shapes vanish into the darkness. Then, with a wailing cry, he flung himself away from the stone and ran after them. "Wolf!" he cried into the night, beseechingly. "Wolf!" He ran, heedless of the coarse bushes that caught at his feet and the sudden hummocks of grass he stumbled over. He might yet catch up with them. He might yet have the chance to place his hand between those yellow eyes and claim a spirit brother. He could still hear the rising howls, the chorus swelling as voices joined it. He lifted his own voice in a pitiful wail, heard it blend for a moment with those other cries in the night. Then he tripped and fell, landing full length upon the ground. As suddenly as the howling had begun, it ceased. His beacon had been extinguished. Kerlew rose to his knees, blind in the absolute darkness, bereft of sound or sight to guide him. He had failed again in his quest for a spirit brother. In despair he howled again, listened vainly for some reply in the vast night. And when none came, he fell forward into the hollow that had tripped him, and gave himself up to the empty night.

chapter six

THERE WAS SO little to go on. Heckram touched a patch of crushed forget-me-nots. Was it the size and shape of a small boy's foot? Or had some rabbit crouched here? He squeezed his weary eyes closed, shook his head, and then opened his eyes again, to concentrate doggedly on what might be Kerlew's trail. Or might as easily be a thing he imagined, a string of coincidental indentations in the earth, of broken tips of bushes and slightly bruised grasses. How far back was that one clear imprint of a foot in the soft earth near a spring? He paused again, straightened, and rubbed at his aching temples. Useless to ask himself, useless to wonder if he followed a real trail.

Once more he made a slow scan of the tundra in every direction. He wished the boy wore a bright wool cap like the herdfolk youngsters did. A spot of bright color would show up against the tundra's wide patches of color. Even a bit of bright trim on his tunic would have helped. But, no, he remembered Kerlew's clothes; the simple leather shirt and leggings would blend in well. If the boy were flat on the earth, he could not ask for better camouflage. Even standing still in the distance, he would not be easily seen. He should have given the boy a bright cap. He would, he promised himself. If he could.

He lifted his voice in another hoarse cry. "Kerlew!" He let the last syllable draw out and hang in the still air. Some distant waterbird honked in reply. Nothing else. He swallowed in a throat gone raw, and lifted his waterbag for a small sip. He wished again that he had brought a pack-harke with him. He had a feeling that if he did find Kerlew, the boy was not going to be in any condition to walk. But it had been difficult enough to slip past Joboam on the trail. The flat tundra offered little cover for a man his size, even in the dark. If it had not been for Ristin and Tillu alone in the camp, he would have taken a harke, and relished the encounter with Joboam. But it had not been the right time to anger the big man. He would wait until he was sure that the boy was safe, and that he alone would be the target of Joboam's anger. But his patience was wearing thin.

Tillu. He had all but promised her he would find the boy. And if he didn't, what then? He slapped wildly at the insects that had found him, venting his frustration. For a moment he thought of what it would be like to return and tell her he had found nothing. His eyes narrowed as he stared into the distance. Then he turned his eyes back to the ground again, looked for the next trampled patch of moss, the next snapped stem.

Step by slow step, he followed the meager trail. He did not like the direction it was taking. The seite skulked in the distance like a great gray beast. Surely the boy would not have been drawn to that chill thing. But here were small indentations in a muddy place that could have been three of his toes. Not two hands away were the well-defined tracks of a wolf. Heckram crouched to touch the clean edges of the imprint. It was fresh, no older than last night at most. It, too, headed for the seite.

The seite. He forced himself to look at it. It hulked in the distance, gray and cold. He shivered to look at it, with a chill that had nothing to do with temperature. How many years since he had last stood in the shadow of the great stone? The great gray stone reared up out of the tundra, a natural monument erected by nature herself to the forces that ruled men's lives. More ominous and implacable than any idol shaped by the hands of humans, the seite brooded in the midst of the tundra. He had wondered then what was the sense in chanting and dancing for so immense a power.

As well to be a mosquito buzzing about it, a beetle crawling across the surface of the stone. What was a man to a thing as immense and old as the power-stone? He remembered the chanting of the herdfolk's last najd, the great fire built to honor the seite, to ask it to free the herdfolk from the plague that decimated their herds. Instead the najd's drum had split, and swallowed the luck-symbol of the herdfolk that had been dancing atop it. Heckram squeezed his eyes shut. The memories of his childhood were bright and sharp-edged, cutting into his adult mind. Hard days had followed the herdfolk's pilgrimage to the seite. Hard days, and many of them.

He stood up, frowning. Every muscle and joint in his body ached, his eyes were sandy from lack of sleep, and the horrid guilt of responsibility weighted his heart. He forced himself to gaze ahead, to look for what might be the next clue to Kerlew's trail. Two or three steps at a time he went, never certain that he was following anything. Except for the wolf. Here were more tracks. It meant little. Wolves crossed and recrossed the tundra this time of year, looking for the lagging calf or the old sarva that could be cut from the herd. They seldom bothered people. Some even said that they never did. They had found the bones of that one man, with the teeth marks of wolves plain upon them . . . but that had been three years back, during a hard year. Even then, most of the herdfolk believed that wolves had but found the body and dragged the bones about as they fed on it. Wolves had a natural wariness of men. Why bother a human boy when there were easier prey in abundance? Young rabbits, fat ducklings that could not yet fly, sickly calves wearied by the long trek . . . Heckram found he had increased his stride. He forced himself to slow down, to watch the ground carefully. But as soon as he did, he found again the tracks of wolves, this time obviously two. And there were a third set of tracks now, smaller than any of these. A pack on the move. And here, where he least wanted to find it, a single clear footprint. A boy's innocent bare toes, outlined plainly in the soft earth. A wolf's tracks overclawed the heel-print.

Again Heckram lifted his eyes and voice. No reply. The seite loomed closer, and the boy's tracks seemed bound there. He scanned ahead anxiously, looking for the crushed and rumpled vegetation that usually marked a pack's kill site. He could see nothing. The temptation to stop tracking and run ahead to the seite was strong. But if he missed Kerlew's steps veering aside? The habits of caution were strong. He moved on again slowly, watched with dull horror as the tracks of the pack converged on the boy's trail. Here were the marks of a running foot; so Kerlew had tried to flee them. Heckram swallowed drily, raised his water-skin, but could not drink. What would he take back to Tillu? A scrap of the boy's shirt? If he turned back now, he could tell her truthfully that he had not found her son, didn't know what became of him. He wondered if that would be better. What little he knew of Tillu told him it would not. She would not rest until she knew her son's fate. And neither, he realized, would he. He had sent Kerlew out to whatever had found him. He would face up to that, now.

He pushed the pace of his tracking, followed the wolf tracks now as much as the boy's prints. Straight to the seite they led him, and he watched it grow larger before him. Yes, It would be there, he thought to himself. He was surprised how closely it resembled the seite of his vision. But a child's memories were clear ones, he told himself. He thought again of the old najd dragging the clacking antler around the gray stone flanks of the stone. If he blinked his eyes, he could see again the bright emblems painted on its rough sides. And a hand-print? He told himself that if there were a hand-print on the seite, it would mean nothing. Only that he had seen the mark as a boy and remembered it. No more than that. He shook his head, trying to rid himself of the uneasiness he felt whenever he recalled his dream. The vision had come to him the same night that Carp had found him. Whenever he recalled it, he tried to believe his meeting with Wolf had been a dream, a product of a cold and lonely watch kept through the night. It seemed a thing apart from the rest of his life, an experience that had no common grounds with his reality. "Such is the spirit vision of a man," he heard the voice of the old najd echo down the years in his mind.

"Kerlew!" he bellowed, as much to fill his own ears with a real sound as to call the boy. But there was no reply, and his voice bounced back to him from the great gray stone that now reared up before him. He halted, no more than the length of two men from the stone, and looked up at it.

The seite. It radiated a powerful holiness, a sacredness that transcended the puny passage of men upon the face of the tundra. The seite had been here, had raised itself out of the earth's belly and stood up beneath the sky. Its godliness had nothing to do with the pitiful homage of the passing herdfolk. They might pay their respects to it with an offering of meat or fur or gleaming amber, but their honoring it did not alter or affect it in any way. It was the seite, implacable and unyielding in its awesome power. A man might visit it once or twice in his lifetime, coming in secret to offer thanks for a healthy child or a good year of calves. That women came here as well, he did not doubt, but he had no idea what they asked or offered or thanked for. He didn't want to know. The terrible ceremony of the antler and the drum had been the only formal gathering he had ever seen at the seite. Surely folk had visited it since then, from his own herd and from others. But he had not been among them, and he did not come willingly now. As if the seite knew that, it turned a chill gray face to him and greeted him with stony silence.

"Well, Kerlew, you were here. Where did you go?" His own words sounded thin in his ears, their casualness forced. The boy had paused here, letting his weight sink his tracks into the earth. And then, and then, he had walked over this way, circling the seite, now pausing, now dashing on. Heckram frowned to himself. This was not the behavior of a boy pursued by wolves. He had thought that Kerlew had run toward the seite hoping to clamber up it and escape the pack on his heels. But perhaps the wolves had not been pursuing him. Perhaps he could hope still.

And so around the seite, and then, here, the boy had turned and backed up to stand flat against the stone itself. Heckram scowled at the lush, crushed leaves and petals of a ranunculus. Kerlew had stood squarely atop that plant, not stepped on it in passing. Why? What had held his attention so?

Then, as he stepped back from Kerlew's marks and glanced up, Heckram felt a sudden wave of dizziness sweep over him. The hand-print was red, the wolf's track below it black. Like a pledge marked together, like an agreement sealed with the gripping of hands. He swayed where he stood, denying it. Someone else had done it, he told himself, in some ancient time, and he had remembered it from his childhood in a bizarre dream. But another part of him laughed wildly inside his skull, demanding who else would have a handspan that wide and would set his mark so casually high. Who else would have been drawn, through a dream and across an impossible distance to Wolf and the Seite, to strike a bargain: Heckram's loyalty to Wolf, if Wolf would bring justice to Elsa's killer?

Without will he lifted his hand and spread the fingers wide, held it before him to compare it to the mark. It would fit. It was on a level with his eyes, an easy touch for him, but a difficult reach for almost anyone else. He didn't need to fit his hand in that print to know it for his own. But like an insect drawn to a flame, he took the steps that carried him into the seite's cool gray shadow. He set his hand in the print, saw the precision of the mark. Ice and fire in the touch of his flesh against the stone, and when he drew his hand back to himself with a cry, he was surprised to find the familiar calluses and lines of his palm intact. Yes, the hand-print was his.

Whose, then, the wolf-print?

Every hair on his body hackled, and he stumbled away from the seite's shadow, back into the sunlight and soft wind of the tundra day. But for long moments the warmth of the day couldn't reach him, and it took even longer before he recalled his present errand. He let his eyes scan the earth again, and his belly churned at the multitude of wolf-tracks that arched around Kerlew's track. There he had stood at bay, then, while the wolves circled round him. And then? And then any wolves he had ever known would have pulled down their cornered prey and torn each his share of flesh and bone. But there were no signs of a grisly feast. Instead, there were the marks of the wolves packing up and moving off again. And among their tracks and on top of them, the bare prints of a young boy's feet.

Heckram let out a shuddering breath. What manner of boy ran with wolves by night? And what manner of wolves allowed it? His eyes strayed once more to his hand-print, and the wolf print below it. The sudden kinship he felt for Kerlew astounded and overwhelmed him. He set out in the wake of the pack's tracks, suddenly certain the boy would be alive and well when he found him. That he never need have worried at all.

He trotted along, the wind and sunlight fresh against his face and hair. And there was Kerlew, tousled but whole, rising suddenly from a hollow in the earth. The boy's eyes were wide, pale as a wolf's, and the greeting he called to Heckram chilled his bones: "Brother Wolf, I knew you would come for me!"

But Heckram found no surprise in himself at all.

❯ chapter
seven

SHE DID NOT sleep, but morning came anyway, and with it
a semblance of normalcy that chafed Tillu's nerves. She
and Kari rose, they ate, and Lasse came for the harkar.
They spoke very little and of Kerlew and Heckram not at
all. Heckram had not returned, Kerlew hadn't wandered
in. If Kari and Lasse knew of Heckram's plan, they did
not betray it. The only sign was that Ristin's rajd had
grown. She passed them with a solemn nod. Carp sat
astride the last harke in her rajd. Tillu stared at him as he
rode past, hating his unperturbed manner. She didn't blame
Ristin for putting him on the last harke; from there he
couldn't speak to her.

The harkar and their loads were gone, the fire burned to
embers, and still they lingered. Families and rajds moved
past them as the temporary camp broke up and resumed
the migration. Tillu wandered aimlessly in the trodden
circle that had been their camp last night. The place held
her; leaving this spot and moving on would be abandoning
Kerlew. Surrendering him to death.

"I thought you would come to ask for word of your son.
I see you were not as worried as you seemed." Cool
words, edged words. Tillu turned her head slowly. Joboam
stood at the edge of their camp, his fists on his hips. His
jerkin was open halfway down his chest, displaying hair.
His arms were bare and muscle bulged on them. She found
the sight repellent.

"I never thought to seek you out," Tillu said softly,

truthfully. "I thought you would come to tell me if you had found anything."

He shrugged. "Well, if you're interested. I found bones spread about, still red with clinging flesh. At least a dozen wolves had nosed and pawed through them."

Tillu's throat clenched. Kari's voice was shrill and raw in the chill air. "And?" she demanded.

"And I suppose they must have found a calf that straggled away from the main herd. It was probably half-starved by the time they pulled it down. There is a kindness in the savagery of wolves, making sure a lost calf does not suffer too long."

"But Kerlew? Did you find any sign of him?" Either Kari's voice shook, or the humming in Tillu's ears made her think it did. She hated Joboam and his ghastly teasing. He smiled so kindly as he sliced her with words.

"The boy? No, I saw no sign of the boy. I called, but he neither answered nor came." Tillu looked at him dumbly, unable to reply. His eyes met hers, and for an instant the anger and mockery in his died away, to be replaced with pitying condescension. "It seems hard, I know. But only the strongest are favored on the tundra. Life is for the strongest. But mercy's teeth are sharp and swift."

"Perhaps. But not all strength is easily seen," Tillu found herself answering. Her voice was surprisingly steady and she lifted her chin as she spoke. He stared down at her, and she saw his determination to master her grow. What had he imagined last night? That she would come to him in tears and pain, and he would comfort and distract her? Did he believe that with Kerlew gone, she would forget her son, and accept Joboam?

"You had better get started, if you are to keep up with the caravan today. Capiam would be very angry if he had to send me back to look for you also." The words were formed as a suggestion, but spoken as a command. Tillu and Kari stood insolently still, staring up at him.

"And Carp told me last night that if you ignored his summons again, there would be little he could do to help you." Bright color dotted Kari's cheeks as she suddenly flung the words at him. Tillu wondered what she was talking about.

With a snort of disdain and anger, he spun away from them. He yanked the lead harke's head around, and dragged the rajd off at a lagging trot, hastening up the moving line of folk and beasts to take the place his status required.

"What does Carp want with Joboam?" Tillu asked distractedly.

Kari looked at her for a long moment, the secrets behind her eyes looming large. Her eyes were black as she said, "All my life, Joboam has been making me do things. Things I did not want to do. Just once, I should like to be able to make him do something he didn't want to do. When I was small and he came to drag me back to Ketla, I used to scream and scratch at him. I remember screeching, 'You can't make me do it. You can't make me.' But of course he could. And did. He has been the biggest for so long, he has come to believe that gives him the right to command. My father does not see it, but I do. It chafes him that he is not herdlord, but he dares not dispute it yet. One day he will. In the meantime, he does not tolerate any defiance."

Kari turned to Tillu, a sad warning in her eyes. "Don't defy him, Tillu. Give in to him, for awhile. And then, after a time when you do not resist, he will think he has mastered you. Then he will leave you alone. Pretending to give up is the only way to win with Joboam. Giving in is easier and hurts less than fighting him. You can't win."

"Kari," Tillu began wonderingly, but the girl only shook her head angrily and turned away. She snatched up her gathering bag from the ground and set out after the caravan. Tillu followed silently, a dreadful suspicion gnawing at her heart.

Tillu tried to focus her mind on the plants she passed. Her pharmacopia was complete now, or nearly so. These last few days of gathering had been mostly for Kari's education, and to provide fresh greens for their meals. Today they both moved slowly, pausing often to stoop and dig for roots. Rajd after rajd moved past the grubbing

women. Both took exaggerated care in cleaning the roots
and cutting them in manageable pieces. Old Natta finally
passed them, limping and huffing, but too proud to let her
grandson lead her rajd while she rode. Tillu had met her
once before, when she had come to her for a liniment for
sore joints. She slowed and then halted her two moth-eaten
animals.

"Healer?" she called in her cracked old voice.

Tillu looked up from the roots in her lap. The old
woman's eyes were set deep in her wrinkled face, and one
had begun to film with age. She spoke slowly, pausing
often.

"I'm sorry about your boy. I lost a little daughter that
way, years ago. Just a wee one, just old enough to run and
play with the other children. But when they came back to
the fires at night, she wasn't with them. They tell you not
to grieve, there will be other children for you. And there
will. But I know that none will be like the boy you lost,
and you will never cease missing him. So grieve away,
and know I grieve with you. But don't do what you're
thinking of doing. Don't go back down the trail, looking
and calling. You'll only be lost as well, and if you do find
him, you'll wish you hadn't." She paused a long time,
taking quick, shallow breaths, and Tillu thought she was
finished. But then Natta flashed a look to her from old
eyes that suddenly brimmed with tears. "I know. Don't go
back to look." Her old mouth folded in on itself and said
no more as she turned her face away from them, looking to
the far horizon.

Then she was stumping on her way. She did not lead her
head harke, but leaned one hand on its shoulder. Its muzzle was rimmed with white, and the pace they set suited
them both. Silence flowed in slowly after' they passed.
Tillu squatted on her heels, staring after them. She started
at Kari's touch on her shoulder.

"She's right, you know." Kari spoke simply. "If he
can be found alive, Heckram will find him and bring him
to you. You have to trust that task to him. And if he finds

him otherwise . . . he will do all that can be done for him; you could do no more by being there."

Tillu tucked the roots into her shoulder bag, and rose. She looked back the way they had come. The passage of the people and hooved beasts had leveled a swath through the tundra's face. Her eyes followed it back to the horizon. Within her sight, nothing moved. No one followed. She trudged after Kari, and for the first time in days her legs ached with the long walk. The mosses and grasses of the tundra grabbed at her feet and slowed her.

They were last into camp that night, arriving even after old Natta. Great worn gray boulders and outcroppings of stone characterized their stopping place. In the long gray twilight, the camp was visible as small red fires and children outlined against the sunset as they clambered and leaped from the stones. Tillu felt exhausted. Her head throbbed and her entire body ached with unrelieved tension. She knew she should be hungry, but the thought of food choked her. As they trudged into the camp Lasse slid down from a large boulder. They knew he had been keeping watch for them.

Without preamble he told them, "Ristin has cooked more than enough for all, and bids you join her. And if you say you would rather be alone now, I'm supposed to tell you that she would, too. But being alone right now is not good for you, and besides, if she has to share her fire with Carp, she'd like some other company as well."

Kari looked uncertain of the invitation, but Tillu was too tired to resist. She followed Lasse and Kari came behind her.

Ristin had set her tent between two great boulders, and it gave an air of privacy to this home in the middle of the tundra. Her fire burned cleanly, reindeer dung and twigs turning to glowing coals. A pot of bubbling stew was wedged into the glowing embers, and flat cakes baked from reindeer moss were heaped on a flat stone where the fire could warm them. Skins were spread on the soft grasses between the boulders, and roofed with a slanting of hides. Ristin sat by her fire, her eyes narrowed as she stitched away at some project. Of Carp there was no sign.

"Wash your face and hands," she told them as they began to settle near her fire. "You'll feel better." And though Lasse was the first to obey her, it was clear she addressed them all. It was the first time Tillu had really looked at her since Elsa's death. Strange, how long ago that seemed now. This woman looked older than Tillu remembered. Older and stronger. There was sorrow and serenity in her features, and they somehow combined to suggest wisdom. Tillu wondered if her own mother would have looked like this, and behaved this way, calmly assuming dominion over anyone the same age as her son. Kari came to sit beside Tillu and as Lasse moved to sit beside her, Ristin calmly observed, "I fetched a bucket of water for your grandmother, Lasse. She said that one would be plenty, as she eats alone now. I tried to get her to join us this evening, but she wouldn't. I think she thought we would be bored with her."

The stricken look on Lasse's face was not something he could control or hide. Without a word he rose and hurried away.

"He's a good boy," Ristin observed to no one in particular. "But sometimes he needs to be reminded that there are responsibilities to being loved."

Beside her, Kari stiffened. Tillu did not know if the words had been aimed at her, but they had certainly struck. "But sometimes one does not choose to be loved. Then does that one have a responsibility?"

Ristin stared at the girl across the fire. Tillu could almost see the thoughts in her head being reorganized. She thought she looked surprised. "Then one can always choose to be kind," she suggested softly. "It costs little enough. Come. Let's eat, and let words wait for later. I was waiting for Carp, but if he chooses to stay away, he chooses to eat after we have."

"Where did he go?" Tillu asked as she accepted the bowl of soup and the warm cake of bread.

"I don't really know. He saw Joboam pass. Or rather, Joboam made sure we saw him, for he stood and stared at the fire and shelter quite rudely. Then, as he started to walk away Carp rose and followed him. But maybe it only seemed that way. He could have gone for a walk, or to see the herdlord, or just to relieve himself. He'll be back when it suits him.''

"You seem to know him well already," Tillu agreed with a mirthless laugh.

"Better than I care to," Ristin admitted, and a tension that had hung in the air melted. Kari smiled uncertainly and accepted another round of bread from Ristin.

"Do you think he'll find him?" Tillu found herself asking the older woman, and then could scarcely believe she had spoken the words. But Ristin accepted them calmly.

"If anyone can, Heckram will. He's a good hunter and tracker. I have always believed he was better than most, because he hunted so often alone. The lone hunter cannot afford to make a mistake, or to rely on others to see what he has missed. If anyone can find the boy, he will." Ristin leaned forward to poke at her small fire. The yellow light played over her features, and Tillu saw Heckram's cheek-bones, Heckram's brows on her face. Then she leaned back and turned to face Tillu squarely. "Don't hide what you know from yourself, Tillu. With each hour that passes, it is more likely that Heckram will find only the boy's body. I know how my son works. He will go back to where he last saw the boy, and track him from there. But this time of year, tracks do not long remain on the ground. Moss springs up in the morning dew, and one bare footprint looks much like another. He will be thorough, and I do not think that he will return until he has found something. But what he finds may not be what we hope for.'' Ristin took a breath, and suddenly looked away into the darkness. "Do you blame him?"

"I . . . no. No. I can imagine how it would have been. Perhaps I would not have let the boy go, but men always are eager to help a boy prove himself. Any man would have let him go.''

"Good. I mean, I am glad that you do not blame him. He blames himself for it. And for Elsa. And I had thought, perhaps, that you blamed him for Elsa's death in some way.''

The air in Tillu's lungs turned to stone and sank down to press on her belly. She kept her voice steady as she asked, "Why would you think that?"

Ristin looked over at her, holding her eyes but not speaking.

"Everyone knows who killed Elsa."

Tillu and Ristin turned incredulous eyes to Kari. Her feet were flat on the ground, her knees gathered to her chest. Her shoulders were hunched against the night, and in the wide black eyes that stared into the fire, she could almost see Owl.

"What are you saying?" Ristin asked in a horrified whisper.

"Wolverine. Wolverine did it. Who else comes so softly, who else creeps so silently? You know how they kill, Ristin. They wait until the reindeer has scooped out a hollow in the snow to bare the moss. Then, when the deer puts its head down to eat and cannot see anything but snow, the wolverine streaks forward and tears out its throat. That is what happened to Elsa. When she knelt to dip her bucket in the water, Wolverine was waiting. He was angered, as he often is, for no reason at all, and poor Elsa had no spirit beast to protect her. Wolverine sprang out and seized her spirit and ran away with it into the dark lands, to drink its blood. That is why Tillu could not make her live. Her soul was gone. If Carp had been with us, he could have drummed and chanted and followed Wolverine into the earth. He could have fought Wolverine for Elsa's soul, and when he came back, he would have brought a spirit beast to protect Elsa. But we had no najd, and so she died."

"Who tells you these things?" Tillu demanded when the silence had grown long.

"Carp. Old men sleep little, and night is the time for owls to be wakeful. It was not your fault, Tillu. No healer could have saved her from Wolverine. Only a najd."

"No wolverine attacked Elsa. I've seen women beaten before, and Elsa was beaten to death. By a man, not a wolverine spirit!" Tillu added emphatically. She felt sudden disgust.

"And you have never met a man with the spirit of a wolverine?" Kari asked coldly.

"Joboam." Ristin dropped the name, and it fell like a heavy round stone into a still pool. The ripples of the implication washed over Tillu, and dizzied her. Heckram's behavior suddenly had a logical pattern.

"If this is known," she asked weakly, "why is nothing done about it? Do your folk have no punishment for those who kill?"

"No proof," Ristin said heavily. "But I am not the only one who thinks it so. There is Missa, Elsa's mother. She dares not speak, for fear Kuoljok would be driven to do something. He has not been the same since the death. Stina and Lasse suspect him, as do Heckram and I. But the herdlord is blind to Joboam's faults, and will not even . . ." Ristin's voice ran down, and she turned to Kari apologetically. "I did not mean to criticize your father, Kari. I forgot to whom I spoke."

"Too many forget to speak at all. To whisper the truth is better than to not speak it at all. I take no offense, Ristin. If I thought I could make my father hear, I would scream it to him myself. But his ears are closed." Kari's voice was bitter, and brought no reply from the other two.

Tillu sat silent, too many thoughts whirling through her head to make sense of any of them. It seemed possible that Joboam had beaten Elsa to death, and no one had spoken out against him. Kari had dropped enough hints that she thought she knew what Joboam had been able to "make her do" when she was a child. And Carp was using his strange influence over Kari to pull her ever farther from the normal paths of life. Kerlew was likely dead; or so Ristin believed. And her own ambivalence toward Heckram was not as secret as she thought; his mother at least had sensed it. The food she had eaten was a sodden lump in the pit of her stomach, and she felt drugged with exhaustion.

Into the midst of the fire-light and silence, Carp came stumping. He sighed noisily as he eased himself down onto the skins, conveying both weariness and satisfaction. "I need food," he announced to no one in particular.

Ristin and Tillu exchanged glances. Neither one spoke nor moved. But Kari was unmindful of them as she rose to fetch cakes and soup for the old man. He took it from her without thanks, and sipped at the stew noisily. He smacked his pale tongue against his gums and remaining teeth and sighed again. "It's all been arranged," he said with smug satisfaction.

Kari fell into the trap. "What has?"

He gave her a scathing look. "Women. Always babbling and prying. The work of a najd is not for you to ask about, girl. Bring me some water."

"Let him get it himself," Tillu cut in angrily. His manner rasped on her like sand against a wound.

"There speaks an ungrateful woman. What does she care about her son, or the one who will bring him safely home to her? Oh, she likes to mope and drag about, so that all will pity her for her loss, but when one does something to bring the boy back, does she thank him? No, she will not even fetch him a simple dipper of water."

Instead of maddening her, the words only made her weary. She ignored him, didn't watch Kari as she rose to get him a drink. To Ristin she said, "I think I will sleep now. I want to thank you for your hospitality this night. And for making me understand things I had not known before."

"What things?" Carp instantly demanded.

"Only women's natterings. Nothing to interest a najd." Ristin assured him blandly. In spite of her sorrows, Tillu felt a small smile twitch the corners of her mouth. She liked this Ristin. She found the bundle that held her sleeping skins, and took them to the far side of the shelter, as far from Carp as she could get without leaving Ristin's hospitality. She unrolled the hides and rolled herself up in one. The spring nights were getting warmer. But it would still be cold for a boy out alone in the dark. She tried to push the thought from her mind and sleep.

> chapter
eight

WHEN TILLU DID sleep, her dreams were of cold dark places, where wolverines snarled at her from cracks in shattered cliffs and moldering bones pushed greenly from the earth. Tillu wandered in a long ravine she could not climb out of, her feet sinking into freezing mud. The passage was narrow, and she could barely avoid the wolverines as they lunged at her from their lairs. She tried to run, but terror folded her legs limply beneath her. She dragged herself on, moving so slowly that she knew she would never escape. Far away, someone called her name.

Then someone took her shoulder and tugged at her, pulling her free. She awoke to cold hands on her arms, and Kerlew tugging at her. She clutched at him wordlessly. Only now, when the pain of loss stopped, could she comprehend how bad it had been. The boy yelped as she hugged him and struggled against her, but she didn't care. His skin was so cold, his clothing soaked with dew.

"Oh, it's warm in here!" he suddenly exclaimed, and burrowed into her sleeping hides and pulled them around himself. The cold night slapped Tillu, but she laughed. As she reached for another hide one fell over her. Heckram knelt down stiffly beside them, to tuck the hides more closely around Kerlew.

"Are you asleep already?" he asked softly, but the boy didn't answer. He chuckled quietly. "I guess he'll be fine."

Tillu reached up to grip his cold hand. He looked down

and swayed slightly where he knelt. "I'm so tired," he said, as if it were all the explanation she needed.

"And cold." She sat up as she spoke and wrapped her sleeping hide around his shoulders. He sank down beside Kerlew. "Do you want something hot to drink?" she asked.

He nodded, rubbing his face with both hands. "I haven't slept since the last time I saw you." His voice was hollow with weariness. He spoke softly, and the others in the shelter never stirred. Tillu moved to the fire, to poke up the embers and add a little water to the soup left in the pot.

"I went back over the trail. At first I didn't call, because I didn't want to alert Joboam. I don't mind trouble with Joboam, but I didn't want it to delay me just then. So I went back a long ways through the dark as quietly as I could. I figured that if Kerlew were in sight of the camp-fires, he would find his way to the camp. When I couldn't see the fires anymore, I began to call. No answer and no sign of the boy." He paused for a tremendous yawn, and to scratch at his tousled hair. Tillu stirred the soup and waited impatiently for it to heat.

"I went all the way back, to where I had last seen him. I thought that he would be somewhere between there and the camp. But I was wrong."

"What?"

"I had to wait for dawn, but as soon as there was light, I looked for his trail. There wasn't much to go on, so many had passed that way. I decided to watch both sides of the trail for signs of anyone leaving it. I didn't have hope of finding much. A barefoot boy doesn't leave much mark on the land." Heckram's voice ran down. Silence fell.

"Are you asleep?" Tillu asked softly.

"Mmm? Oh. No. Thinking. I'm too cold to sleep yet. No. Kerlew didn't leave much of a trail. All I could do was guess which tracks were his. They seemed to follow the trail. Then I came to where a laden rajd had left the caravan and stood for awhile. Their tracks were sunk deep in the moss. And a big man had been leading them. His sign was plain, also."

"Joboam." Tillu wasn't asking.

"So I guessed, and so Kerlew told me when I found him. He had been hurrying up the caravan, and had come to Joboam relieving himself. And he told Kerlew that if he was looking for you, he was going the wrong way. He said you and Kari were off the trail looking for plants. So Kerlew looked where he pointed, and set off that way. To nowhere."

Tillu felt cold. "Maybe Joboam had seen us off the trail. Kari and I walk well to either side of it, to get plants that have not been grazed or trampled." Her voice faltered to a halt. She glanced over at Heckram. He lay on his side, staring at her with red-rimmed eyes.

"You, too," he said in soft accusation. "I don't know why everyone refuses the truth about Joboam. He tried to kill your son, Tillu. Just as surely as if he had beaten him to death."

She dipped a spoon into the soup and tested it against her lip. It was warm enough. She scooped up a mugful and crossed softly among the sleeping folk. Heckram leaned up on one elbow to take it from her. He wrapped his cold fingers around the mug, glad of the warmth, and drank it down as if it were not hot at all. He set the empty mug off the spread skins, and then rolled back to face Tillu. She knelt between him and Kerlew, one hand resting on the boy as he slept. It was so good to touch him, to know where and how he was. Heckram gave a sudden shudder of cold. Without thinking about it, she took a hide from the floor and tucked it closely around him. She sat between the two, touching her boy and staring at the man.

"Perhaps," she said, "we are all afraid that if we believe these things about Joboam, we will have to do something about him. And what we might do might make us no better than he."

"Capiam should act," Heckram muttered. "We call him herdlord. Why doesn't he behave as one?"

"Perhaps he doesn't want to believe he could have a man like that among his folk."

"Whether he wants to believe it or not, it's true. I told

him what I knew when Elsa was killed. Instead of looking into it, he became angry with me. As if I were the cause of it. Joboam could not stand that Elsa had chosen me over him. He hamstrung Bruk. He battered Elsa. And now he has tried to do away with Kerlew. What will it take to convince Capiam?''

Tillu had no answer. Despite his anger, Heckram's eyes were sagging shut. "I'm so tired," he muttered. "I wanted to get here sooner. When Kerlew gave out, I carried him until he could walk again. He's a game little man. He never complained of being cold or hungry." His eyes were closed now, his words slurred so that she could barely understand them. "When I found him," he said, and she leaned close to hear, "he was hunkered down in a little hollow, like an abandoned nestling. He wasn't looking for the trail or calling or crying. He was just sitting with his legs folded and his arms wrapped around himself. He was shaking with cold. He looked up and saw me and said, 'I knew you'd come for me, brother wolf.' He wasn't surprised at all.''

"Thank you." The words seemed small. She wanted to say more, but didn't know what it was she needed to say. He was sleeping now, anyway. Wasn't he? "Heckram?"

His eyes didn't open. But he lifted the edge of the sleeping hide and held it open for her. She hesitated. But he did not clutch at her. He only held it up and waited. Every muscle in her body was tense as she crawled in beside him. His heavy arm fell across her, drawing her close until she rested against him. He seemed not to notice her stiffness. "I've been so cold," he said. His beard was against her forehead. "I thought I'd never feel warm again.''

She drew in a deep breath, and found she could relax. He smelled of sweat and reindeer and life. "Me, too," she said quietly. She settled against him and put her hand on his chest, feeling the steady movement of his breathing. Behind her, Kerlew muttered in his sleep and twitched deeper into his covers. He was safe, and she could rest now. They were all safe. She felt her eyes sagging shut and let them. Beside her, Heckram slept.

Tillu awoke to spring rain drumming on the shelter roof, and someone tugging her arm. Pirtsi had her elbow and was shaking it like a dog worrying a rabbit. She jerked her arm free of him and sat up groggily. She didn't want to be awake. Sleep had been a warm, deep place without problems. She was comfortable, her son was safe, and it was early yet. There was time to sleep a little longer, to savor the warmth of Heckram's body close to hers, to enjoy the peace of knowing Kerlew was safe.

"Ketla's sick!" Pirtsi hissed frantically. "You've got to come right away. Now!"

Tillu rubbed her face, feeling her skin come alive again. She gazed around sleepily. Everyone else still slept. Why was he bothering her? Pirtsi crouched by her. His eyes darted from Heckram to Kerlew, but his curiosity could not match his mission's importance. He only repeated, "Ketla's sick!"

The meaning finally penetrated her mind. "I'm coming," she hissed back. It wasn't even dawn, only the long dark-gray false dawn of spring and summer. Heckram stirred as she took the warmth of her body from his. She had been pressed against the length of his side, and he muttered grumpily at the touch of cold. She pushed the cover down snugly to take her place and touched Kerlew briefly as she stepped over him. He slept deeply, unaware of her passage.

"Hurry!" Pirtsi whisper-screeched.

"Calm down!" Tillu commanded in a low voice. "And tell me what's wrong so I know what to bring."

"Capiam awoke me. Her moaning had wakened him. Her skin is hot, but she complains she is cold, no matter how we wrap her. She says her head aches; she weeps from the pain, and cries out if we make the least sound."

Tillu sloshed water over her hands and face. She smoothed her damp hair away from her face. "Does she vomit? Is her stomach tender?"

"No . . . I don't think so. I don't know! I came away as quickly as I could to fetch you."

"I will want a bucket of fresh, cold water. Run and fetch it and bring it to Capiam's shelter."

She did not watch him race away. The boy was more human in his fear than she had ever seen him before. But even as she selected willow bark and root, and reindeer moss, dried goldenrod and yarrow, burdock roots from the dwindling supply gathered last autumn, and long dandelion roots still crisp and fresh, she wondered at Capiam's blindness. Who could look at that boy and see him as a mate for Kari? Kari would as soon take a dog. She shook her head and sighed as she stood. Half the problems she treated were brought on by the victim's own foolishness. Ketla had probably eaten too much, or perhaps eaten spoiled meat. The willow bark, and perhaps—she paused to dig through her herbs—some of the inner bark of the black spruce would take care of the fever and headache. A tonic of some of the other herbs would wash out whatever was troubling her. Or so Tillu hoped.

She arrived at Capiam's shelter just as Pirtsi did, his bare legs splashed with water where his hurry had sloshed it from his buckets. The panting boy followed her in.

The domed tent looked as if it had never been moved. The same rich hides coated the floor, the same tools and cheeses hung from the arching tent supports. The shelter was warm, but Capiam was putting more fuel on the fire. In one shadowed area, Rolke slept on, unmindful of his mother's distress. Tillu had no doubt of her discomfort. The smell of her labored sweat stained the air, and her low moans came and went with every breath. Blankets had been heaped atop her until her form was barely discernible. Capiam rose as Tillu entered, and stepped hastily out of her way to allow her to kneel by the woman's side.

Setting down her pack, she asked abruptly, "How long has she been this way?"

"I . . . " Capiam made a helpless gesture. "At first, last night, when we lay down to sleep, she complained of the cold. So I covered her with an extra hide. But her body was giving off so much heat, I could not sleep beside her. And still she said she was cold, so I brought her more hides. And then she slept, for most of the night. I woke up, not long ago, when she started moaning. Her skin is so hot, but she keeps on shivering. . . ." His words mired down in his helplessness, and he fixed Tillu with a pleading glance. She turned from him to Ketla.

She placed her chilled hand against the woman's hot, dry forehead. Ketla's eyes flickered open. "My head hurts so," she said weakly. Over her shoulder, Tillu ordered Pirtsi, "Put some water to heat." Turning back to Ketla, she firmly pressed the woman's temples. "Does this help?" she asked.

"Aah. Yes. Some. But I'm still so cold." She opened her eyes again, and recognized Tillu. Sympathy wandered across her pain-lined face. "I'm sorry about your boy. So sorry."

"Don't be sorry. He's found. Late last night, he wandered into camp. He's sleeping at Ristin's tent right now." Just sharing the news made Tillu smile again. She trailed her fingers lightly over Ketla's brow, and watched the lines of pain smooth away. Touching could often ease pain, even if it could not erase it completely. "Does your belly hurt?" Tillu asked gently as she stroked Ketla's face. "Do you feel like vomiting?"

"A . . . little." The woman panted the words. "I'm just so cold." Her eyes opened again. "Kerlew's safe. So glad . . . for you." She tried to smile, but her pain pushed it away. "Can't you help me?" she asked piteously.

"In a moment. Just a moment. As soon as the water is hot. Capiam?" Tillu glanced over her shoulder to find the herdlord standing anxiously over her. "Can you do this? Touch her face like this while I'm mixing the medicine? It helps the pain. See. You press gently on her temples, and then stroke your fingers across her brow. Like so."

The man knelt awkwardly and reached with gentle hands for his wife's face. But his thickly calloused fingers rasped as they slid across her dry brow, and Ketla winced at the touch. "I should have thought of it before," Tillu said aloud, wondering at her own stupidity. "I should have wakened Kari and brought her with me. Pirtsi! Fetch Kari. Tell her I need her right now."

The boy looked at her, puzzled. He made no move to obey her, but only turned questioning eyes to Capiam. It was the herdlord who asked, "Why do you send for Kari?"

"To help me!" Tillu exclaimed impatiently. "Do you think I can grind and mix herbs and rub your wife's face all at once? If Kari wants to be a healer, here is her beginning. She has the mind for it. Now let her try her hands at the work."

"No." Capiam's voice was firm. "I'll not have that girl becoming any stranger than she is already. You are the healer. You take care of Ketla."

Tillu raised incredulous eyes to him. "Stranger? How is becoming a healer going to make her stranger?"

Capiam shrugged uncomfortably, looking like a reindeer shuddering off stinging flies. "It isn't what she needs. If she becomes a healer, she will use it as an excuse to be alone, to wander apart from everyone, to sit and stare and be idle. I won't have it. That's no life for a young woman. When we reach the Cataclysm this year, she will take Pirtsi for husband. A man and children—that's what she needs. A married woman can't always be wandering about with a strange look on her face, can't be saying rude and nonsensical things to her folk. She will learn to lead a rajd, to pitch her shelter and to sew clothes and cook and weave. She will be useful. And she will be happy."

Too late Tillu recalled her promise not to speak of Kari's apprenticeship. Now she understood the reason for the promise. "How can she be happy in a life she doesn't choose, with a man she doesn't love?" Tillu asked recklessly.

Capiam's eyes were cold. "Choose? Haven't you lived with her? How can you talk of her choosing? She makes no sense, she runs about like a little child, she has no pride, no ambitions, none of the hopes a young woman should have. She would choose ridicule and poverty for

herself. And so I choose for her. I chose Pirtsi for her,
who will make her a woman and a mother. She will learn
to be happy. She will.'' He turned aside from Tillu's
unbelieving face with a gesture of rejection. ''Do not talk
about it. Don't ask me about what you cannot understand.
She is my daughter, and I won't see her throw her life
away.''

''Please. Please stop!'' Ketla sobbed suddenly, clutching at her temples. It seemed to Tillu that it was not the
pain in her head that grieved her now, but the pain in her
heart. The healer turned aside, dippered up boiling water
from the pot, and set out her herbs and roots and grinding
tools. She said no more of Kari. How could her parents be
so blind? Kari would never be happy with Pirtsi. As she
chopped roots and crumbled leaves into steaming water
she tried to imagine Kari with children clinging to her,
needing her attention. Would she suckle a babe at a breast
marked with Owl's claw? Tillu shook her head as she
mixed and measured. They should let Kari go, let her be
what she needed to be. She was not an animal to be broken
and harnessed.

When the ingredients steeping in the hot water had
released their benefits, Tillu dipped up a measure of the
tonic.

''Help her sit up,'' she told Capiam. Without a word he
slid an arm under Ketla and wrestled her to a sitting
position. She wailed in discomfort as the covers fell away
from her fevered body. ''Come now. Drink this. It will
help,'' Tillu coaxed, and got her to sip at tonic. As
Capiam eased her down Tillu added, ''Bring her an empty
bucket. Just in case.''

He had barely handed it to her before it was needed.
Ketla coughed, gagged, and rolled up suddenly onto her
knees. Tillu thrust the bucket before her just in time to
catch the spew of vomit. Gush after gush of foul liquid and
chunks of half-digested food spewed from her nose and
mouth. Tears rolled down her cheeks with the force of the
paroxysms that wrenched her. Sweat burst out on her face.
For a moment the spasms eased, and Ketla took great,

shuddering breaths. Then, again, it hit her, and once more her body ejected gouts of vomit. This time she continued to gag long after her stomach was empty. Tillu damped a handful of moss in water and gently sponged her face.

She eased the quivering woman down. Pirtsi took the bucket away, his nose wrinkled with disgust. Ketla's eyes were already closed, her breathing deepening. Tillu touched her face. The fever was lessened. A few moments later Ketla pushed irritably at her burden of skins. Tillu took some away. In moments she was sleeping, her lips puffing in and out with each breath.

"She'll sleep now," Tillu told Capiam. "If she awakens and is feverish, come and get me right away. But I think she'll be fine now. Perhaps she ate something spoiled? Was there anything she ate last night that no one else shared?"

Capiam shook his head in bafflement, glancing from the healer to his peacefully sleeping wife. "Nothing. Nothing I know of. She cooked some ducks that Pirtsi brought, and we shared those. Then later Joboam brought a dish of new greens and chopped meat that we shared. I did not care for it, but we all ate it, and juobmo and cheese. Sometimes she eats again, later, after our meal, but I do not recall that she did last night. She will be fine now?"

Tillu shrugged. "After she rests. Whatever poisoned her, her body has thrown out. I will leave a packet of herbs with you. When she awakes, brew her a tea from them. It will cleanse her body, and renew her strength. And let her sleep, as long as she likes. All day, if she will."

Capiam shook his head slowly. "Soon, the folk will be waking, and preparing for the day's travel."

"Cannot we stay one day in one spot, while she rests?" Tillu asked incredulously. "What harm is there in one day's delay?" She held the packet of herbs out to him. He took it absently.

Then Capiam shook his head, his decision hardened. "The stinging flies will come soon. I am surprised they have not come already. They come in clouds, they bite the reindeer and drive them mad. Many will die, or race away and be lost unless we are at the Cataclysm by then. We cannot delay, not even for a day." Then, in a gentler voice, "Did you think I would refuse to wait for your lost son, but halt the caravan for my sick wife? I know some speak against me, but no one would say I am as poor a herdlord as that." He glanced over at Ketla, and worry creased his face deeply. "If she cannot walk," he said, more to himself than to Tillu, "I will make a drag for her to ride on. It won't be a pleasant journey for her, but she will not be left behind."

There seemed nothing for Tillu to say. She nodded gravely, and crossed the tent to lift the door flap. Just as she ducked down to leave, Capiam's voice halted her. "About Kari."

Tillu paused, looking up at him blandly.

"I am glad she has had this time with you. Whatever you have taught her will not go to waste. You must understand that you cannot know her as her own father does. You may think me cruel, but I am not. It would be crueller to let her go as she has. I will die before her. I don't want to die knowing that she will grow old alone. Kari will always need a family to care for her. If not a father and mother, than a husband and children. Ten years from now, she will not be able to imagine a different life. She will be happy!" He spoke so fiercely that Tillu dared not dispute it. She only looked down at the trampled wild grasses that poked up between the skins flooring the hut. She heard him sigh. "And I am glad that Kerlew was found. You might tell Heckram that a younger man than I might be angered by one who sidestepped the herdlord's authority. I am not."

Just as Tillu softened toward Capiam, the man added, "I will take his willfulness as a warning. Such sly dealings do not restore my trust in him. They make a leader wonder if he has not judged him too gently in the past. I must be wary of him now. I regret that, for his father I would have trusted with my life."

She lifted her eyes, to stare at him without speaking.

Finally, she took a deep breath. "I did not know his father. But I would trust my life, and my son's, to his son." She let the door-flap fall behind her.

Outside, in the still, cool air, the world teetered on the brink of true dawn. A misty rain was settling on everything. The clustered tents and shelters of the herdfolk created a sense of closeness that the wide gray sky above her denied. Beyond the immediacy of the temporary village, the tundra rolled away in a merciless wave of flat land. A low gray smudge, perhaps clouds, marked the edge of the sky. She stared at the far horizon; the edge of the world fled away from her. The hills and forests of the winter had faded to a dark green smear along the edge of the sky. The world flowed vast around her, and she was in the center of it. If she chose to leave the herd now, she thought, she would go alone into all that openness. She thought of herself and Kerlew trekking across the flat vastness, like two tiny water-bugs on the surface of a wide pond. She shivered.

As she hugged herself against the chill, she caught a furtive movement from the corner of her eye. She clutched herself tighter, and hurried away from the herdlord's tent. She did not look back, but she wondered why Joboam loitered outside Capiam's tent so early in the day. Had he heard of Ketla's sickness? Then why did he not go in? She shrugged the question away and hastened through the wet grasses. She should be grateful he had not seized the chance to bother her. The rain fell harder and Tillu shivered in its chill touchings.

At Ristin's shelter, Heckram and Kerlew slept on. Of Kari and Carp there were no signs except their rumpled bedding abandoned in the shelter. Tillu wondered with distaste if they were together. Little she could do about it if they were. Ristin sat by the fire, poking at coals that sent up a thread of white smoke into the damp air. She looked up at Tillu's light step. Their eyes met, two mothers whose sons had come home from the cold and the dark. What they felt was bigger than a smile, and Tillu found herself dropping her bag to embrace the older woman.

They stepped back from each other, and both glanced over to where Heckram and Kerlew slept. The heaviness of their sleep was almost tangible. Tillu wanted to go and kneel by them, to touch them both, to feel the reality of their safety. She sighed away her impulse, knowing how much they needed whatever rest they could steal.

"Find a bit of fuel for us," Ristin suggested, "and we'll have a quiet meal."

"That sounds nice," Tillu agreed, and set out to scavenge fuel for the fire. The tundra did not offer trees and fallen branches, but here were handfuls of twigs, clumps of dead moss and grasses and dry pellets of reindeer dung to burn. Tillu built up the fire while Ristin sorted through her food supplies. She set six goose eggs in a pot of water on the fire.

"I found a new nest yesterday, by that lake," Ristin said. "There's nothing I like better than a fresh egg or two." She added small cakes of the moss-bread to the meal, warming them on a flat stone near the fire. "Where did you go, so early this morning?" she asked casually.

"Ketla was sick. Spoiled food, I think. She vomited, and I think she will be better now. But her fever was high. Capiam would be wise to let her rest for a day or so."

Ristin slapped at a mite buzzing in her face. "He can't. In another day or so, we'll be at the Cataclysm. Then she can rest all she wants, to the end of summer if she desires it. But if we stopped here, we'd soon be sorry."

"So Capiam said," Tillu confirmed softly. "But I thought he was just being stubborn."

"There's a lot about Capiam I don't like," Ristin said bluntly. "But he has reasons for what he does. Good ones, usually."

"What is it, this Cataclysm that everyone speaks of?"

Ristin looked at her, startled, and then gave a snort of laughter. "Strange, to think that there are folk that do not know the Cataclysm. And then, I have to think, 'well, of course, she doesn't know.' Come here. Come over here, and look over there. A little more east. There. See it?"

Tillu nodded uncertainly, staring in the direction Ristin

pointed. The rain dotted her face and clung to her lashes. All she saw was a bluish shadow on the horizon, vague in the drizzle.

"That's it. That's the Cataclysm. It doesn't look like much from here. But as we get closer, you'll be surprised. It's as if the giants of the earth crumbled and stacked the tundra. Like a smooth hide suddenly pushed together so it wrinkles up." Ristin watched Tillu's face for understanding as she made vague gestures. "Or the ice of a stream, when it thaws and breaks and floats downstream to pile up in jagged layers."

"You mean it's frozen?" Tillu asked hesitantly.

"Yes. That's part of it. There are great sheets of ice trapped in the upheaval of the Cataclysm. The reindeer go up onto the sheets of ice to escape the insects. But it is more than that. There are steep cliffs, tall as the sky, of bare gray and black stone. Cracked pieces of the world, stood on end . . ." Ristin's voice trailed off and she gestured helplessly. "You will have to see it. There is no other place like it in the world, I think. And it is a place of power. All the najds have always said so. It is a place for beginning and endings. A lucky thing to birth a baby in its shadow, and a good place for an old one to set aside life. A place for joinings, too." Her voice broke suddenly. She leaned forward to poke at the fire.

"Capiam says that Kari and Pirtsi will be joined there."

"Does he? Of course. I had nearly forgotten, for they do not act like a couple anxious to be joined."

"They aren't. Not Kari, anyway," Tillu said softly.

For long moments, Ristin stared into the fire. Sighing, she roused herself, and took the bubbling pot of eggs from the coals. She set it on a stone to finish cooking. "The things we do to our children, all with loving hearts." She glanced at Tillu. "It can't be helped. If you try to intervene, you will make it worse. Pirtsi will go through with it, to be husband of the herdlord's daughter. They will be joined, and for some short time, he will have to share her tent. Maybe even father a child. But he hasn't the strength to stand up to her for long. She'll drive him out. What will happen then, I don't know."

Tillu nodded slowly. Ristin dippered up the eggs from the hot water and set them to cool on the moss. She paid no attention at all to the drizzling rain. She scooted the moss-cakes away from the fire before they scorched. She looked up suddenly at Tillu. "We mothers can be so anxious for our children to be safe that we don't consider what will really endanger them. The wrong mate can be as dangerous to a person as a cornered wolverine." Tillu had the uneasy feeling that she was no longer speaking of Kari. "Sometimes," Ristin said awkwardly, "we should allow them to make their own choices, and then welcome whoever they choose. No matter how strange that choice might seem." She turned aside abruptly. She tested the eggs' shells with her fingertip, then passed one to Tillu.

They were shelling the eggs when Carp and Kari returned to the shelter. "Bring me two eggs and two of the cakes," Carp told Kari as they passed the fire. He retreated from the rain into the shelter. Seating himself, he tugged one hide up to cover his crossed legs, and pulled another around his shoulders. Kari hastened to fetch food for him, while Ristin sat silently with compressed lips. When the old man was settled and casually dropping fragments of shell on the hides that floored the shelter, Kari came to sit with them. Her cheeks were flushed with excitement, and her leggings were damp to the knee. She took the moss-cake that Ristin offered, but shook her head to the egg. "I may no longer eat eggs," she said, blushing with pride. Tillu and Ristin exchanged puzzled glances. Kari looked from one confused face to the other, and unleashed a laugh of pure joy. "Oh, Tillu!" she exclaimed, leaning forward to clutch her shoulder fondly. "I would tell you if I could. I really wish it were a thing I could share. But it is forbidden, so I can only say that today I am happy and complete. As you should be, for has not Kerlew returned from a long and dangerous journey?"

"That he has," she agreed, unable to keep from smiling as she glanced over to her boy. But as she looked back to

Kari, her smile became more fragile. "I do not know what has brought you such happiness," she said carefully. "I only hope it is something that will last more than a day or two."

"Forever!" Kari promised her, glowing. "Forever."

"Forever is a long time," Ristin said in a pragmatic voice. "I'm afraid all I know of it is today, and the day that will follow it. But only if we get this day started. I hate to wake them, but I must, unless we wish to be last in the caravan."

She tossed her eggshells into the fire, and rose stiffly. Tillu jumped up to follow her. She felt almost shy as she knelt beside Kerlew and shook him gently. He stirred and complained, and opened his eyes. For a long instant he regarded her sleepily, his long silky lashes framing his odd, deeply set eyes, reminding her of a wondering babe. Then his eyes widened, he sat up, and flung his thin arms around her neck. Tears stung her eyes as he choked her with his hug. She held him tightly, feeling his thinness, the warmth of his small body through his light shirt. How close she had come to never holding him again. Her son. She loosened her grip when he released her neck, and leaned back to look into his face. Like Kari, he glowed with suppressed amazement.

"Mother, I have seen so much! I know so much more now, I have been so far! And I have come back, alive! He said I would, and I have done it! Carp, where is Carp? I have so much to tell him, there is so much he must explain now." And in one wrenching instant he scrabbled clear of her, crawling across the hides to fling himself on the old man with cries of delight. Tillu looked after him in disbelief. She felt gutted. She stared at them, watched the old man's heavily veined hands pat her son's back as they embraced. Then he was sitting at Carp's side, taking the food that Kari offered, stuffing it into his mouth without thanks or hesitation, and talking to Carp, heedless of the food that muffled his words. He spoke in a rapid, excited whisper she could not decipher, his thin hands waving egg

and bread in wild gestures. His eyes never left the old
shaman's face.

But Carp's eyes strayed. His gaze lifted over Kerlew's
head in a flash of vindictive triumph. Tillu recoiled as from
a physical blow. For one brief instant she had held her son
in her arms. Now he was gone. She could see him, she
could touch him, but they no longer walked in the same
world. He was Carp's now. She stared at him with hungry
eyes, unable to turn away even though she knew Carp
gloated at her. It was no comfort to see Kari sitting
patiently, close enough to hear any request of Carp's but
not so close that she intruded on the najd and his apprentice.

Strong hands fell on her shoulders, pulling her to her
feet and turning her to face him. She had to tilt her head
back to look into Heckram's eyes. They mirrored her loss.

"Why don't you walk with me today?" he invited her
quietly. She nodded dumbly.

> chapter
nine

KARI LED THE harke that Carp sat upon. Tillu watched them as they moved into place in the caravan line, heard the greetings the folk called as he passed them.

"So the young apprentice found his way back to you! Good luck upon us!"

"I told his mother there was nothing to worry about, didn't I? Glad to see your boy is safe and fine."

"Look, there, the najd's boy is back."

Carp grinned his gaping smile and nodded down on his well-wishers, while Kerlew trotted beside his knee unaware of the attention. The sprinkling rain misted Tillu's eyelashes and made rainbows as she longed after him.

She walked beside Heckram, listening to the creak of the harness leather and the deep thrumming of his voice. The rain damped her face and gradually soaked her clothing until the weight dragged on her. Tillu felt that she must be staggering along like a gut-wounded animal. The oddest part was that no one else noticed any change. Carp had taken her son, wrenched Kerlew from her as she had occasionally wrenched a rotted tooth from a man's jaw. He had said he would, that Kerlew would be his when the migration of the Herdfolk began, but somehow she had not believed it. She had been deceiving herself all these days of traveling, pretending that because she could see Kerlew and speak with him he was still hers. It wasn't so. She tried to tell herself there was no difference between this day and other days when Kerlew had walked beside

Carp instead of her. But there was. Today she knew what
the others had recognized long before. Kerlew belonged to
Carp. He was the najd's boy, not the healer's son. He
would not be coming back to her tonight, or any other
night.

The sun came out, sending vapors streaming up from
the earth. And rising with the vapors came the midges.
They hovered over Tillu as she walked on the other side of
the harke Heckram led. They walked thick around the
harkars' eyes and shrilled in Tillu's ears. They were not
enough to distract her from Kerlew's loss. Heckram spoke
softly over the moving back of the harke about the things
they passed, telling her the herdfolk names for the plants
and grasses. Kari had already taught them to her, but she
let him speak on. She let her mind drift on the flow of his
words.

The bright sunlight soon dissipated the midges. "But
they'll be back come evening. We'll make fires tonight,
and heap green moss on the flames to keep them away.
Their humming can drive a man crazy, let alone a reindeer. I'm glad the Cataclysm is in sight. Watch it today; it
will rise up before us, and tomorrow night we will camp at
its feet."

She nodded to his words, unable to keep her mind on
them. Somewhere ahead of them, Kari led the harke that
Carp rode on, and Kerlew walked beside it. Tillu would
have given a great deal to know what had happened to
Kari. The change in her was plain to everyone. Many had
turned to watch her as she took her place when the caravan
formed up that morning. Even Ketla, bundled up on a litter
dragged by two harkar, had lifted her head to stare at her
daughter in perplexity. Tillu had met Capiam's glare with
a blank stare. This was none of her doing; let him speak to
Carp if he did not approve of it. Strangest of all was the
oddly neutral look on Joboam's face. He showed no surprise at Kerlew's reappearance, nor at Kari's caretaking of
Carp. He passed Tillu and Heckram without a word or a
look, letting his rajd fall into line behind Capiam's. She
watched the bunched muscles of Heckram's shoulders slowly

relax as he stared after Joboam's retreating back. So he, too, had expected a confrontation. He turned questioning eyes to her, but she could only shrug. She understood nothing of what was happening today, except that she hurt. She stung as sorely as if Kerlew had been skin stripped from her body. To have him be returned and then once more taken from her doubled the hurt. She walked in a daze.

Sometimes she let her hand rest on the warm shoulder of the harke. The smooth shifting of the muscles beneath her palm loaned her strength. There were moments when the fragrances of the warming earth pushed their way into her attention. Twice the cries of birds drew her eyes skyward to a territorial battle in the air. But as quickly as she roused, she lapsed again, sinking back into her own morass of abandonment. She felt Heckram watching her, heard the gentle stream of his words, but could find no replies. Her mind was too full. From Kerlew to Kari her mind wandered, and then to Ketla on her litter. Why was Carp so satisfied, Joboam so aloof of them? Her steps slowed as she tried to juggle all the pieces, and Heckram slowed the rajd rather than rush her. Other animals and folk passed them. She did not even watch where she was going, but walked with her one hand on the reindeer's shoulder and her eyes turned inward.

"I want to show you this," she heard him say. She was aware that they were veering gradually away from the caravan's path. The only difference it made to her was that the ground they trod now had not been packed into a path. Bushes caught at her feet, and low growing brambles scratched her bare ankles. The ground became rough where the unevenness of frost and thaw had heaved and broken it. Huge raw boulders had been squeezed up by the tortured earth, and in other places great sinks had been formed by lingering pools of water. It was the most uneven bit of ground they had encountered on the tundra, and its irregularity seemed restful after the eternal flatness and retreating horizon of the plain. The rest of the herdfolk detoured around this disturbance, but Tillu was glad that

Heckram chose to lead his rajd over and through the
buckled upheaval.

The land rose around them. They traveled between the
crumbling walls of an arroyo. In the lee of upthrust earth
and stone, bushes grew boldly, standing taller than they
did on the tundra proper. The flowers were larger in the
collected heat of the hollows, and their fragrance hung in
the still air. Thaws and running water had gullied the earth
before seeping away. The edges of the ravines were bright
with moss and dangling flowers. Ice-bright ranunculus
dripped down a cleft. Small, fragrant anemones bloomed
in the sheltered areas, and tiny blue forget-me-not cloaked
the ground.

"Stop," Tillu said softly. Heckram muttered to the rajd
and the animals halted and gazed around them, their ridiculous ears spread in perplexity. "It's so quiet," she whispered to herself. The depression of the ravine hid the
herdfolk and their beasts from her sight, and muffled the
steady tread of their passage. The soft soughing of the
eternal wind was broken by the earthen barriers, letting the
warmth of the sun settle and stay. Tillu swayed, feeling
almost sleepy. Here, in this hollow of earth, the sky
retreated to its proper distant blue, instead of pressing
down on her as it did on the great flatness of the tundra.
The world became smaller, cozier, and safer. She sank
down to the earth and leaned her back against a mossy
boulder that jutted from the verdant floor of the hollow.
She watched silently as Heckram moved among the rajd,
unfastening lead ropes. The animals quickly stepped away
from him, to nuzzle and snuffle through the grasses and
bushes. She heard the rip of their teeth and their grinding
jaws as a peaceful sound.

"We could rest here, for awhile," Heckram said. The
closeness of the earth swallowed his words. She nodded.
A small wariness grew in her as he came closer. Well, he
had brought her son back to her, hadn't he? She supposed
she owed him something. And she was not reluctant, she
admitted to herself. She realized she would welcome the
closeness, the touching. Unless. The pit of her belly felt

hard and cold. She tried not to imagine his suffocating weight atop her, her body pinned helpless beneath his. He probably won't be rough, she told herself. But . . . her teeth clenched as he lowered himself to the ground beside her. And lay back.

"I know I slept last night, but I don't feel like I did." His eyes closed as he spoke. "We can catch up with the others this afternoon. They swing wide of these ravines and hummocks, but there's a way through. Long time ago, when I was a boy, I found it." The edges of his words were softening. He spoke without opening his eyes. "They'll never even miss us." He breathed out, long, and settled his shoulders into the cushioning earth. He stretched his body in the sun. Tillu sat an arm's length away, looking down on his lax face. He turned toward her, his eyes opening a crack. "This is the beginning, you know. The Cataclysm starts here." Then his eyes closed and his breathing became deep and even. She shook off the unreasonable shiver of dread that his words had caused and lay back on the earth. She closed her eyes, but the bright light through her eyelids still made her eyes water. She rolled onto her side, cradling her head on her arms, facing Heckram. The warmth and fragrance of the earth blanketed her. His brow was smooth in sleep, his beard more rust than his hair. His sleep roused an elusive feeling in her. She bit her lip, examining it. It was . . . annoyance.

She had to smile at herself. So it was a just debt she must pay? She had wanted him to reach for her, wanted him to have planned this interlude alone with her. Instead he had planned a nap. Her separation from Kerlew had weakened her. Something in her cried out for warmth and touch, demanded that someone want and need her. She realized she had been counting on him to voice a desire; she had been reluctant to be the one that reached out. But the warmth of the sun on her body and her new aloneness unfastened the reserves of her soul. She needed someone to want her touch. She needed warmth to ease the ache in her heart, like a poultice soothing a twisted joint. But she would let him sleep. For awhile.

*   *   *

He swam into consciousness like a swimmer rising to the top of a warm, deep pool. Her body was warm against his side, and after a moment he realized that her breath against the side of his neck had wakened him. She lay on her side atop his outflung arm, and her eyes were wide and close to his. He crooked his arm, pulling her closer, and found her easing her body atop his. Her desire warmed him, but he hesitated. Slowly, he told himself. Slowly. He forced himself to lie still, staring up into her face.

"Tillu?" he asked, but her fingers softly stopped his words. She shook her head at him, and took a short, quick breath, like a diver facing cold, deep water. Close as she was, vulnerable as she was making herself to him, there was still a feral quality to her eyes. Like a wary vixen, he thought. He lifted one hand to the angle of her jaw, half-expecting that she would turn and snap at him. But she did not. Instead she leaned into his touch, letting her eyelids droop down over her watchful gaze.

But even half-lidded, there was something unreadable in those eyes. A reservation. She wanted to be where she was, just as she had that day in her tent. Yet he was certain that if he made the wrong move now, she would flash out of his reach and be gone. It made the simple act of mating a complicated game with rules he didn't know. He would move with care, letting her make the decisions.

He put his arms around her and was still, feeling her weight atop him as a near unbearable pleasure. She rubbed her face against his, her mouth trailing across his beard to his lips. He opened his mouth to hers, felt her hesitation before her tongue darted briefly between his lips. He smiled around her kiss and ran his hands gently over her back. In response she pressed fiercely against him and her breath was suddenly hot against his mouth. Emboldened, he pulled her suddenly tight against him, kissed her deeply.

And felt her go suddenly still in his arms.

He released her immediately, and she rolled away from him, and sat up. Heckram stared into eyes that were full of

both desire and fear. "Tillu?" he began, but "I'm sorry,"
she said, and turned swiftly aside from him.

His mind scrabbled for reasons, could find none. The
mother of Kerlew could not be a frightened maiden. And
there was a fierceness to her reluctance, as if it angered
her, not toward him, but toward herself. He did not understand it, but a sudden fierceness rose in him to match it.
He wanted to be close to this woman, and he would be.

Tillu heard him stand. She could not look at him, could
not find any words to explain. She wanted him as she had
never wanted a man, for she wanted Heckram as himself.
Yet his size terrified her, and when his arms closed around
her every savage memory had risen, screaming. The raid-
ers that had taken her from her village had been hard men
and cold. They had laughed when she had screamed,
standing in circles around the captured women, watching,
waiting a turn. So long ago. But they were still there,
watching and waiting, always, hiding in the shadow of
every man who touched her, waiting to hurt and shame
her. She put her forehead on her knees and rocked in
miserable wanting that she was afraid to satisfy.

"Tillu." His voice was soft with want. She shook her
head, refusing to look up.

"Tillu. Come here." It was neither a request nor a
command. She could not name what she heard in his
voice, but it echoed something that spoke within her. She
could not deny it. She lifted her head and looked at him.

The mosses were green and the sky was blue, and
between them Heckram stood. He was naked, his bundled
clothing kicked aside. She stared at him as if she had never
seen a naked man before. Nor had she, Tillu thought.
Quick couplings in a darkened tent or in the shadows away
from a fire had not shown her a man this way, nor had
men stripped for healing, writhing in their pain. Nothing in
her life had prepared her for a man who stood naked and
unashamed in the bright sunlight. His face and arms were
bronzed, but his chest and thighs were pale where the sun
seldom touched them. He was thinner than she had ex-

pected and more muscular, his chest deeper, his legs long and straight. His manhood . . . she pulled her eyes away from that jutting accusation, and made the mistake of meeting his eyes.

His gaze was as naked as his flesh. He wanted her, and yet he stood, waiting for her to come to him. She knew in that moment that she could turn aside and walk away from him without fear. He would let her, would let her carry this tale back to the campfires of the arrotak, let her giggle with Kari over this. This tall strong man had made himself vulnerable to her. Vulnerable and naked as she had once been. It broke her heart and her eyes stung. How could he put himself at such risk? Could he believe in her that much?

She walked to him slowly, her heart thundering more loudly with every step. He was too tall, too male. The sun made planes of light on his muscled arms, delineated his flat belly, glinted on the hair of his chest. Too much of him. Too male, too strong. Unthinkable to go on, impossible to stop. Smell of male musk, warmth of his bared body crossing the small space between them. "I'm here," she said softly.

She was content to let her hands rest on the smooth warm skin of his sides as his big fingers worked the laces of her tunic. He stripped her clothing away, letting the sunlight touch her skin as warmly as his frank stare. Then he knelt slowly, and the soft rasp of his beard against her breasts was more than she could bear. An animal sound pushed out of her as she pressed suddenly against him. She guided his big hand between her legs, demanding his touch. Together they sank onto the soft mosses. The pressures of his body atop and within her were sweet and strong. In her demanding, Tillu forgot to be wary, and when the tide of passion rose to engulf her she clung to Heckram and pulled him under with her.

The second time he awoke, the afternoon sun was losing its warmth. He came fully awake in an instant, knowing with great clarity exactly where he was. The warm weight of her arm and leg flung across his body in possessive comfort were welcome. He eased his hands over her back and shoulders, crushing the mosquitoes that had come to feast on unprotected skin. The heat of the day was seeping away from the earth. He shivered deliciously, and tried to reach his tunic without waking her. But when he shifted, she stirred immediately. She opened her eyes and stared silently into his.

"It's late," she said, and reached across him for her shirt, not casually, but contained. She sealed off their hours together as a thing accomplished. He sensed that she neither needed nor wanted love words and compliments. Her calm acceptance made him wonder if he had not been cheated somehow. She leaned against him casually as she pulled her shirt on, but he felt she was no closer to him. Ten years ago, he thought to himself, a woman like this would have left me sulking, wondering if I had satisfied her, desperate to know what she thought of our mating. But today . . . He shrugged inwardly as he found his own shirt tangled with her leggings. Given time, he thought, she would let him know exactly what she desired from him. In her own good time. Shaking the garments apart, he offered hers to her, and then donned his.

"It's late. We'll have to hurry and hope we catch the end of the caravan. I've a feeling I've called enough attention to myself lately."

"Capiam said as much when I was healing Ketla this morning. He said . . ." She paused, ashamed to repeat the hard words.

"The thing about my father," Heckram filled in calmly. "Again. I've heard it before, and the first few times it stung. Sometimes I think he resents a man he cannot control. At other times, I realize that in my own way I am a danger to his authority."

"I think he would rather you lusted after his power as Joboam does, instead of ignoring it," Tillu observed.

She did not walk blindly among the herdfolk, he reflected. Would it please Capiam to know how easily this woman read him? He watched her as she dressed and pulled the hair back from her face. For a brief instant he remembered the silkiness of her hair across his face, different from the coarser tresses of the herdwomen. More like his own. Absently he touched his hair and watched her as she gathered the straying harkar. Was this the woman who, days ago, had looked so shaken at the prospect of leading one harke? He watched her speak coaxingly to one, and grip the next by the coarse hair of its lower jaw. She would make a fine herdswoman. The thought displeased him. He didn't want her to merge with the herdfolk and lose her foreign ways. She was not curd to be packed into a cheese mold and shaped like a hundred others. He pulled his boots on and rose to help her.

They formed up the rajd and left the little glen. Shadows were lengthening across it. It was a different place from the sun-filled hollow where they had paused earlier. Tillu strayed away, gathering sorrel, roots and all. He knew from his mother that it made a refreshing tea. But, "What's that for?" he called as she dragged several ranunculus plants from the earth. Tillu cut the roots free of the greenery and flowers and wrapped them in moss before adding them to her pouch.

"For nosebleed," she told him. "And some use the root to blister the skin. They say it soothes the muscles beneath. But I think . . ." She paused a long time, and then said softly, "I miss Kari. She wanted to know so much. I felt as if I knew more, because I was sharing it with her. I don't understand why Capiam won't let her be a healer."

"You said it yourself, earlier," Heckram answered. "It would make her less vulnerable to his authority. Others would be listening to her, following her advice. He likes control."

Tillu said nothing more, but followed silently as he led the rajd on the winding path between boulders and gullies. Here a shelf of earth had been thrust up, there a wash of water had left bare a swatch of gravel down its face. He hurried the animals as the shadows lengthened and the warmth of the day slipped away. The overcast crept over the sky again, promising another night of rain. With the clouds came a wind that slunk amongst the broken earth to spring on them at unexpected moments. Whenever a drift of earth thwarted the wind, the midges and mosquitoes found them. The reindeer flapped their clownish ears in annoyance, and tugged their heads about to nip at sudden itches. Tillu stopped to gather anemones and stuff the whole plants into her bag. Then she ran to catch up, the shoulder pouch bouncing against her hip. She ran well, as if running swiftly were more natural to her than the bearing of heavy burdens. He realized he was comparing her to the herdwomen again. Her bones were longer and thinner, and her hair floated airily in the wind of her passage. Like foxes and bears, he told himself. Speed and grace against strength and stamina. It eased his eyes to watch her.

She came up, not on the other side of the harke, but beside him. She walked close to him, matching her hurrying strides to his. He glanced down and across at her and smiled, but said nothing. Instead, he imagined. He and Tillu were journeying alone on the tundra. Their own small herd of reindeer followed them, and they were journeying, not to the Cataclysm nor to the talvsit, but to lands beyond, to a place where the people were taller and slender and lived a settled life. To places where folk spoke a different tongue and . . . his imagination faltered. And what would he do among such a people? And there was something else. Kerlew, they would have to have Kerlew with them, to be complete. Both of them, he realized, he wanted both of them, as if together they made up the whole of a new world for him.

Stars were dim against the still blue sky when he led the rajd from the rugged upthrustings of the earth and back onto the tundra. The lights of the night camp were lower stars against a blacker sky of tundra. "No sense in hurrying anymore," he muttered. "We're coming in late and everyone can talk." They slowed to a comfortable walk and looked ahead to the lights, not at each other, and suddenly she spoke.

"About Elsa."

The name hung between them like smoke blowing from

a moss fire. With its utterance, she seemed to move apart from him without changing her position at his side. He didn't know what she expected him to say, but the silence grew until he felt compelled to fill it. What was he to say about Elsa? He took a deep breath through a tight throat. Was he supposed to say that he understood why she had given Elsa the medicine that let her slide from sleep to death? Was she asking for forgiveness? Or was she asking how he could lie with her so soon after his loss?

"Elsa was my friend," he said slowly. He paused, and was ambushed by the sting of tears. His throat went raw. He gasped for air and was blind as the sudden tears ran. He put his hand on the harke's shoulder. The depth and suddenness of his grief made him powerless before it. He stumbled beside the harke, his words running as freely as his tears. "I don't know . . . what is the use of my tears now? I don't know why I cry. I didn't weep for her then. I couldn't. If I wasn't going to kill Joboam for killing her, then I had no right to mourn. Do you see? If I was only going to miss her as a friend, not as a husband should, then . . . she wasn't mine to mourn. The night she died, when I slept by her and held her hand, I dreamed of her. Not as 'Elsa my wife' but as my friend. I was on a hill, watching her, and she was going off to hunt, with her bow on her back and her hair blowing in the wind. I was glad to see her go, because she enjoyed hunting and was good at it. I didn't run after her, or call to her. I let her go." He swallowed and dragged his arm across his eyes. "I never told anyone about that," he said in a strangled voice. "I let her go."

"Hush." He felt her hands, touching his arm, and then her arm twined around his waist as they walked together. "You didn't want her to die. You only wanted her to be free." She spoke hesitantly, as if convincing herself.

Fury stormed up in him as suddenly as grief had. "I should have killed Joboam. I didn't have to see him do it to know that he's the only one who could have done it. He cut Bruk's tendons, he killed Elsa, he tried to lose Kerlew

and leave him to die. Why don't I kill him?" Bafflement
filled his voice.

Her voice was calm beside him, coming out of the
darkness. "Is it so common, then, for your folk to kill
each other?"

"No." The idea disgusted him. "It may happen, sometimes in an accident. Once, when I was small, Nes shot an
arrow at what he thought was a bear near his vaja and calf.
It was Oso, in a bear coat. Nes was sorry, but Oso died."

"They do not fight, then, to the death? Over women or
status in the tribe?"

Heckram peered at her through the gathering dusk. Her
face was unreadable. He shrugged. "Do other peoples do
so? I've heard of such things but . . . Why fight over a
woman? She will mate where she will. One may be sor-
rowed by it, or angered. But he is only a bigger fool to let
others know of it. And a man's place in the herdfolk is the
place he grows to. Capiam is the herdlord, and Rolke will
be so after him. Unless his line dies out, so will the
position be passed. And if the herdlord has no child to take
leadership, then the elders choose a new herdlord. But no
man can say, 'I am the leader now,' and have it be so.
Followers choose a leader; a leader cannot choose followers."

"Some folk choose their leaders that way. The biggest,
the strongest, he who can knock down all the others."

"Not the herdfolk."

"But your folk . . ."

"My folk. Hm." There was a bitter edge in his short
laugh.

"What?"

"Sometimes I think they are not my folk. That blood
has more of a say in me than my rearing. Like a fox cub
raised with puppies, I may run with them and try to bark,
but it does not make me one of their pack. No, nor
Joboam. I can say, they should rid themselves of him, he
doesn't belong, he is hurting them. But what of me? What
of a man who feels pleasure when he thinks of killing
Joboam. Does he belong among the herdfolk?"

"Your heart is here."

He was silent, his long strides eating up the trail. "Some-times. I like the calving times, I like putting my mark into a new animal. I like watching over my feeding rein-deer and keeping them safe from wolverines. But when I dream . . ."

"You dream?" Tillu broke the dangling silence.

"I wonder about my grandfather's folk. I remember the trading trip I made with my father. I think of their bright bronze tools, and the strange tales they told of the folk that lived to the south of them. And I feel like the marsh birds feel when the edge of fall is in the air. The young ones stand on the rocks and stretch their necks and lift their wings and yearn. And when the pull gets too strong, all of them rise and go. The pull is getting very strong, Tillu. Perhaps it would be a way for me. To leave, before I kill Joboam and shame my mother."

Tillu nodded reluctantly and the conversation lapsed. The night closed softly around them as the last of the colors left the day. The midges hummed and the hooves of the reindeer clicked in their eternal rhythm. Heckram felt drained, body and soul. There was no part of him that Tillu had not explored today. She knew him now. It troubled him that he knew so little of her in return. But time would lower her barriers. Time or pain. If she had not been so hurt today, she might never have let him near. He wondered how the night would shape itself.

He decided he would pitch his shelter beside Ristin's. He would leave it up to Tillu where she slept, in his shelter or Ristin's. He wondered where Kari would set up her tent for Carp. Had Kerlew missed his mother yet? He doubted that the boy realized her pain. Then he wondered if it would make any difference if he did. Kerlew would regret causing her pain, he knew that much. What he didn't know was if the regret would be enough to make him reconsider the path he had chosen. He doubted it.

Tillu had become very quiet. Was her head busy with the same thoughts? His free hand had been resting on her shoulder for some time. Now he snugged her closer for an instant, acting before he could wonder if she would resent the action. She didn't. Her own arm around his waist tightened, and for a few strides they walked that way. Then, with a soft shrug, she freed herself, and walked unencumbered at his side.

The fullness of night had caught them. The wind that slipped the clouds past the stars blew the midges away as well. "There's rain on the wind," he said softly.

He felt her assent, although he didn't see her nod. "I hope we can get the shelter up before it comes down," she said, and a small tension that had been riding on his shoulders lifted away. She would be with him tonight. He felt her cool fingers touch his hand briefly. He smiled without looking at her and walked on toward the lights of the camp.

But just when the lights became fires, and the crouching shadows tents, a shape reared suddenly from beside their path and stepped between them and the lights. Shaggy but manlike it stood, too tall to be a man. He heard Tillu gasp and without thought he swept his arm wide to carry her behind him. It spoke.

"If the herdlord's wife and son die, we won't have to look far to fix the blame."

"Joboam," he hissed, and set his feet.

"Yes. Joboam." A sneering satisfaction in the reply.

The shagginess resolved itself into a hide flung across his shoulders against the night chill, the hugeness became merely Joboam's usual height and bulk. Revulsion swept through Heckram, and for the first time, he thought he might be right to kill this man. It would not be like killing an animal, where the challenge was in the stalking and the satisfaction in the meat afterward. No. Here the challenge would be in matching his strength, and the satisfaction in wiping the blood from his hands. A shiver ran lightly over his shoulders and back, readying him.

Did Joboam sense it? He held out one hand in a gesture bidding him wait.

"I haven't come to challenge you, Heckram. Though we both know the time for that comes soon. I've heard the things you've said about me, and I'll make you answer for them. But not yet. Capiam sent me, to find the healer he has so generously fed and provided for. Where is she, now that there is something more than a splinter or a rash to cure? When both his wife and his son toss in a fever and vomit and shiver with pain? Has not he upheld his end of the bargain, even taking in her half-wit son and the trouble-making najd that teaches him? The healer has a few questions to answer. And you, too, Heckram. Capiam wonders about a man who does not feel bound by the herdlord's word or the customs of his people."

"He will have his answers," Heckram replied evenly. "If the healer is late, it is no fault of her own. I will answer for it. And any other questions he may ask me. But only if they come from his mouth, not from a dog that grovels on his threshold."

Joboam growled and his shoulders hunched with his anger. Heckram waited calmly for his rush. But it was Tillu who pushed past him brusquely, saying, "And will not the herdlord wonder what delayed the healer even after she was found? Snarl and savage each other at your own leisure. I won't have time to bandage you tonight. Let's be on our way. Ketla is in pain."

Joboam straightened slowly. "Yes," he agreed with slow satisfaction. "Hurry, Healer. Or you may be too late."

Something in his voice triggered Heckram. He surged forward, and his fist carried the momentum of his movement as it hammered into the center of Joboam's chest. It was not the most telling spot to hit a man. Even Heckram knew that from his childhood tussles. A blow to the face would have hurt more and been more debilitating. But the force of his fist was enough to sit Joboam down flat in the mud-churned moss. Heckram braced himself for Joboam to rise and attack him. Instead, Joboam sat, head bowed, trying to pull air back into his lungs. Heckram stared at him, amazed, as he realized that Joboam wasn't going to get up. This was it. It was over.

"That was stupid!" Tillu's voice sizzled like snow spilled on a fire. She started to crouch down beside Joboam, but

Heckram surprised himself by taking her elbow and pulling her to her feet.

"He's not hurt, and you don't have time. Run ahead, toward the fires. I'll bring the harkar as fast as I can. Here," he turned and fumbled at the bundles one harke carried. "This is your healer's pouch, I think. Do you need anything else?"

She shook her head, staring up at him in the darkness. On her face was a strange mixture of anger and admiration. He nearly smiled.

"Well, go on, then. And when you are finished, you'll find my tent near Ristin's. I'll check on Kerlew for you. You go to Capiam and see what you can do. Hurry, now."

She took a few steps, and then looked back at him. "Well, go on!" he urged her, and she turned and ran. He took up the lead rope of his harke. As he started the rajd forward again, Joboam had gotten to one knee and was trying to stand. Heckram looked down on him as he passed. The hatred he had felt for the man so long was suddenly lost. Instead, he remembered Wolf, in what might have been a dream, and a bargain. There was another task for him this night, one that had nothing to do with Joboam. He uttered the thought aloud, without thinking. "I don't need to worry about you. You're Wolf's meat."

Joboam gaped at him, his face awash with feelings. Incredulous, angry, and somewhere in a corner of his soul, afraid. Heckram didn't look at him. Instead he fixed his eyes on the fires and the small silhouette with the flying hair. He walked on.

chapter ten

TILLU WALKED RESOLUTELY down the row of shelters and fires of the camp. Conversation died as she walked past each fire, to be taken up in whispers after her. But what had she done that was so terrible? She and Heckram had been late coming in. That was all.

A large fire blazed before Capiam's tent, and gathered about it were the elders of the herdfolk. As she approached, all eyes turned her way. Acor stared at her accusingly and Ristor's black eyes peered at her from their nest of wrinkles. Pirtsi moved about the fire anxiously, crouching to poke at it, and then rising to glance at her. She met his eyes, and he turned aside quickly, to lift an armful of moss and dump it on the flames. Smoke billowed, and the midges drawn to the firelight dispersed. She strode up to the fire, still panting from her run.

"Isn't she here yet?" Capiam's voice preceded him. He thrust his head and shoulders from the tent and glared balefully about. No one else spoke. As his eyes settled on Tillu, they widened in a look between relief and anger. "Get in here!" he commanded her harshly. He jerked himself back into the domed tent, and she followed apprehensively.

Within the tent, a bright fire blazed, making the interior so hot that Tillu felt breathless. Ketla was swathed in blankets on a pallet beside the fire. She rolled her head restively, murmuring discomfortedly. Not far away, Rolke moaned inside a huddle of hides. He lay very still. Capiam

stood glaring at the healer. His face was etched deep with
worry. "When her fever first came back, I sent for you.
No one could find you. So we pressed on to this stopping
place, and again I sent for you. And again no one could
find you. By then Rolke was sick, too."

"What have you done for them?" Tillu interrupted
brusquely. She dropped her pouch and knelt beside Ketla.
The rank smell of fever sweat and urine rose from her.
Tillu placed her hand gently on the woman's face, felt the
fire that burned within her.

"Ibb remembered that our old healer, Kila, used fire to
drive out fever. Like fears like, she used to say. So we
built the fire, and bundled them close to it. Where were
you?"

"With Heckram." Tillu spoke tersely, and when she
looked up to the anger in Capiam's face, she was tempted
to let the words stand alone. But that would focus his
anger on Heckram. She bit back her annoyance. "I was
very tired, after rising so early to see to Ketla. Heckram
noticed it, and took his rajd to one side of the trail and
stopped so I could sleep for awhile. I slept longer than I
meant to. Have they taken any water?"

"No. I didn't want to interfere with the fire driving out
the fever. Heckram knows better than to leave the trail.
This makes twice he has defied my rules. Does he think I
will ignore his insulting behavior?"

"I don't know what he thinks." The heat of the fire had
already given Tillu a pounding headache. She pinched a
fold of Ketla's flesh. "Bring them water. As much as they
will take. The fire may drive out the fever, that is true. But
I've had more luck using water to wash fever and illness
from a sickly body." She turned her attention suddenly
from Ketla to Capiam. "And although I don't know what
Heckram thinks, I know that I am responsible for my own
acts. If I hadn't rested today, do you think I'd have the
strength to be tending Ketla and Rolke now? I don't want
to talk to you right now. Perhaps what I did was irrespon-
sible. But right now, I must give all my attention to these
two. Get me water. Please."

He might have argued, but at that moment, Ketla gave out a long, cracked moan. Capiam stepped to the flap of the tent, and ordered Pirtsi to bring water. Tillu pushed the hair back from her face and considered. This was no longer a simple case of gut ache from overeating. She didn't know what it was. Was it spreading? Or had Ketla and Rolke shared some food or drink that had poisoned them both? She moved from Ketla to Rolke, and cautiously lifted a corner of his blankets. The fever burned as hotly in him as it did in his mother. Worse, perhaps, for he did not toss and mutter, but lay still and only moaned. His lips were swollen and shiny. The skin of his hand was dry and brittle as birchbark. As she moved to tuck his arm back under his blankets, she felt a swelling inside the bend of his elbow. She prodded it gently. He pulled away from her, whimpering. She flipped the coverings back and examined him more closely.

He had been stripped naked before they had bundled him in the hides. His hairless chest was narrow and childish. There were swellings inside the bends of his arms, and in his armpits. She prodded them, and his cry of pain was like the hoarse caw of a crow. "Like boils," she mumbled to herself. "Or cysts. But I don't think I'll try to lance them." She covered him again. A noise behind her was Pirtsi. Water dripped from his buckets.

"Where'd you fetch it from?" Tillu demanded as she ladled the yellowish water into a cooking pot.

"A pond at the bottom of a sink near here," he replied uneasily. He glanced about restlessly, lines of distaste between his brows. Like many folk, he was uncomfortable around sickness.

"It will do. But moving water is always better. Is there a stream?" When the boy nodded unhappily, she gave one of the buckets back to him. "Dump this outside. And bring me another bucket from the stream. Hurry." He left, pouting. She measured willow bark and a few yarrow leaves into the warming water. She pulled the sorrel from her pouch, cut off two of the wilted roots and wiped most of the dirt from them. She cut them into tiny bits into the bottom of a cooking pot and added a splash of water. This she set to simmer, and then rocked back on her heels. The heat in the tent was stifling. She rubbed her eyes and looked up to find Capiam watching her. He had been so quiet, she had all but forgotten him.

He was sitting on one of the traveling chests. His back was hunched and his hands cradled his jaw. Carefully he lifted his face from his hands to return her gaze. "Well," he asked her after a moment of silence.

"You don't look much better than they do. Have you a fever?" She rose and put her hands against his face despite his look of annoyance.

"No fever," he grunted, pushing her hands away. "Only a headache. As any man would have who faced my problems."

Tillu ignored his scowl and ran her fingers under the angle of his jaw. No swellings there, but he might have a slight fever. In the sweltering tent, it was difficult to tell.

"Will you leave me alone, and treat the sick?" he growled irritably.

"I'll leave you alone. But when that tonic has boiled, I want you to drink a cup. It cannot hurt you, and it may keep the fever from you." She moved away to stir first one pot, and then the other. She added another splash of water to the sorrel roots. She wanted them to boil down into a salve she could put on Rolke's swellings. A sudden frown creased her brow. She crossed to Ketla, and pulled the covers away. Kneeling, she examined the woman's arms. Fat hung from them in a thick fold, but the swellings inside her elbows and armpits were still easily felt. Capiam came to stand over her. Tillu looked up at him.

"Do you have any swellings like these?"

Capiam shook his head slowly. "I told you. Only a headache. And aching back and shoulders. But those are nothing new to any man my age. Where is Heckram? He should be here by now. And the najd. I sent for him long ago."

"Heckram will probably see to his animals and set up his tent before he comes. And Carp . . ." Tillu shrugged.

"He pays no attention to what others want. Why did you send for him?"

Capiam gave her an incredulous look. "When folk are sick as these, with no cause, then is the time to call for the najd. The old najd would come with his drum and his soft chanting. His voice alone could bring rest and ease." His voice trailed off, and Tillu felt the depth of his helplessness. This was a man who liked to be in control. He'd try anything to master this situation.

The door flap was pushed aside, and Pirtsi staggered in with the dripping bucket. He set it down by the fire, wiped his forehead on his sleeve, and then stood uncertainly looking at Capiam. "Herdlord?" he began hesitantly.

Capiam nodded to him as Tillu lowered a dipper into the water. This water was clear, and cold. Tillu grunted her approval. "Lift Ketla so she doesn't choke," she instructed him.

Pirtsi edged around the woman's bulk and knelt by her. His hands wavered helplessly as Tillu held the dripping dipper of cold water. He didn't want to touch her.

"Move, puppy," Capiam said contemptuously. "I'll do this. You go find the najd and hurry him this way. And Heckram. I've words for him." As the youth scrambled out of the tent, Capiam knelt by Ketla. He eased an arm under her shoulders, muttering to her softly. Her head lolled on her shoulders. Tillu supported her head and held the dipper to her lips. The cold water lapped against her chapped lips.

"Drink," Tillu urged her softly, and as if the words wakened her, Ketla surged against the dipper. "Slowly, don't choke," Tillu cautioned her as she gulped the water down. She gave her another dipperful, and then motioned to Capiam to ease her back down. "That's enough for now. We shouldn't give her too much cold water on an empty stomach." A sudden thought occurred to her. "Has she or Rolke eaten anything today?"

He tucked the soft hides around her. "Earlier Ibb came in and made broth of the rabbit meat for them."

"And you? Have you eaten anything?"

He made an irritable gesture of dismissal. "Yes. Joboam and Pirtsi cooked earlier, and I had some. I'm not sick."

"Not yet," Tillu agreed sourly. She stirred the two simmering pots, and then scooped up a fresh dipperful of water. "Rolke," she said, nodding toward the boy. Capiam moved to support the boy's shoulder and head.

But as Tillu held the dipper to his lips, she felt that sudden coldness in her belly. She was seldom wrong. Maybe it was his sunken, darkened eyesockets or the indifference of his shallow breathing. She tipped the dipper, so the water lapped against his dry lips. "Rolke," she said softly. "Drink this. You'll feel better." He didn't move. "You must be thirsty. Drink." Capiam watched his son's face intently. With her free hand, she parted Rolke's lips, spilled water between them. He aspirated it in, choked slightly, and let the rest dribble from his mouth. Without a word Capiam eased his son down into the hides. He covered him very carefully, snuggling the blankets around him. Then he sat down on the traveling chest and stared long at the tent walls. Tillu didn't lie to him.

The sorrel had simmered into a thick mass. She set it aside to cool. The tea of willow and yarrow was ready. She added cool water so it wouldn't scald the lips, and ladled portions into three cups. Taking the first one to Capiam, she said softly, "Drink this." His black eyes were empty. He took the cup from her silently and drained it. Then he helped her with Ketla, who gulped the tea thirstily. And on to the sham of trickling a little into Rolke's lax mouth. Capiam watched silently as she smoothed the sorrel paste onto Rolke's swellings. She was treating Ketla's when the tent flap was lifted.

Pirtsi came in cautiously. Heckram was behind him. And behind him came Carp, with Kerlew on his heels. The boy's eyes were wide with excitement. He clutched a small skin drum and stared at everything with interest. He was the only one who looked pleased to be there. Heckram looked both wary and stubborn, while Carp wore an expression of resignation. Capiam's assessment of them was plain.

"Pirtsi. You may go now, back to your own tent and fire. I thank you for your aid this night. Carp. When you joined my herdfolk, you said you would be najd for us. Little have I asked of you. I now ask that you speak to the spirit world on behalf of my son and wife. Heckram. You have both grieved and offended me. You seem to think that my authority is not . . ."

"I will need the liver of a newly killed reindeer," Carp intoned across Capiam's words. "And its caught blood and marrow bones. I will need the fat of a bear, and the smoked flesh of a river fish."

For a moment Capiam's jaw hung ajar with outrage. Then his eyes hardened and he demanded gruffly, "What for?"

Carp sighed theatrically. "Has it been so long since you had a najd among you, Herdlord? The spirits are not dogs to come wagging at my call. I must invite them as honored guests. Your daughter Kari must cook the liver and prepare the fish while I chant to my spirits and ask them to honor your herdfolk with their presence. When they come, my apprentice and I will eat of the food to show them how good it is, and how well the herdlord treats their friends. Then I will drum and chant, and ask that they find out what troubles Ketla and Rolke."

For a long moment Capiam was silent, considering. He frowned, the lines in his face going deeper. He looked from Carp's mask of earnest sincerity to Kerlew's stare.

He spoke slowly and heavily. "Tell Pirtsi to give you my harke, the one with the streaked tail. He knows the one . . ."

Carp shook his head sadly. "No, Capiam. That will not do. The spirits must know it comes from you. You must lead the harke to the slaughter place, you must kill it and take the liver and blood and marrow bones. Leave the rest. Then you must bring them to Kari's fire, where I will be drumming and chanting."

"But . . . Ketla. My son." Capiam gestured helplessly. "I cannot leave them alone."

"The healer will be here," Carp pointed out implacably. "And she can send Heckram running if you are needed. What good can you do here? Watch a woman boil herbs, watch your wife mutter and toss? No, Capiam. Your time would be better spent in killing a harke. Or do you wish to sit and watch as their spirits are stolen away from them?"

Capiam shook his head like a reindeer beseiged by gnats. He glanced at Kerlew and away, his distaste plain on his face. "No. I will come." His voice was dull. When he looked at Tillu and Heckram, the command had gone out of his eyes. "You will stay?" he asked uncertainly. "You will come for me if I am needed?"

Tillu nodded solemnly. She did not enjoy seeing the man humbled so suddenly. Heckram spoke softly. "I have always been ready to do whatever the herdlord needed and asked of me."

Capiam didn't reply. He moved like an older man as he pushed aside the tent flap and went into the night. Carp followed him, and Kerlew, clutching the drum, drifted after them.

"Kerlew?" Tillu asked as the boy brushed past her. Then, as his eyes found her, she asked awkwardly, "Were you all right today? Did Carp and Kari look after you?"

"Yes." He lifted one hand to scratch the back of his neck, and then looked suddenly at the drum he held.

"Did you . . . ," Tillu began, but Carp thrust his head back into the tent. His filmed eyes were narrow with anger.

"Kerlew! Will you keep your master and the herdlord waiting? You have more important things to do than babble at a woman. Come along!"

"I have important things to do," Kerlew echoed without apology. He hurried after the old shaman.

Silence thick and choking as moss-smoke wafted through the hut. For a long time Tillu stared at the door-flap, willing it to open, willing Kerlew to come back and speak to her, if only a word. But he didn't. There was only Ketla's mutter and the shallow rasp of Rolke's breath.

"I've never known anyone like him," Heckram said quietly.

"He's always been strange." Tillu worked the words past the knot in her throat. "It's not his fault. He's only a boy, in many ways little more than a baby. The last thing he hears is the first thing out of his mouth." She sagged down beside Ketla.

"I didn't mean Kerlew. Carp. No one has ever spoken to Capiam like that. Yet Capiam meekly obeyed him. I don't understand his power over men. You know what I found when I went to check on Kerlew this evening?"

Tillu gave no sign of interest, but Heckram went on speaking. "Kari was cooking a kettle of meat. Fresh meat, not dried, with big globs of white fat floating in it. I must have looked surprised, for she smiled and said to me, 'See how generous Joboam has learned to be with the new najd? Soon all will come to respect him.' I can't understand it. I thought Joboam hated Carp and Kerlew."

"Hate and fear. Carp's best tools, always. Among Benu's folk, there was not a man who dared to forbid him anything. Let a man find good luck, and Carp demanded a share of his fortune as thanks. Let tragedy strike, and Carp was there to wring whatever was left from him, lest something even worse happen. There was no secret shame that Carp had not found out, no hidden treasure that he did not take his share of. His magic is built on pain and greed. You have seen how he mastered Capiam. I have no idea how he has threatened Joboam. No one will ever know, unless Joboam brings Carp's displeasure on himself. Then Carp will ruin him, with no remorse at all. In some ways he is like Capiam. He cannot tolerate one who does not fear or grovel before him."

"Like you." Heckram said softly. He looked at Tillu across the fire, his eyes soft and grave. "What is it he wants from you? What would you have to give him to get Kerlew back?"

Tillu shook her head slowly. "More than I could give him."

"Hides? Meat? Reindeer?" Heckram pressed. "I am not a wealthy man, but I have . . ."

"No." The weariness in Tillu's voice silenced him. "It is too late. I know Carp. He will never give Kerlew up. Nor will he stop until he finds a way to bring me under his command." She lifted her hands and rubbed hard at her face. "I have always known that. There is no way that I can regain Kerlew."

Heckram crossed the tent and sat beside her. He didn't touch her. She held herself too tightly; if he touched her, she would break. "What if you took the boy and went away?" he asked.

"He'd follow again," she said dully. "And he is always with the boy, and Kerlew would never willingly leave him. I've lost him. My son is lost to me. He will be what Carp shapes him to be, a man as conniving and vicious as Carp himself."

The depth of pain in the small woman's voice broke Heckram. He reached for her, then drew his hand back. "Don't give up," he whispered. "Let me think about it. But don't give up yet."

She looked at him, and through him. Something hardened inside her, some small bit of resistance that she had not known she possessed. Heckram saw it in her face and dared to smile at her. Almost, she smiled back. Then she gave herself a small shake and rose suddenly. "Can you help me give Ketla a drink of water?" she asked him. He nodded.

Tillu pulled her sandy eyelids open. A gray dawn had infiltrated the hut to put a merciful end to the night. She lifted her head, felt the jab of a kink in her neck. She had been sleeping with her back braced against a carved chest. Now as she stood up, the ground seemed to rock under her feet. She leaned a hand on the chest and looked around her.

Ketla and Rolke lay exactly as she had left them. She should check them again. In a moment. She scrubbed at her face. Capiam lay with a single hide tossed across his still-clothed form. A line divided his brows and his face was gray with the fever he wouldn't admit. Heckram was gone. She tried to remember his leaving and couldn't. She remembered the cup of soup and piece of cheese he had brought from Ristin's hearth. She had eaten it, and then he had said something about watching Kerlew and Carp. He must have left then. She rubbed at her eyes and temples, willing the dull pounding inside her head to stop.

All night she had moved from Ketla to Rolke and back again, keeping water in Ketla, and endeavoring to get Rolke to drink. The stench of sickness was thick in the tent. Sour sweat and urine blended with the aromatic potions she mixed. Tillu felt soaked in the smell. And the drumming and chanting hadn't helped. It had begun soon after Capiam left with old Carp. The varying beats of the drum had continued until Tillu felt it beat within her head, thudding against her temples. More muffled was the chanting, first in Carp's wavering old voice, and then in Kerlew's uncertain tenor. Heckram had left then, to return with food for her and news of the shamanic efforts.

"Kari has rubbed her face with soot, except for tall ovals around her eyes. She cooks the offering meat for them, while Carp sits on soft hides and drums. He is dressed in white fox skins and wears many necklaces of amber and bone. Kerlew is at his knee, and repeats every chant after Carp."

He had whispered the words softly, their heads close together as he supported Rolke and Tillu spooned willow bark tea between his shiny lips.

"Where is Capiam?" Tillu had asked.

"There, at Kari's fire, as are most of the herdfolk. Those who do not sit about the fire to watch find an excuse to walk past and stare. Capiam sits across the fire from Carp, and watches him silently. I believe it is what Carp told him he must do, if Carp is to present his requests to the spirit world."

"Spirit world!" Tillu had spat out the words and Heckram had looked at her with surprise. Her anger had risen as she met his stare. "The 'spirit world' to Carp is an excuse to take what he wants. He will drum and chant and demand

the best food and drink and soft hides to sleep on. Then, if
Ketla and Rolke live, he will say it was his doing, and
demand gifts of thanks. And if they die, he will say it was
Capiam's fault, that he was not generous enough to satisfy
the spirits. He lives like a great black tick fat with blood.''
Her voice had dropped as she added, ''And that is what he
will teach my son.''

Heckram had reached across Rolke, to grip her shoulder
for an instant. She had felt her eyes drawn to his. His
voice was grave as he asked, ''And you have no belief in
the spirits at all? I know you have no faith in Carp. But
what of your son? You do not think that Kerlew can be a
true najd, one who honestly helps the herdfolk to honor the
spirits of the earth?''

She answered unwillingly. ''Kerlew believes what Carp
tells him. He honestly thinks his chantings and dreams can
change the world he lives in.'' She shut her eyes tightly
for an instant. ''Carp could not ask for a better tool. Take
a boy who has never been accepted, and tell him it is
because he is special, that he is destined to be a shaman,
that magical powers will be his. . . .'' Her voice trailed
off in helplessness. ''What can I offer him that is better
than that? I tell him that he must work harder, try harder.
And no matter how he works, he will always be different.
There will always be those who taunt him, shame him.''

''Not if he were najd,'' Heckram had said softly. ''None
would dare!''

''But that isn't what I want for him!'' Tillu had insisted.

''But it may be what Kerlew wants for himself,'' Heckram
had reminded her.

That must have been when he decided to go to Kari's
fire himself, to watch the boy. Not that it could have done
much good, Tillu told herself. She straightened slowly,
feeling her vision darken and then clear. Never had she felt
so drained by one night's vigil.

Ketla was breathing well. When Tillu offered her water,
she opened her eyes briefly and even murmured thanks.
Tillu covered her again. With time and rest, Ketla would
recover. Her knees creaked as she rose again. Rolke was

next. She stooped over him, feeling the grim fear rise in her. But his chest still rose and fell in brief breaths. She lifted him easily from his nest of blankets and held the dipper of willow-bark tea against his lips. A little trickled into his mouth. He swallowed once, twice, and then the rest trickled out the corner of his mouth. Tillu sighed and eased him into his bedding. She damped her hands in cool water and sprinkled it over his face and chest. His skin was hot and dry, and the lumps inside his elbow joints were now painfully obvious. She covered him again.

Suddenly the tent stifled her, the smells of her own herbs and roots rose to choke her. She stumbled to the door and pushed her way out into the cool morning air. Already the rest of the camp was wakeful. A considerate quiet was kept outside the herdlord's tent, but elsewhere folk were taking down their tents and loading up their harkar. The thought of travel made her feel queasy. She sank onto the thick hides on the doorstep and breathed in the cool morning air. There was a full bucket of cold water outside the tent door. Tillu plunged her hands and face into it, feeling the icy contact as a painful pleasure. She drank from her cupped hands, washing away the clotted taste of the night. She sleeked her hair back and lifted wakeful eyes.

The Cataclysm leaped up before her. She gasped in the impact of its presence. No description could have prepared her for it. After the long trek across the tundra, the up-thrust of the Cataclysm was startling. The clear light of morning brought it closer to the cluster of tents and animals. Her eyes traced the ragged edges of rock, schist, and soil. Layer upon layer of the earth's skin had crashed together in mammoth confrontation, had pushed each other into vertical ramparts of stone. Bluish white slabs of ice and snow were trapped in pockets of the Cataclysm, contrasting with the stark gray and black of rock and the verdant greens of plant life. She guessed that the moving dots on the high ice fields were the wild herd.

"By tonight, we'll camp in the shadow of the Cataclysm." There was smug satisfaction in Joboam's voice. Tillu

turned to him, trying not to show her uneasiness. This
jovial greeting from the man Heckram had knocked down
last night? She held her body in alertness, ready to leap
away in an instant.

He looked down on her and smiled. It was not the easy
smile of friendship, but the smile of one who knows he has
another at his mercy. The smile made Tillu feel both ill
and angry. She made no reply to his comment, but only
looked up at him warily.

He stepped to the door of the tent and thrust his head
inside. "Capiam! Shall I bring your rajd up for you?"

"Shush!" Tillu hissed angrily, but Capiam was already
stirring. In a moment the herdlord was swaying in the
entrance of the tent. One hand gripped the door-flap; the
other rubbed wearily at his blood-streaked eyes. Tillu saw
the fever's track in his shiny lips and grayish skin. His
years sagged upon his body like ill-fitting clothing. He
reeked of sweat and sickness. And Joboam, flushed with
life and health, smiled down upon him and said, "All the
herdfolk are ready to leave, Herdlord. I thought that with
Ketla and Rolke sick, you might need help to take down
your tent and load it."

Capiam stared past him, fixing his eyes on the Cataclysm. After a long moment, he nodded jerkily. "Yes . . ."
His voice was thick. "Take it down and load it up. I will
take Ketla and Rolke to the coolness of the Cataclysm. We
will all feel better in the cool winds off the ice-packs." He
turned bleary eyes on Tillu. "All the herdfolks come
together at the Cataclysm. Did you know that?"

Tillu shook her head numbly. Joboam's voice was gay
as he picked up the tale. "Yes, Healer. They all come,
following their herds. At the Cataclysm, there will be
dancing, and many weddings to celebrate. How Ketla does
love to dance for a joining! And perhaps this year there
will be a girl to catch Rolke's young heart. One with long
black braids and a merry hat atop them. Calves will have
their ears notched, sarva will be nipped into harkar, and
boys and girls from all the herds will smile at one another.

It is a good time, Tillu. You will enjoy it." His smile was cold.

"Rolke needs rest." She focused her words on Capiam. "And Ketla, too. Let me stay here with them, bring them later."

Capiam turned from her plea, to stagger back into his tent. Tears of frustration stung Tillu's eyes. He would kill his son. When she felt fingers on her arm, she whirled angrily, ready to claw Joboam's face. But he jerked himself back from her touch and stood grinning down on her.

"I wanted to ask you if you had heard what the najd said? Surely you should be interested in the doings of the najd and his boy?"

"His . . . boy." The words hit her like a blow. She stepped away from the man who hurled them. "Leave me alone."

"But, Healer, wait! Just let me tell what the spirits told the najd last night. They were not pleased with Capiam's gift. The harke was too old, the meat tough. But still Carp chanted and drummed. Then the spirits told that in the shadow of the Cataclysm, Ketla and Rolke will be freed from their sickness. Why else would Capiam be so anxious to press on?"

She turned her eyes from him in disgust, sickened by Carp's remorseless greed, shamed that her son was connected with it. "I suppose he told Capiam that he must make a larger, better offering to the spirits tonight?"

"Of course. The spirits ask Capiam to give his best. Tonight Carp will come to Capiam's tent, to drum and chant and drive away whatever evil sucks the life from his wife and son."

"Where is the najd?" Tillu kept her voice level, but fury seeped into it.

"At Kari's tent, of course. Though that will not be so for long. The spirits would like the najd to have a tent of his own, a large one, where he can chant and drum and make sweet smells for them away from the eyes of ordinary men."

Tillu did not wait to hear more. She spun away from

him, hastening through the disappearing village. She wished she knew where Kari had pitched her tent last night. She hurried on, head pounding and eyes stinging in the bright morning light. All around her, folk were dismantling tents and loading their harkar. Children finished hasty breakfasts while adults folded tent hides and strapped loads on patient harkar. Bror stopped Tillu to show her an infected blister on his thumb. She lanced it hastily and recommended he wash more often. The old man's grumblings and his wife's triumphant cackle followed her.

But Kari was not to be found, nor Carp nor Kerlew. Angry and frustrated, Tillu hurried back to Capiam's tent. She'd see Ketla and Rolke were handled gently, if nothing else.

But when she reached the place where Capiam's tent had stood, she found his rajd loaded. A bleary-eyed Capiam knelt by a drag fashioned of tent-poles and hides. He was talking softly with Ketla as he held her hand. A few paces away a very still Rolke rested on a similar drag. A short distance away, Kari stood, wearing a face both sullen and worried. Carp was already astride her lead harke, Kerlew at his knee. No time to have words with him now. Tillu gave her son a sharp look. His eyes were blank, almost dazed, and his face pale. Up half the night, drumming and chanting when he should be sleeping. She hoped he was not sick. Heckram stood some distance behind them, watching the goings-on quietly. And standing over Capiam, as if supervising him, was Joboam. His affable manner irritated Tillu.

Tillu saw Ketla nod carefully. Capiam stood with a sigh and, glancing around, suddenly gestured to Tillu. "There you are, Healer. You always seem to be gone when I need you. Do you think you can lead the harke that draws Ketla? She says she would not mind. I myself will lead Rolke's. And Kari," he lifted his voice, commanding, not asking, "will lead my rajd."

Kari's eyes blazed. Evidently she had already had words with her father. But she led her own two harkar forward, and took up the rope of her father's lead harke to fasten it to the harness of her second harke. But her father's gray-muzzled harke objected. Accustomed to leading, he refused to be tied behind another harke. He shook his head vigorously, brandishing his short velvet-covered stubs. The more insistent Kari became, the more the old animal objected, resisting so vigorously that her harke danced away from him, unwilling to have his rump so near the horns of the incensed lead harke. Stifled laughter greeted her efforts, and Kari's face flushed with anger. Joboam stepped into the middle of it.

"Lead your father's rajd, Kari," he suggested smoothly. "My lead harke will not mind following your rajd. And it will give me pleasure to care for the najd for a day."

Tillu's mouth gaped at his offer. For a moment Kari stared incredulous. Then outrage filled her face and voice as she replied, "But I think the najd would take more pleasure in my company, Joboam. I have been the one who has . . ."

"But Joboam is most kind," Carp cut in sharply. "And I would be pleased to go with him. It is time we knew one another better, Joboam. My ears have grown weary of chattering women."

If he had struck Kari publicly, the impact could not have been greater. The gathered herdfolk were too shocked to murmur or take sides. Kari dropped the lead rope of the najd's harke as if it were hot. For an instant she stood stock still, staring with anguished eyes at the najd. Carp sat impassively, as if unaware of the insult he had given her. Kerlew stood at his knee, blinking. Even Capiam stood with his eyes cast down, unwilling to witness his daughter's humiliation. Kari's eyes roamed slowly over the crowd. Then suddenly she lowered her eyes and silently moved to her second harke. Swift and silent, her fingers freed his rope. She left the harke that carried the najd standing unattended and moved to add the harke that carried her belongings to the end of her father's rajd. There was resignation to her gesture, but also dignity, and Tillu heard murmurs of approval. She watched Kari fasten her harke into the rajd and then come to the head of the line. Tillu tried to catch her eye, but the girl was studiously looking at no one. Tillu turned her head just in time to see Joboam lead away the najd's harke. Kerlew followed at his heels.

"Kerlew!" she called. Surely her son would not follow the najd now, would not put himself under Joboam's control. The boy glanced at her, but Carp turned and said something over his shoulder. For an instant longer Kerlew looked at his mother; then he turned and trotted hastily after the najd's harke. Tillu was transfixed. He had looked at her as if she were a stranger; or a tree, perhaps. She took a step after him.

"Tillu!" Capiam reminded her. Kari had started the rajd, Capiam had fallen in behind it, and the gap between her harke and Rolke's drag was widening. She stared in agony after Kerlew. And saw Heckram, drifting silent as a ghost as he shadowed the boy. Their eyes met and his reassurance was silent but unmistakable. Tillu breathed out in relief. She pulled gently at her harke's rope, and it stepped out, dragging Ketla easily. In a moment she was where she was supposed to be. She glanced over her shoulder, saw the caravan forming behind her. Families and reindeer drifted into place, took up the steady pace that Capiam had set. She stumbled, and turned her eyes forward again.

The Cataclysm rose before them, impossibly huge. Far ahead of them, the domestic herd was moving steadily toward the upthrust of earth and rock. In the distance, Tillu glimpsed other moving shapes. She counted three other herds and two other caravan lines. All seemed to be converging at the Cataclysm. She tried to imagine all those people and animals gathered in one place, and couldn't.

Yet as the day advanced, both the Cataclysm and the other caravans drew nearer. Several times Ketla lifted her head, to smile weakly at Tillu. Each time Tillu gave her water. And each time, she afterward edged her harke forward, to look down on Rolke's grayed face. Rolke did not refuse water; he was impassive to it. Tillu smoothed it over his face and lips. His breathing had a hoarse, wet sound.

"Tonight," Tillu said softly to Capiam, "I will make a steam of pine needles and birch cones. It may clear his breathing."

Capiam nodded wearily. His own breathing was raspy, and his face too flushed for the coolness of the day. Tillu folded her lips and said nothing. Useless to argue with this man. He would not rest until he had reached the Cataclysm. Perhaps then he would behave sensibly. She flicked a tick off her arm, and let her harke ease back into line. She, too, was looking forward to the cool of the Cataclysm and the easing of the insect problem. She stared forward, to Kari's straight little back as she led the herdfolk onward. The thought crossed Tillu's mind, that in the final assessment, Kari was Capiam's daughter. Leading her folk onward, finding the courage to keep her dignity in the face of Carp's insult. Tillu wondered if Capiam could see that. Probably not. He was probably too caught up in the illness plaguing his family to notice the one who carried on. But Tillu did. Maybe tonight she would have time to speak to Kari. And Kerlew. And Heckram.

"Heckram." She murmured his name like a charm, let her strange feelings for him rise unchecked. For an instant she saw him again, naked in the sun. She stumbled slightly and the harke snorted rebukingly. She patted his neck and walked on. For many years, it had been others who needed her and took comfort in her skills. She had not known that needing could throb unremitting as pain. A pain to savor.

> chapter
eleven

Two DAYS AFTER arriving at the Cataclysm, Tillu was still
not accustomed to it. It was, she thought, like camping by
river rapids. The flow of people and sound never ceased.
The reindeer clustered on the sides and flanks of the vast
upheaval of earth and rocks, watched over by the young
boys and girls of the herdfolk; it was taken for granted that
more than reindeer herding was taking place on the moun-
tainsides. Many a joining and lifelong partnership had
begun in such innocent trysts.

Folk were equally busy below. Many a joining ceremony was being prepared. Women were sewing and weav-
ing, comparing garments, and trading bridal trims and
gossips, speculating about which couples would be joined
next year. Some were assessing animals, their own and
others. In a makeshift corral of stone and brush, vajor
were separated from their calves. The owner of each calf
then moved in, to swiftly notch his mark into the calf's
ear. Each small flap of skin was strung on a tally line to
keep the count. Bull calves were bloodlessly castrated.
One herdsman would hold the calf down while his partner
carefully took the calf's scrotum into his mouth. Two
quick nips of white teeth severed free the testicles inside
the pouch without breaking the skin. A brief massage of
the pouch, and the calf that had lain down a sarva stood up
as a harke, to run back to its frantic mother.

Goods and animals were traded and compared, children
fought, screamed, and played, and all folk continually

visited one another. Their voices were lifted in a sound as constant as the patter of rain. The whirl of people and activity flowed past Tillu's awareness, washing from her mind any personal thoughts. A blanket of noise and movement insulated her from her problems.

Of Heckram she had seen little; of Kerlew, even less. She was healer now for all of her day, and Tillu only in odd moments. She felt as if her personal life and problems had been set aside, like a piece of sewing that could be completed later. Dimly she was aware that this was not so; that the lives of Kerlew and Heckram and Kari went on without her intervention. But in the herdlord's tents the threads of lives lay in her hands. She was all that held them intact, and she could not let them go, no matter what pain goaded her.

Although Ketla was feeling better, she was not well. Even a few steps made her lose her breath, while Rolke did little more than breathe and moan. The fine bones in his hands and feet stood out clearly, and his skin burned under Tillu's hands. Capiam refused to admit his illness, but Tillu added ground willow bark and birch root to his tea at every opportunity. She stayed in the herdlord's tent, Rolke's constant nurse, though there was little she could do for him. She trickled tea and broth into his lax mouth. She rubbed water and oil into his papery skin and endured Ketla's predictions that any hour now he would be better. Hadn't the najd said so? All the boy needed was rest.

Rest. She would have liked to take it for herself. But there were always distractions to claim her energy. Capiam's najd and healer had attracted attention in the summer settlement. Folk from another herdlord brought her a boy with a broken arm. Her setting it unleashed a stream of visitors to Capiam's tent, most with minor ailments, but some with bad teeth, infected cuts, or injuries from the scuffles in the reindeer pens. The warm weather brought tick bites, many of them infected or abscessed. Some complained of a fever and headache that came and went. The symptoms were too like Rolke's and Ketla's for Tillu's liking. She treated them all, and wondered when she could sleep. Despite his feverish headaches, Capiam seemed to welcome the attention his new healer attracted. Even Ketla sat up in her robes by the fire, and chatted with the folk that came for healing.

Evening brought the najd with his incessant drumming and chanting before the herdlord's tent. Then folk came in threes and fours, to gawk at Capiam's najd and whisper of other najds they had known. A fire would be kindled for the najd, and savory offerings set out on wooden platters. There would be a spread of soft hides where he might sit or stand, and a sweep of clean earth where he might dance. At those times Tillu might get a glimpse of Kerlew. He squatted at Carp's bony knee, swaying with the rhythm of the small drum he patted in time to Carp's chanting. Carp attired himself in Joboam's best tunics and his neck and wrists hung heavy with strings of amber and ivory beads. From time to time he drew strange and grisly objects from his pouch and chanted to them softly, or made mysterious passes that brought the flames of his fire leaping at his command or sent gouts of yellow smoke pouring up into the night. Then the gathered folk hummed and muttered to themselves and stared fascinated at the najd who chanted for Capiam's son.

Tillu watched only Kerlew. The boy would be near naked but for a twist of leather about his loins. His hair was longer and unkempt, hanging about his narrow shoulders. His pale-brown eyes seemed overlarge in his gaunt face. His chest was ribby, his knees and elbows painfully large in his thinness. Only once had Tillu tried to speak to him. During a lull, when Kerlew's fingers whispered against the drum as Carp muttered to a tangle of teeth and feathers, she had crept closer to him, reached a hand to brush his back. Her fingers had felt the knobs of his spine, the high warmth of his skin. "Kerlew," she had whispered.

Carp had sprung at her, shaking his talisman at her frantically as his chanting rose to an angry scream. A man from another herd had dragged her roughly back into the crowd, but for long moments Carp had pranced his stamping dance and rattled his talisman angrily at an awe-stricken crowd. Kerlew had given no sign he was aware of her. She had crept back to Capiam's tent, hiding her thoughts from herself in the chattering of the women who clustered about Ketla's hearth, drinking tea and sewing. Later Capiam had observed, "A boy of Kerlew's age is not a child anymore. Parents must know when to let go of their children." Tillu had only stared at him, hard and silent.

She could have turned his rebuke back upon him. She could have asked why he and Ketla forced Kari to this joining. But she did not. She didn't want to do anything to make the girl any more miserable. When they had arrived at the Cataclysm, Capiam had ordered his daughter to move back into his tent. Tillu had expected her to protest angrily, but Kari had obeyed with uncharacteristic meekness. The fire had gone out of her eyes since the day Carp had gone with Joboam. Nothing seemed to interest her anymore. Kari spent most of her time staring into her mother's hearthfire. Tillu's efforts at rousing her were ignored; she no longer asked questions about healing. She reminded Tillu of a mother who had lost a new-born child. She had that same baffled look of shattered expectancy. Tillu wondered what promises Carp had made her and forgotten. Once she dared to speak to Capiam of his daughter's withdrawn silence. Puzzled, he had replied, "But Kari has always been that way; quiet, idle, dreaming. It is why Ketla and I have decided that marriage is best for her. With a hearth and a man, she will have to talk, to take care of things. She will be a different woman."

Tillu wondered. She suspected marriage would not change the girl. When Kari was not staring into the fire, she busied herself with needlework. From somewhere she had acquired baskets of black pinion feathers. Row upon overlapping row she stitched to a cloak of calf-leather. Ketla seemed proud of her new domesticity, but wrinkled her nose at the work, declaring it would smell horrid the first time it was rained on. Kari never replied. She only bent her dark head closer over her work, sealing out their words with her tiny even stitching.

And so the days passed, one after another, as alike as beads carved painstakingly from bone. Rolke was no better, Kerlew seemed only thinner, his eyes more vacant. Of Heckram she had but a few guilty words a day, whispered at the door-flap while Capiam stood watching as if he begrudged every instant Tillu did not give his son. Heckram's news was sparse and not comforting. Kerlew lived in the najd's new tent, and should be eating well, for Joboam furnished the najd with fresh meat daily. Heckram and Ristin were fine; they missed Tillu's company. And sometimes there was the touch of his hand on hers, sending her strength and warmth before she had to return once more to the herdlord's son.

But the days did pass, with or without Tillu's cognizance of them. There came an evening when the tent seemed full of women, clustered about Ketla, making merry chatter over their sewing. Rolke was sleeping, and Capiam out. Kari sat apart from the others, her lap cloaked with the black feathers, her shoulders hunched to her endless task. Tillu slipped quietly from her place by Rolke, to hunker down beside Kari. She glanced at the girl's dull eyes. Their edges had been reddened by the close, meticulous work. Tillu put out a cautious hand to stroke the evenly set feathers. "It's a lovely piece of work, Kari," she ventured gently.

Kari lifted her face slowly. Their eyes met. "It's useless," Kari said dully. "He'll refuse. He won't have me." Then she abruptly stood, letting her work slide from her lap, and walked over to her bedding. She lay down and pulled the hides up over her head. Tillu was stricken with terror. Death had looked at her from Kari's eyes.

Ketla had noticed her daughter's rebuff of the healer. "Don't mind the girl," she had called laughingly to Tillu. "She is only nervous and thoughtful, as any girl is the night before her joining. Come and help us with the sewing."

Tillu felt buffeted by the commiserating laughter that rose from the other women. How could they be so blind? Her own voice sounded thin to her as she answered.

"Thank you, but no. I think I shall go outside into the cool for a while. If Rolke awakes, call me."

"Let him get his rest," Ketla clucked fondly. "Soon he will be better. The najd has said so."

Tillu bit her tongue and left the stifling tent. Outside, the soft twilight and the cool air off the Cataclysm soothed her. She would enjoy this quiet time. Soon enough Carp would arrive with his acrid smokes and monotonous noise. She sank slowly down onto the hides and tried to let go of her worries. If Kari worried that Pirtsi would not have her, then surely she had changed her heart about this joining? Why could not Tillu lift her own spirits, be happy that Kari had decided to take a man?

When Heckram stepped out of the darkness to stand over her, her heart leaped with gladness. His quiet strength drew her like the warmth and light of a fire. She reached up easily to seize his hand and draw him down beside her. He smiled at her and kept her hand in his. But his first words were "I cannot stay long."

"Why not?" Sharp disappointment.

He hesitated. "So much must be done in the next few days. I've been at the reindeer pens all day. My calves and Lasse's are marked now and castrated. But there are still Ristin's, Missa's, and Kuoljok's to do." He laughed softly, without humor. "Sometimes I feel I am marking half the herd. I don't know how many calves carry my teeth marks."

Tillu nodded. "Sometimes I feel I have healed half the people here. And more are coming every day. Ticks. Most of them have infected tick-bites. Or a fever that comes and goes, and then comes again." Tillu stopped, tried to veer her mind from her own secret fears of plague. "Or a calf's hoofprint somewhere. Never have I seen such a people for breaking bones and twisting joints."

With the ghost of a smile, Heckram held up his free hand. Three of his fingers were bound together. "I wasn't going to mention it, but . . ."

With an exclamation, Tillu seized his wrist and pulled the hand to her. She unwrapped his crude bandaging and gently felt, then manipulated each finger. "Not broken," she said as he flinched and pulled his hand away. She recaptured his hand and massaged it softly. "Heat a pot of water tonight, as hot as you can stand, and soak your hand in it. Does Ristin have alder bark or yarrow? If so, grind some and add it to the water. And wrap the fingers again tomorrow, before you try to work."

Heckram listened gravely, but amusement danced in his eyes. "I came to see Tillu, not the healer," he observed quietly.

Tillu laughed, but didn't stop massaging his hand. "I think the healer is all I am these days." Her smile faded suddenly. "Unless I want to sew on Kari's wedding clothes. Her joining tomorrow is all they talk of within the tent. No matter how often I tell them they must be quiet, that Rolke must rest and Ketla should lie down, they do not listen. I will almost be glad when it is done. Perhaps then there will be enough quiet for Ketla to get better."

"And Rolke?" Heckram asked.

Tillu turned worried eyes up to him. "I don't know. He lives, but seems no better. Whenever Ketla looks at him, she turns pale. Capiam will not talk to me about it. All he says is 'the najd said he would be better when we reached the Cataclysm. We are here. You are the healer. You know what to do for him. Do it.' Then Ketla goes back to planning Kari's joining, and Capiam goes off to count reindeer, or take Carp another gift. No one listens to me."

"It is the way of the herdfolk. And Capiam most of all. What he cannot fix, he will not worry about. Instead, he does the things he can. He marks calves for himself, and Ketla, and Rolke, and even Kari, who should be doing her own. He increases the stature of his folk by letting all know what a good healer he has. He catches fish to dry for the long winter, and does all a man can do to see that his family is provided for. If death comes, he will mourn. But he will not mourn before then."

After a moment, Tillu nodded. "I see." She paused. "Without realizing it, I have been doing the same myself." She turned beseeching eyes on him. "I haven't seen Kerlew today. How is he?"

Heckram looked uncomfortable. "I haven't seen him either. But he seemed fine the last time I did. Thinner, but perhaps he is growing taller."

"Is he eating well?" Tillu asked anxiously.

"I . . . I would suppose so. There is never a lack of food in Joboam's tent."

Tillu stared at him without speaking. Heckram sighed. "I can do little about it, Tillu. I do not like him to be there, but he stays where the najd stays, and Carp stays with Joboam. Capiam has given hides and paid women to sew him a fine new tent. The tent is up, and the najd likes it, but he also likes to stay in Joboam's tent. There he does not have to build his own fire or cook for himself. Joboam does it all, but not as willingly as he did at first. Still, in that tent Carp has much to eat, rich furs to sleep on, and many gifts. I wonder at the things Joboam has given him. Yesterday I saw the najd wearing a bronze neckpiece that was Joboam's favorite. He dressed in Joboam's best tunics, for all that they hang to the ground on him. Yesterday Pirtsi was butchering one of Joboam's calves; the najd wished to eat calve's heart and tongue. I cannot walk into Joboam's hut and demand the boy; Kerlew would not leave the najd, and Joboam would cause an uproar. But I do not think the najd would allow Joboam to hurt the boy."

Tillu had listened in silence. "I understand," she said. "There is little either of us can do right now. When Rolke is better, then I will find a way to speak to Kerlew." She suddenly looked up at Heckram. "I may have to take him away with me," she whispered. She fumbled suddenly for words to express her sudden resolution. "I do not want him learning what Carp is teaching him; that a friend is the one who gives you the most. Look at poor Kari, and how he repaid all her care and hospitality. Since the najd tossed her aside, she has grieved like a heart-broken child. She scarcely speaks at all. Tomorrow they will join her to Pirtsi, as if they were giving him a puppy from their best bitch. No one asks her what she would like to wear for her joining, what she would like to eat, let alone if she likes the man. It all goes on without her." Tillu's outrage broke into her voice as she asked. "They do not even know who she is. How can they decide what is best for her?"

"They are her parents," Heckram reminded her gently. "They do not see her as she is."

"Perhaps no parent sees when a child is grown. You do not wish to give Kerlew to the najd. You would choose differently for him. But he has chosen for himself that which makes him happiest. I know you do not care for Carp; nor do I. But he is teaching Kerlew what the boy wishes most to learn. There is something I have come to believe. In time, Kerlew will be a powerful najd."

A coldness came into Tillu's voice. She released Heckram's hand. "Powerful, yes. He will excel at taking from folk their food and clothes and shelter, by threatening them with his mystical powers. He will trick the clothes from their backs, threaten the food from their children's mouths. What do you think Carp does right now? He has found a weakness in Joboam, a way to threaten him. And he will use it, until he has taken from Joboam all he can give. Or until he finds a wealthier victim. Already he drains Capiam. Carp is a sucking tick, Heckram. Do you wonder that I do not wish Kerlew to become one?"

Heckram retreated from the bristle in her voice. "Tillu, I did not mean that . . ."

"Healer!" One of the women leaned out the tent flap. "Ketla bids you come and see! Kari has tried on her clothes for tomorrow's joining."

"Tillu," Heckram began again, but she cut in, "I have to see to Rolke. Be careful of your fingers. Remember what I told you to do for them." She rose, and the back she turned to him was stiff and straight.

"I'll be back tomorrow," he said to the falling tent-flap.

Within the tent, Kari stood like a stretched hide. She wore a jacket of soft leather with half-length sleeves, trimmed with amber beads and Ketla's woven work. Her knee-length woolen skirt was decorated with fringe around the hem. Bracelets of bronze wrapped her arms. Carved bone combs restrained her sleek hair. And her face was yellow and stiff as poorly cured leather.

"Have you ever seen her so beautiful?" Ketla demanded.

Tillu couldn't speak, but her silence wasn't noticed in the general assent. "I must see to Rolke," she said, and slipped to the back of the tent where the boy lay. She stooped over him, to trickle willow bark tea into his mouth, while the women clustered about Kari, removing her finery and chattering of tomorrow's joining. Tillu shut them from her awareness. The boy wasn't getting better. He clung to life but each day he was weaker. "Rolke?" she called gently. His eyelids twitched, but didn't open. The fever burned him like a flame consumes oil. He was melting away before her eyes. Her own pallet was not far from his. She lay down on it, wondering if there was any way she could help any one.

The tent had been long dark, the chants and drum stilled for hours when Kari nudged her. "Wake up," she pleaded, tears in her voice. "Please, Tillu, you have to help me." No sooner had Tillu sat up than Kari had her by the arm, tugging her to her feet and out of the tent. The flap fell behind them and Tillu rubbed her eyes in the mellow undark of the summer night. The sun hovered still in the sky, making night a pale parody of the day. The camp around them was still.

"Here is the knife," Kari said, pushing the sheathed blade into Tillu's sleepy hands. "Do you need a light to do it?"

"What?" Tillu felt trapped in a dream where none of the events were connected.

"My nose. Remember, you said you would help me notch my nose and ears so Pirtsi wouldn't want me. Hurry."

"Kari," Tillu began in confusion. "I can't. I'm a healer, not one who . . ."

"No one will help me!" Kari's whisper screamed. "Not you, not Carp! You will not keep your promise to scar me. He will not say that I am Owl's, and not to be given to Pirtsi!"

Tillu suddenly realized who had refused Kari. Owl, not

Pirtsi. "Is that what Carp promised he would do?" Tillu interrupted. "That he would say you were Owl's, would give you to Owl?"

"Yes!" Kari sank to her knees on the hides before the tent. Her hands rose to claw at her breasts. "Yes. He said that if I would do favors for him, find secrets for him, he would see that I belonged to Owl alone. He said that when I served him, I served the spirits and they would be pleased with me. He promised that as long as I served him, I would be safe. But then he left with Joboam! That wasn't my fault! I didn't leave him, he left me. But when I went to him tonight, to ask him to tell my father that Pirtsi must not have me, he laughed at me. He laughed. He said the spirits cared little about women, that I was not fit to be Owl's. He told me to go home and do as I was told. And then Joboam came into the tent. He was angry to see me there. He asked, 'Is this how you keep your promises, Najd?' And Carp said, 'Men do not direct me, Joboam, but the spirits. So far they have asked me to be kind to you. Do not risk angering them with wild words.' Then Joboam got very angry, but Carp only laughed more, and said to me, 'Run back to your tent, little woman. Sleep well tonight, for tomorrow is your joining day.' And Joboam looked so angry that I ran back here. Thinking you would help me. But you won't."

"Kerlew. Where was Kerlew?" Tillu demanded, grabbing Kari by the shoulders as she knelt down to face her.

"I . . . he wasn't there, I didn't see him. Tillu, you must help me. I cannot be joined with Pirtsi. I will not let him touch me. I can't."

"Why?"

Kari only stared at her, her eyes going bigger in her face. Then her mouth crumpled like a little child's and she pushed into Tillu's arms. She held the girl, feeling the sobs that shook her. "Why?" Tillu asked again, gently, but Kari shook her head. The words finally came in hesitant gasps. "When I was little. He used to say he'd kill me. So I couldn't tell. Then, last time, he said. If my father challenged him about it. He'd kill him. It would be my fault. Everyone would say I was a liar and a trouble-maker. No one would believe me, ever. No one. Joboam was always bigger, always stronger. Rolke knew, but he wouldn't tell. Because of the presents. Never again. Never."

"Hush. Hush." Tillu rocked her as if she were a small child. It was the only comfort she could give her. Some-how she had known all along and was not surprised. What bandage could be put on an injury like this? What poultice could draw the poison from the past?

"Listen," she said, whispering over Kari's sobs. "Listen to me. Tomorrow morning, I will go to the herdlord. I will speak up for you, I will say . . ."

"No! No, then my father would attack him, and he would kill my father. No. No one must know. And I must not be joined to Pirtsi, either. No. No."

"All right. All right," Tillu agreed frantically. "We'll think of something else, then. We'll think of something else." She hugged the girl tightly, then released her. "Kari. Listen to me. I want you to go inside, and lie down and sleep. Get some rest. By tomorrow, I will have an idea, and we will not let them join you to Pirtsi. Will you do as I ask? Will you?"

Tillu leaned closer to peer into her face. Kari had sud-denly gone slack in her grip, as if she had lost all life. Slowly the girl lifted her dark head. Her eyes caught the starlight as she asked, "Do you think I am unfit to serve Owl? Or do you think Owl might help me?"

"Of course. Of course Owl will help us," Tillu lied to ease the girl's pain. "Go inside. Sleep now. I have much to do before morning. Please."

"Owl will help me," Kari said softly. Her voice was suddenly relaxed and trusting. "I should have thought of it before, Tillu. I can go to Owl and ask for help. He came to me first when I was alone, by my father's fire. Carp was not with me then, yet Owl came to me. And I may yet go to him."

"Yes, yes. But sleep now, Kari. Sleep."

Tillu forced herself to be still as Kari rose and lifted the tent-flap. "It's going to be all right," she assured Kari once more as she stooped to enter.

"Yes," Kari agreed, and the tent-flap fell behind her.

In an instant Tillu was on her feet. Kerlew. Where was Kerlew? And what could be done for Kari? The trodden earth was cool beneath her bare feet as she trotted down the path between the tents. She peered at the tents as she passed. There was Ristor's, that one Acor's. On. There was Stina's tent, patched with a new hide sewn pale against the old ones. And Ristin's. And beside it, a pale new tent she didn't know. She hesitated.

"Tillu!"

Her name from behind her. She was caught in a fierce embrace. An instant she struggled, until the rasp of his beard against her face and familiar scent calmed her. She clutched back at him, abruptly became aware that she still gripped Kari's knife. She wriggled from his grasp, thrust Kari's knife into her belt. At least she wouldn't cut her own face before morning.

"I was coming to find you," Heckram was saying. "When I saw you on the path."

"I was coming to find you, because . . ."

"Listen to me, first. Kerlew is gone. I hadn't had a sight of him all day, so I finally made an excuse to call on the najd. I took him a nest of eggs I found this morning. He seemed glad to see me, but Joboam was not. They had words about it, and Carp said he would invite whomever he wished. Joboam became silent, then, but his eyes were full of anger. Carp is not wise to bait him. But Kerlew was nowhere in sight. And when I asked about him, Carp said that he had gone to seek a vision. I asked more questions, but all he would say was that he could not speak of it, but all would soon be clear."

The words had tumbled from Heckram's lips without pause. Now he stood before her, his eyes black in the night. He lifted a hand toward her, as if asking forgiveness. She seized it.

"He's sent Kerlew on a vision-quest. I know that much of the shaman. He spoke of it often when we lived among

Benu's folk. He encouraged the young men to fast for long periods, and then to isolate themselves from the tribe and seek a vision. It was a way of gaining spirit protection.''

''That would be why the boy looked so thin lately,'' Heckram said slowly. ''A long fast and then . . . but Kerlew is not old enough to be sent out alone for such a thing. Nor wise enough.''

''It matters little to Carp. Unless the boy comes back with a vision, he cannot be a shaman. If he isn't a najd, he's no use to Carp. Kerlew used to mutter about it when he thought I was asleep. Visions and guardian animals. Where would he go?''

Tillu's question was despairing, not seeking an answer. Silence stretched long and brittle. Then Heckram spoke in unwilling answer. ''To the Najd's Steps.''

''What?''

''I had not thought of it in years. It is a dare game that some boys still play at. There is a part of the Cataclysm that is all buckled stone. Not a grain of soil, not a stem of grass grows there. It is all a tumble of black sharp-edged stones, like a torrent of rock down the Cataclysm's face, and above it a sheer rise of stone, broken only by narrow ledges. When I was very small and there were summer storms, the old folk used to say the ancient najd was angry. The tale was that he had gone up the steps to speak with the sky spirits and never come back. That he was up there still, and looked down on the herdfolk and would know if one was less than honest or brave.''

He looked down into Tillu's face. She came into his arms, shivering at his words. ''The other boys used to challenge one another, when adults weren't around. No one was supposed to climb the Najd's Steps. To do so was . . . more than unlucky. The najd might send something to steal you from your tent if you dared his steps. So, of course, boys did.'' He paused, then added, almost ashamed, ''Except for me. I heard about it, but my days were too full of chores to run and play with the others. Then I heard one day that Joboam had gone higher than anyone else had ever gone, to the very top. And to mark the top of his climb, he had left on the highest step a bronze wristband that his father had just given him. All the boys could talk of nothing else, for days. Joboam went about saying that he had proved forever that he was the bravest of us all."

"It must have chafed you, to hear them brag of what you could not even try." Despite her worries, Tillu had been caught up in the story.

Heckram choked down a laugh. "It did. It did for days. Until one drizzly morning, I rose before anyone else, and tried myself against the Najd's Steps. They were slippery in the damp, and once I looked down and all the camp was hidden in mist. As if I climbed through the very clouds. But I was stubborn and pushed on. At first I had had some vague dream that the other boys in the camp would look up and see me high up the Najd's Steps. Now I knew they couldn't, that I would be hidden by the mist and the steepness of the climb. But I went on. For myself. And I discovered two things."

He paused, forcing Tillu to ask, "What?"

"There is a place where the steps narrow and work out across the face of the Cataclysm. Too narrow a place for me to safely go. Or Joboam. A place a smaller boy might walk, but not he or I. And at the narrowing place is where I found his wristband. Not at the top of the Najd's Steps. So I took it. And then I pressed myself flat against the rock face, and I went beyond it. Five steps beyond it. I counted them. And then I discovered the other thing. At the end of the Najd's Steps."

Somewhere a small animal screamed as talons found it. Tillu started as if she felt the claws in her own back. Heckram held her closer.

"The najd is still there," he whispered. "The steps stop. But beyond them is a tiny niche, less than a cave, in the cliff's face. And in that place, with his basket and his magic tokens spread before him, is the najd. Crouching and grinning out over the Cataclysm and the herdfolk below."

Tillu gasped in horror, then asked, "What did you do then?"

"I left it alone. Even I was smart enough to know no good could come of meddling with a najd's bones. But I scratched my mark there on the wall of the Cataclysm. And I worked my way back off the narrow place and back onto the steps. And I came down. That evening, I went to Joboam's father's tent. With his father looking on, I said, 'I found this today. Isn't it yours?' And I gave him back his wristband."

"And you wonder why he hates you," Tillu said softly.

"Not really. He had his revenge. He told the herdlord that I had been making mock of the Najd's Steps, playing there. He was very angry and scolded me before all the elders. Ristin was furious that I had taken such a chance, and made sure my chores kept me too busy to try it again. But I did not mind. For all that, Joboam and I both still know that his wristband was not on the top step. That he was not as brave as he had said he was."

"And you think Kerlew would go there?"

"I do. Joboam would make sure of it, if he thought of it. It is not an easy place to return from."

A silence fell, but when Tillu opened her lips to speak, Heckram bent to swiftly kiss her. He held her close as he spoke. "But we will both come down, tomorrow. The night is mild, and the lower steps are easy for a boy Kerlew's size. I will let him have his night on the Najd's Steps. He won't go very high. I know you will worry. But you must understand these dares are important to a boy. And he has his own kind of wisdom. He will be safe. And tomorrow I will bring him down to you."

"You are sure of this?"

Honesty saddened his eyes. "No. But it is the best I can do. In the dark, a man my size would not get one-third of the way up the Steps." He could see her thoughts. "And you yourself would not even get that far. One has to have seen it by daylight to climb it. In this false light, it would be suicide. Besides . . ." He paused. "To bring Kerlew down now would be to take something from him, something he might never find again. He has to have this night alone, on the Najd's Steps, Tillu."

She understood, but unwillingly. There was nothing she could do for her son this night. Tillu sighed deeply and leaned into Heckram's chest. Kari broke suddenly into her thoughts. "Heckram. What do the herdfolk say about a woman being forced into a joining she does not want?"

His brows knit at the abrupt change of subject. After a moment he replied, "It very seldom happens. Sometimes, a woman desires a man who is already joined to another. So, she takes another man instead. It is sad, but it happens. Sometimes they learn to get along, though. Look at Ibb and Bror. It is gossiped that Ibb took him only because no one else asked her. But they are long and happy years they have shared."

"But if the woman did not want the joining at all? If she hated the idea, but her parents insisted?"

His mind leaped the gap. "Kari is that unhappy?"

Tillu nodded. "She wanted me to cut her nose off this evening. So Pirtsi wouldn't take her."

Heckram's expression reflected his dismay at the idea. "But she is right," he conceded. "Pirtsi is too vain to take a disfigured woman. He'd find a way out."

"Then you think I should do it?" Tillu asked in horror.

"No!" Heckram was vehement. "She should go to Stina or old Natta. One of the older herdwomen. Or several of them. She should say she is being forced, and that she is truly unhappy. They'll be swift to take her side. They've been on their own long enough to know that sometimes a woman is better alone than bedded with someone like Pirtsi. And neither of them like the boy, anyway. Capiam will be very unhappy when they come to him, and greatly embarrassed. But he can't stand against them, nor can Ketla. If he did, those women would raise such an outcry as would have every woman in the gathered folks angered and impatient with the men. Better embarrassment than the whole folk disturbed. Old women will not be ignored."

"You mean this? This is true, among the herdfolk?"

"So it has always been. Didn't you know that? I recall Ristin mentioned some time ago that she thought Kari was

unhappy. But no one was sure. Sometimes a woman pre-
tends reluctance to make a man more attentive. Send her to
Ristin, if you wish. She'll know which matriarchs will
scare Capiam the most.''

She hugged him suddenly, tightly. With her face pressed
against him, she said, "I did not even know why I was
running to you tonight. But you had the answers, to all my
fears. I think I shall even be able to sleep a little this
night.''

He stooped suddenly, lifted her off her feet. The strength
of his arms around her, the ease with which he held her
made her feel, not weak, but protected by his strength. She
put his arms around his neck and hugged him close. He
nodded toward the new tent. "Sleep? I have a better
idea,'' he whispered.

She clung to him, teasing herself with the idea. "I
can't,'' she murmured against his neck. His skin was salt
against her mouth. "I have to go back to Capiam's tent. I
have to talk to Kari.''

"No,'' he chided her. His hands supported her against
him, sent warmth flowing across her skin in waves. "Don't
tell Kari now. She'd run right to Stina and Natta, wake
them from a sound sleep, and sound like a foolish girl with
marriage jitters. Have her go in the cool gray of morning,
dressed sensibly and talking calmly. They must see her as
a determined woman, not as a willful teasing girl.''

"Mm,'' she said into his neck. She could not decide if
his reasoning was sound or if she merely wanted it to be so
that she could linger here with him. And Kerlew . . .

"And stop fretting about Kerlew. If you will not believe
as I do, that there is something about the boy that brings
him through danger unscathed, then have faith in what you
yourself have taught him. The boy is cautious to a fault.
Let him have this bit of a dare; the other boys will hear of
it, and respect him for it. But not if his parents run to fetch
him down.''

A great stillness spread through Tillu's body. He could
not have meant what he had so casually implied. He had
been speaking in generalities. But never had any man ever

spoken so of Kerlew, thoughtfully, as if he were a boy to be raised instead of a problem to be solved. A small part of herself hackled possessively; but within bloomed the perception that Heckram might know more of being a boy than she could.

He took her silence for assent. The top of the tent door brushed her head. He set her gently on her feet and stood in silence. She looked around. It was a man's tent, sternly practical. The one traveling chest in it was dark and scarred and plain. She wondered what had become of Elsa's unfinished trunk, then pushed the thought away. There was nothing here that was not Heckram. She saw him in the tidy pallet and the simple implements of his life. Then he touched her, his callused fingers running softly down her bare arm and setting her skin singing. The simple touch, the smell of man in the tent, the gentle glow of the coals on the hearth undid the catches on her self-control. The frustrated imaginings of the last few days rose rampant. Urgency seized her.

There was no time for careful undressing. She sensed his surprise as she tugged his shirt open and ran greedy hands over his chest. Her mouth followed them, and the taste of his skin made her dizzy. His tiny nipples stood up beneath her tongue. She felt him take a sudden breath. His hands ran down her back, slipped up inside her shirt. Callused fingers stroked her breasts. She wondered who this woman was, who did not hesitate under his touch, but only felt her heat rise higher. Fear this man? His body seemed a part of her own already, hers to touch and use. It was natural to show him her wants, to guide one of his big hands down her belly. His hand slipped lower, exploring, and she held suddenly still, her mouth on his skin, her eyes closed. He moved so slowly, so carefully. But she was suddenly ready, more ready than she had ever been and unwilling to wait any longer. So a herdwoman could say who she would join? A woman could decide such things? Then . . . She fumbled at the fastening of his trousers, dragging them down to expose his readiness. "Tillu," he murmured in pleased rebuke as she pushed him toward the bedding. She heard herself laugh softly, the sound of a woman who had taken possession of the moment and knew no fear. Her own boldness and his delighted response amazed her, feeding her aggression. She pulled him down onto the bedding, but was astonished when he rolled onto his back, ceding control to her. She hesitated.

"Shy?" Laughter behind his challenge.

She met his eyes frankly, found that she, too, could smile. Mating, she realized, did not have to be so serious a thing. Had only to be whatever they wanted to make it. "No," she discovered aloud. "But I'm not going to make all the efforts, either."

"The second time, I'll do the work," he promised, and pulled her down laughing atop him.

Kerlew:
The Vision

HE SAT QUITE still, his knees drawn up to his bony chest. Kerlew's buttocks were cold against the stone, but he didn't move. Moving didn't help. He was cold all over, he ached and his head felt light. Even when he sat still, he quivered. The shaking had been worst during the long climb; now it had settled down to a humming, like bees crawling over his skin. The only thing he didn't feel was hungry. Yesterday he had stopped feeling the pangs and nausea of extreme hunger. That was how Carp had known he was ready. He thought of food, of boiled eggs or meat seared hot. His stomach squeezed with revulsion. No. He wasn't interested in food anymore.

He braced his feet and pushed his back against the cold stone. He wasn't going to look down again. In the dimness of night, he hadn't minded so much. The tiny red fires below had not been, so different from the far stars above. Above. Below. He chuckled foolishly. Here he was, up again when he wanted to go down. Up the stone ridges, to the top of the Najd's Steps, when he needed to go down, into the caverns of the spirit world. He had tried to ask Carp about that, but the old najd had only flapped his question away with his leathery hand. He had been so impatient with Kerlew lately. Chasing him outside so he could talk alone with Joboam, commanding silence when he asked about Kari or his mother. As if Kerlew didn't know what Carp and Joboam spoke of when they were alone. He knew. Spirits whispered to him while he slept, secrets crept into his ears. But Carp no longer wanted to hear what the spirits whispered in his dreams. Carp wanted only to eat, to wear fine garments, to chant and dance before all the people. He had no time for Kerlew's questions or objections.

"Just do," he had said. "Do what I tell you and do not wonder. You will know the place when you see it. When you get there, do what seems right, and wait for a vision. You may have to wait several days and nights. But do not be discouraged, nor afraid. Stay there, and stay awake until your vision comes. Do not sleep, do not eat, drink nothing. Only wait. Then the vision will come. And you will be a najd."

Then he had given Kerlew the little yellow root to chew. And sent him across the hummocky meadows to the base of the stone steps. When? A long, long time ago. He tried to put boundaries on the time. It had been morning at first. Then it had been the warm part of a day. He wasn't sure if there had been evening. But now there was a night. Or was this a morning? He opened his eyes quickly. He had to stay awake. And yes, it was day again, almost. He wondered why this day was still so cold. Down below, gray smoke rose from the domed tents. Tiny reindeer milled around in a pen, chased by a single man. Usually many men chased them. It made no sense to Kerlew, but the herdfolk did it every day, and it was very exciting to watch. The plunging hooves of the animals threw up mud or dust, and the men and women chasing them yelled and fell and wrestled the animals in it. Kerlew wished he could be there now, but Carp had said he must go find a vision. He looked down again at the pen. The man had stopped chasing the reindeer. They churned around in the middle of the pen for a short time, then gathered in a corner. No more excitement. He wasn't missing anything. So wait for the vision.

How long?

As long as it took. There was no going down until he had the vision. Kerlew settled back with vague resignation. He glanced once more at his companion. Was he still waiting for his vision? He hadn't spoken to Kerlew. He simply sat, his knees drawn up to his chest. A basket was beside him. Before him were many fine and wondrous things. There was a knife, with a blade of shining black. Some painted bones. A bundle of draggled feathers, tied in a bouquet with faded string and bright beads still. The shriveled talons of a hawk. But the best of all was between his two bony knees. A small round drum, such as Carp drummed upon. But better. Kerlew had never known there could be a drum better than Carp's. The leather drum head was fuzzed with green mold. But it didn't hide the faded figures in red and blue. Kerlew stared at it enviously. Reindeer. Those were reindeer, and behind them were men, long men painted in blue and red. The small hammer had fallen from the bony fingers that clutched the drum. It lay on the stony floor of the niche. One end was shaped like the curled foot of a bird, the other like a raven's head and beak. Kerlew thought of picking it up. No. This bone najd might be angry if he did that. He glanced warily at the najd, but the najd only smiled the wider.

Kerlew lifted a finger to touch his own teeth, to outline the hidden sockets of bone around his eyes. Yes. His face was like that face, but hidden behind flesh. A mask of skin, he was wearing a mask of skin, but that najd had taken his off and greeted Kerlew bare-faced. Kerlew grinned back at him, trying to show his teeth as wide. When he had first crawled in here, the old najd had frightened him. But he had sat very still beside him, all night long, because this was the end of the steps, there was nowhere else to go, but he couldn't go back without a vision. Maybe this was the vision. Maybe this was what he was supposed to take back with him. No. Carp would have told him more plainly. After a moment, he was sure of it.

"Did you never have your vision?" Kerlew asked the grinning najd. The najd didn't answer, but Kerlew began to feel friendly toward him. He had such fascinating things. And he asked nothing of Kerlew. He didn't eat while making Kerlew stay hungry. He didn't demand he fetch wood or tend a fire. He didn't send him out of the tent into the cold night. He didn't tell him to find a vision. No. This was a very kind najd, who shared his niche with Kerlew. Kerlew liked him. He patted him gently on the shoulder. Dust rose from his feathered mantle, skin crackled and bones shifted beneath his hand. Kerlew took his hand away swiftly. He hadn't liked that sound. Like a bone drum. The old najd was like a hollow bone drum. Bone drum.

He pulled his eyes open again. Had he slept? No. He was sure he hadn't slept. He had only closed his eyes. He leaned his chest against his knees and looked down at his bare feet squinched against the black stone. They looked very far away, as far as the misty tent village below. He reached out his hand, watched it travel a long way until it was beside his toes. He touched one of his toes, pressing his finger down on it. Nothing. His toes were so far away he couldn't feel them anymore. "I can't feel my toes," he whispered. The bone najd looked at him but said nothing.

Giddiness swept Kerlew. He clutched his knees, fighting it. His toes, the edge of the ledge, and the far misty village rippled like stones in a stream. The village washed up against the ledge. He reached past his toes to touch one of the tiny tents. He put his fingers against it, but couldn't feel it. Of course. If his toes were too far away to feel, the tents were, too. He giggled, then leaned back suddenly as another wave of dizziness swept him. The world rocked. He pressed his back to the cold hard stone, pushing hard with his feet, trying to make things be still. Then, without warning, the world tilted sideways and he fell backwards into darkness.

He was in a dark place. Water dripped down the cold stone walls, clung to the roots that festooned the ceiling. He tried to stand up, but could not. He couldn't move at all. He tried to touch his own body, but couldn't find his hands. He couldn't find himself at all. He couldn't even see himself. But he could see the others.

They sat about the small chamber, backs braced against

the stone walls. Two were playing tablo. The other had his talismans spread before him.

"Here's one who hopes to be a najd," said one of the tablo players. He looked over at Kerlew and smiled. He was very old; his face was like a wrinkled hide and his hair as sparse as a dog's whiskers. Even his scalp was brown and wrinkled. "Would you care for a game, first?"

Kerlew kept still. These were the ones who would trick him, the ones trapped between. If he spoke to them, he would be trapped with them. He did not even shake his head.

"Ah, he's too wise to be caught that way," observed the other tablo player. He was much younger than the first najd. He was dressed in sleek otter skins and his teeth were very white. "Carp warned you not to speak to us, didn't he? He's a sly one, Carp is. Did he tell you not to be afraid of anything you meet?"

Just in time he bit down on his tongue and kept it from moving. He wondered how he was going to get out of the chamber. Everywhere was darkness and damp, and all he could see clearly were the three old najds. And he could not find his body to make it walk away. All he could do was keep silent and watch.

"Ah!" muttered the last najd to himself. "This is what was needed. Here he is at last." This najd was a small man, not much larger than Kerlew. A sleek black cloak wrapped his shoulders. Even in the dim chamber, it had a blue sheen. His hair was black streaked gray, and he wore a necklace of bear's claws. He had been rummaging in a small basket beside him. Now he took out something small and brown. He held it in his cupped palm, and turned his head sideways to bring one bright eye close to it. His eyes were very black and shining and when he smiled he bobbed his head up and down. He reminded Kerlew of someone. Something. Now he turned his head sideways and smiled. "Come here," he said. "Don't speak. But he never told you not to look, did he? Come and see what has been missing?"

Then Kerlew was beside the old najd, looking into his

wrinkled hand. The tablo players had receded into darkness. Only this one was left. He patted the soft green moss beside him, and Kerlew found himself. He sat, wondering at possessing a body again. Birds were singing in the willows on the river-bank behind them. The old najd waved them to silence. Eyes shining, the old najd tipped his hand to the boy. His callused palm cupped a tiny wolf of brown bone. Its eyes were black and its tongue was red. As he watched, it sat up on the najd's hand and looked up at Kerlew.

"Ah! Ah!" The shaman made a laugh of the words. "He knows, you see! He should not be in my basket at all. And you have something of mine, perhaps? No? Look in your pouch, young najd. Something there does not belong. Look in your pouch."

Kerlew hesitated. But Carp had told him to do what felt right. This felt right. He unslung his new pouch, the one Carp had demanded from Joboam, from his shoulder. He untied the thongs. Slowly he drew the items from his pouch, spreading them in an arc before him. Knife and bloodstone and piece of blade. Amber and bird's foot and rabbit's tail. Wolverine's tooth.

"Aahh!" The old one sighed, impressed. Then he lifted cunning eyes to Kerlew's face. "You would not trick an old man? The trade must be fair. I have what is yours. But I shall not give it to you until you give me what is mine. These are objects of power, but mine is not among them. Give me what is mine."

Kerlew's eyes wandered over his talismans. But everything here was his, gathered fairly. All of these, he knew, were his. But the old najd only smiled the wider, so many teeth, and said, "Give me what is mine."

Kerlew picked up his shaman's bag to see if something had rolled under it. No. Nothing. But within the bag, something whispered and rustled. Something light and bony. Trepidation washed through him, but he reached into the pouch. Brittle, it rolled under his fingertips, making his skin crawl. He lifted it into the bright sunlight.

"Mine," said the old najd, and the little bird skull

grinned at him. "It is what I have been needing. Just as
you have been needing this." He extended his hand with
the tiny wolf to Kerlew. The wolf sat alertly, his tail swept
neatly around his forepaws. His little black eyes were
bright as he looked up into Kerlew's face. Kerlew's heart
howled for the wolf. He did not need to think. He dropped
the little owl skull into the old najd's hand. And was
suddenly glad to be rid of it. Then the old najd's hand
tipped. But the tiny wolf scrabbled his claws against the
old najd's hand and would not leap to Kerlew.

The old najd looked suddenly troubled. He righted his
hand and the tiny wolf once more sat flat in it. The old
najd looked at Kerlew with his round black eyes. "Something is wrong here," he said gravely. "Something is very
wrong." He tilted his head toward the tiny wolf, listening.
Then he straightened to regard Kerlew stonily. "You are
not herdfolk."

A coldness swept Kerlew that made the hot sting of
tears a sharp pain. The tiny wolf in the najd's hand curled
up, swept his tail over his nose and closed his eyes. Shut
Kerlew out. He would have spoken, forgetting Carp's
warning, if he could have thought of words. He could only
stare mutely into the najd's bottomless eyes.

"Ah." The old najd nodded somberly. "Well, let us
see what is wrong. Let us see why you are not herdfolk."
He closed his hand into a knot around the tiny wolf, and
gestured to Kerlew's spread talismans.

"Ah. See this?" The bony finger that pointed at the
blade fragment had a long yellow nail. It swept suddenly
across the arc of the power items. "See here?" The wolverine tooth. "And see." To the Knife. "And at last."
The amber. "It is all very plain."

Kerlew lifted eyes to the old najd, silently begging him
to explain. He put a cautioning finger against his lips.
"Listen. It is plain. This," a finger tapped the knife
fragment, "is a debt. This," the Knife, "will pay it. The
one who holds the knife will draw the wolverine's teeth.
The stone is on the blood, and the blood is on the stone.

And Wolf will bring it all together." The old najd nodded with immense satisfaction.

Then he looked very stern. "But you are not herdfolk. You have no Wolf, nor do you belong to Wolf. You know why. When you took on the debt of the Knife, you took on a duty to the herdfolk. You have not kept it. You have let harm walk boldly among them. What he does is wrong. Reindeer, who watches over the herdfolk, who feeds and clothes them, is very angry with him. He will demand an accounting. And you. You must arm the Wolf and destroy the Wolverine. I will free what is mine. But you must do the rest, little najd." He leaned very close to Kerlew.

"I could whisper a word to my little wolf. I could tell him that to go with you would be to go with me. That you are to be the najd of the herdfolk. That it is right for you to hold the tokens of the herdfolk in your hands. Ah, but then, but then if you did not keep your duty . . . Wolf would tear your throat out!"

The old najd had leaned ever closer as he spoke, and on the last words his mouth elongated into a snarling muzzle that opened wide and his canines flashed long and white before Kerlew's face. Kerlew tightened his belly muscles but did not draw back. The old najd sat back suddenly and laughed softly. He pulled his lips down over his teeth and resumed his own face. "Yes, yes. You are the Wolf's, yes. But he will not be yours until you are herdfolk. Will you be herdfolk?"

Kerlew hesitated fractionally before bobbing a nod. He would have offered the blood warm from his body to hold Wolf in his hand. His chest heaved with the depth of his wanting.

"Ah. Then. Keep the bargain of the Knife. That is all. She who you freed left a place empty, a task unfinished. Finish the task and take the place. Free your people of that which plagues them. Will you do this?"

Again Kerlew nodded. The old najd copied him. "Good. They have been alone long, and I have suffered with their pain. You take a burden from me. Here." He turned slightly aside from Kerlew, lifted the wolf to his lips, and

whispered over him. Then he reached suddenly to grip
Kerlew's wrist with fingers as cold and hard as bone. He
dragged the boy's hand toward him, pinched his thin wrist
until his coiled fingers opened.

And dropped Wolf into his palm. Kerlew looked down
on the coiled figure.

"He sleeps," the old najd whispered. "But he is with
you. Listen. Once you have earned him, he will help you.
He will make a proper cover for the drum. Then, when
you are alone, you can drum for him and he will dance for
you. But, first!" A cautionary finger in Kerlew's face.
"First, you must listen and obey. This is what you must
do to earn him." The old najd paused suddenly, listening.
His face became very grave and sad. "To the first who
comes, you must say nothing. NOTHING! This will be
hard, and your pain will be great. But Wolf will drink the
blood of your pain, and be satisfied. It is the beginning of
being herdfolk. This you do for Wolf." He nodded to
himself. "To the second one who comes, give this." The
owl's skull rustled icy against his palm. "Say, 'Be free!'
Then that debt is paid." His expression softened. "This
you do for me."

The old najd smiled suddenly, black lips writhing back
from white teeth. "Then comes Wolf. Yes, Wolf comes
and you place your hand between his eyes. And go with
him, to be najd of the herdfolk, and to pay your last debt.
That, you do for yourself." The old najd leaned back with
a sigh of deep contentment. "Long have I waited for you.
Long and long. Now you are here. And I can rest. Gather
your things and come. Take them all, now. All are prop-
erly yours."

Kerlew picked up his power objects, dropping each
carefully into his pouch. Then he watched the old najd
place each of his in a basket. The bright bundled feathers
and the dyed cubes of bone in red and blue; a string of fat
ivory teeth; the black-bladed knife and a talley of calf-ear
bits. He put the lid on the basket and tucked his drum
under his arm. The owl skull Kerlew kept in his hand.
"Come now," the old najd said. He rose with a crackling

of knee bones. "We cannot keep her waiting." Kerlew put his hand in the najd's bony one and they stepped into darkness. And out again.

The bright light of the day blinded him. Tears ran and rainbow colors washed over the village below. Kerlew swayed on the ledge, feeling the fresh winds of the high place brush past him. He was back. He was back and alive. But what of his spirit guardian? What of a vision? He turned to the old najd at his side.

"Comes the first," breathed the najd.

Kerlew looked up. Carp stood before him, smiling, showing the familiar blackness between his teeth. Then the blackness went blue as Carp rippled in the wind. Kerlew recoiled in surprise. "Well, apprentice?" Carp demanded in an airy voice. "Have you no word of welcome for me?" He leaned over Kerlew, smiling insubstantially. "Are you not glad to see me? I have decided to come with you, to guide you to the spirit world. There I. will show you many wonders and gift you with many powers. Give me greeting, take my hand, and we will go together."

Kerlew sat still, frozen with fear. Confusion milled through his mind. The bone najd had told him not to speak to the first one. Carp had told him, many times, that he must find his own path to the spirit world, and enter alone. Something was wrong here, something chilling and evil.

"Do not be afraid, little apprentice." Carp's words were warm and dripping, rich as fresh liver. They reached inside Kerlew, pulled at him. He bowed over his knees with the pain of resisting them.

The bone najd spoke coldly. "There is no place for you here, forest najd. And Kerlew will not take your place nor give you his. Walk the path you have chosen."

Carp suddenly went flat and snarling, his back rippling as angrily as his spirit beast. His growl was the growl of Wolverine enraged. His teeth were sharp and white as he leaned forward and sank them into Kerlew's clenched fist. The blood ran red between his fingers, and the tiny wolf within his fist stirred and growled. Kerlew's mouth stretched wide in soundless agony. Blackness closed in on him. He felt Wolverine worrying his hand from his wrist, felt the parting snap.

"Go back." The bone najd lifted his drum-claw. "Go back and finish dying, forest najd."

There was a sound like an old tent splitting in the wind. The pain stopped. Kerlew opened his eyes. His hand was on the end of his wrist, unmarked. He felt Wolf stir within it. Carp stood just off the edge of the ledge, looking suddenly mournful. "A last word," he begged, and it was the voice of the tired old man Kerlew knew.

"No." The bone najd forbade it, and Carp suddenly tattered to pieces and was swept away on the wind. Something ripped out of Kerlew and went with him, like a hook tearing free of his flesh. He hunched over his knees, feeling his pain run hot down his face. He did not know how many lifetimes it lasted. When he could lift his head, the day was blue and clear before him. He looked down on the tiny herdfolk village below him. Below him, their lives went on. Folk clustered and shouted thinly by the reindeer pens, children raced between the tents, the herd gazed on the meadows and flanks of the Cataclysm.

The ledge was suddenly darkened, the opening to the niche blocked by a dark shape. Kerlew breathed in sudden fear, hid his hands from more pain.

"Comes the second," the bone najd sighed. She filled the opening to the niche, closing the day away from them. Her feathers were sleek and gleaming. She stood, looking down on Kerlew and he almost knew her. But she was not for him. She had come for the bone najd with the bird-bright eyes, and it was for him that Kerlew lifted the tiny skull in his hand. She took the owl talisman into her hand. "Be free," he told her. She smiled suddenly, eyes as black as Raven's feathers. She leaned far out, looked down to the village below. Kerlew followed her gaze. The meadow at the foot of the steps teemed with folk, all crying out in thin voices and waving their arms. Owl gazed down on them for a long moment. Then she spread wide her wings and swooped. Kerlew watched her silent flight. Shrill squeals of terror rose as she descended on her prey. She would feed well. The bone najd looked satisfied. Kerlew leaned back once more in his niche, to await the third. The morning passed its peak, and the warm sun of afternoon touched Kerlew's feet with feeble fingers. And still Kerlew was patient, knowing he would come.

He came as hot panting breath, as the scent of warm life and fresh blood. He felt like a rush of sleek fur under Kerlew's hands, like a tumble of cubs against his chest. He stood before Kerlew, larger than the moon, and his eyes were green. His narrow black lips writhed in a smile that bared brave white teeth, and Kerlew laughed in joy with him. Tears washed his eyes clean and he saw his brother. The hand he reached was not to claim or to subdue, but to touch with fondness. His brother suffered the touch of his human fingers upon his furred brow. "Wolf," he whispered. Joy was hot in him. "At last you have come."

"Kerlew," whispered Wolf, and his voice was a voice to trust at last.

chapter twelve

TILLU AWAKENED SLOWLY. She had drifted at the edge of sleep for much of the night, feeling that she should rise and go back to Capiam's hut, but never finding the will-power to leave the body comfort of the nest of hides and Heckram's warm chest rising and falling beneath her cheek. She pushed a handful of hair back from her eyes. A dim light gave substance to the furnishings of the tent, color to the woolen blanket that wrapped her close to Heckram. Bird sounds, and the mutter of folk moving past the tent. Morning sounds. She sat up abruptly, suddenly awake.

"Kerlew!" she said aloud. And then, "Kari!" At the sound of her voice, Heckram reared up and sat blinking in the light.

"It's morning," he said blearily. For a moment he sat still, catching up with himself. Then he reached across Tillu to scoop up their clothes. "Here," he said, thrusting the wrong shirt at her, "you've got to get to Kari, talk to her. Take her to Ristin, if you want. Or to Stina. Tell them what's wrong, and let them take care of it. But do it quickly, before they start making her ready for the joining ceremony. I've got to get up the Steps, after Kerlew."

Tillu experienced a moment of disorientation. Someone else had taken charge. She smiled a crooked smile as she pushed his shirt back at him and found her own. She wasn't sure if she liked being directed. But as she pulled her shirt on, she thought of the alternative; of being responsible for everything, handling not only every problem

but every decision, however minor. She could find nothing
wrong with his suggestions; it was only that he had voiced
them first. "You'll find Kerlew for me." She said the
words aloud, trying them out. The confidence she felt in
him surprised her.

"Yes. And I'll bring him back to you, not Carp."
Heckram pulled on his leggings as he spoke. He glanced
over his shoulder at her. He stopped suddenly and looked
at her, long. She looked back, wondering what to say.
Nothing, she decided. They would not need to always
explain things to each other. They already understood. So
she didn't apologize as she stuffed Kari's knife into her
belt and ducked out of his tent. It wasn't necessary.

She hurried past children carrying birch scoops of reindeer milk, thick as cream, and women fetching buckets of
water. She nodded hastily to those she knew. "Oh, Healer!"
called one, "My husband's fever is back again and . . ."
But Tillu only nodded quickly and hurried on. Soon, she
promised her guilt, soon. The fevers and headaches that
came and went, the tick bites that suddenly abscessed,
could be tended tomorrow. Kari's joining had to be stopped
today.

"Here you are! I've had the whole herdfolk searching
for you!" Ketla exclaimed, annoyed, as Tillu pushed into
the tent.

Tillu's eyes flew to Rolke, fearing the worst. But his
thin chest still rose and fell, and the fever still tossed him.
Habit made her push past the women to him, kneel to feel
his skin.

"But where's Kari?" Ketla demanded of her back.
"Surely she's been out with you this morning? When we
awoke and you were both gone, we worried. It's like her,
off playing like a child when she should be preparing
herself for her joining. A hundred things to be done, and
she leaves them all for me. But now you are back, and we
can . . ."

"Kari's not with me," Tillu replied distractedly. The
boy's fever was higher today, consuming what little flesh
he had left. But his breathing disturbed her most. It sounded

like water splashing over stones, a nasty, gurgling sound.
She scooped up a dipper of yesterday's cold willow-bark
tea and held it to his lips. He didn't even turn his head
away. He was unaware of her. Tillu closed her eyes
tightly.

"Kari's not here?" she demanded an instant later. Ketla
glared at her.

"Isn't that what I've been telling you? She's not here.
We thought she was with you. I sent Joboam out to find
you both. When he didn't come back, I sent Pirtsi. Don't
think that was an easy thing to do; you tell a young man
that his girl has run off on their joining day! But he took it
well and went." The other women murmured assent.

"You sent Joboam after her?" Tillu asked in outrage
and dismay. "Where's Capiam?"

"Well, of course I sent him after her. What else was I
to do? Capiam would have done the same thing, had he
been up to it. We've always sent Joboam after Kari when
she ran away and hid from us. He was always the best at
finding her. Rolke was no use at all. And he certainly
couldn't be asked to do anything now, sick as he is."
Ketla looked flustered and a little angry. The healer wasn't
listening at all. "As for Capiam, he's still abed. Feverish,
like Rolke, and not feeling well."

Snorting her exasperation, Tillu stepped over to the
pallet Capiam and Ketla shared. The man was lost beneath
blankets and hides. She tried to pull his blanket down, but
he gripped it tightly. His eyes were shiny, his lips papery
as bark, but he spoke in weary command. "I am not as ill
as Ketla thinks I am. I am just tired, and a bit feverish.
Leave me alone."

Tillu pulled stubbornly at the hides, but Capiam was just
as stubborn in retaining them. "Leave me alone," he
repeated obstinately. She sighed and sat back on her heels.

"All right. I'll leave you alone. But I will leave some
tea that I want you to drink, whenever you are even a little
thirsty." She glanced about. Ketla was directing the women
who were setting out Kari's joining clothes and discussing
the food to be prepared. Tillu leaned closer to Capiam.

"Have you any idea where Kari is? Where did Joboam say he would look for her?" Capiam only flapped a hand at her irritably.

"Can't you leave me alone? Joboam will find her, and Ketla will handle the joining ceremony. It isn't until this afternoon. By then, I will have rested, and I will be there. Until then, Joboam will find her. Joboam will . . . he can see to things. Ask Joboam." Capiam's eyes sagged shut with weary finality. His hand fell limply atop the blankets. Tillu rose abruptly.

"Ketla," she said clearly, slicing through the women's conversations. Recklessness settled on her, a premonition of hovering disaster that could be averted only by direct action. She pushed through the circle of women and knelt to put her face on a level with Ketla's. She took the stout herdwoman's hands in hers, noting the fever that still simmered in them.

"Put off the joining," she said in a voice so deadly soft that it filled the tent. "Your husband is ill, you yourself are not well," and, over the beginning of Ketla's objections, "and your son is dying. Dying. Now is not the time for a joining."

"No! Oh, no, not dying, Tillu." Fear and refusal whitened Ketla's face. "You'll see, Healer, he's a strong boy. And the najd has said he'll get better. He's sleeping now, resting, and when he awakes he'll feel better. He'll be up to the feeding grounds, watching the reindeer and the young girls before the end of summer, you'll see." Ketla's voice rose higher and higher as her frantic words tumbled out. Tillu shook her head.

"No. Dying, Ketla, despite the best I can do."

"But the najd . . ."

"The najd has ways of making words say nothing at all. What did he say, exactly? Wasn't it, 'In the shadow of the Cataclysm, Ketla and Rolke would be freed of pain.' Don't you see? He will be right, whether Rolke gets better or dies. That is always how he speaks. With promises that offer nothing, predictions that take no chances. No, Ketla. Listen to me, even though I tell you hard things. Put off

this joining. Don't make me leave Rolke to run and find
Kari. For she must be found before Joboam finds her. She
must be told she doesn't have to join with Pirtsi. You
know she doesn't want to. That's why she has run away.
And you've sent Joboam after her, the very one who has
made her hate and fear the idea of being any man's mate.
And you know that, too!''

Certainty grew in Tillu as she watched Ketla's eyes
widen in horror. She felt a flicker of hope. Ketla would
put off the joining, would hear Kari out. But Ketla's face
set more deeply into stubborn denial. The gathered women,
shocked to silence by Tillu's words, began to mutter among
themselves. Sudden glints of anger kindled in Ketla's deep
eyes.

"Get out!" she shrieked abruptly. "Healer, you call
yourself? And kneel before me and wish death on my son,
and carry wild tales about my daughter! Speaking lies
about the najd who chants for my son, and has taken your
own son into his tent! Get out! Take your evil tongue and
useless medicines with you! Get out of my tent! The najd.
Someone fetch the najd for me! I want him to come now,
to drum and chant for Rolke and Capiam.''

"Ketla!" came Capiam's weary rebuke from across the
tent, but Tillu had already risen. She was not surprised at
Ketla's behavior. It was how she dealt with things she did
not wish to face; she denied them. Tillu stiffened her back
and forced herself to speak calmly.

"I will go. There is little I can do here that you cannot
do yourself. Rub Rolke with water often, and pour tea into
his mouth; even if he does not swallow, it will wet his
tongue. And give the same tea to Capiam. It may keep his
fever down. The sickness is rising in him, as it did in
Rolke.''

"Get out! Get out! Get!" Ketla was shrieking now,
shaking with fury. The healer's calmness only incensed
her more.

"I will. I'm going to find Kari. I'm going to tell her she
does not have to join with Pirtsi, that she can go to Stina
and the older women. They will tell her that she is free to

join or not join. And they will see that no one forces her. Some of the herdwomen seem to have forgotten their old traditions." Tillu's eyes raked the women standing speechless around Ketla. They shifted uneasily, their sudden silence more unsettling than their previous whispering had been.

"Is it true Kari does not wish to join with Pirtsi?" asked one softly.

"Get out!" Ketla shrieked, and Tillu did not bother to reply. She swung her pouch of herbs to her shoulder and left, slapping the door-flap aside. A panting Pirtsi stood before her.

"Well?" Tillu demanded recklessly. "Are you going to say you didn't know Kari didn't want you?"

"I . . . no . . . What?" He took a breath, gathered his wits. "Healer! You are needed at the reindeer pens."

Tillu gave a wordless cry of frustration, stamping her foot. Some fool with a broken shoulder or leg, no doubt. "It will have to wait!" she declared fiercely. "Have him lie still and put a cold wet cloth on it until I can come! Do what you did for a broken bone before I came along."

"But it's the najd!" Pirtsi exclaimed, horrified.

"All the better!" Tillu snarled.

"But he's dying . . ." Pirtsi's voice trailed off. Tillu looked at him hard, seeing the shock in the boy's face, the trembling of his hands. "Like Elsa," he added on a breath.

"What do you mean?" Tillu demanded. She stepped closer to the youth, steadying him with her hands on his shoulders. She locked gazes with him, willing the truth out of him.

"He's crumpled," he said abruptly. "Broken like dry sticks." He shuddered violently and turned from her. She let him go. "Tell Capiam," she instructed him and began to run.

She did not see the tents she passed, didn't hear the folk who cried out to ask what was wrong. Her savage expression was enough to bring men and women running after her, all eager to witness whatever disaster she raced to.

The sorting pens were on a hillside above the camp. Years ago, the pens had been built of boulders and stones. Brush and bushes had grown up around them. The men standing at the open mouth of the pen shouted when they saw her. She pushed past them, ignoring their words. Abruptly she slowed to a walk.

Carp lay like a crumpled doll. A herdsman from one of the other herdfolk stood over him. At the far end of the pen, herders shouted and trotted, keeping the restive vajor and their calves back from the shaman. Tillu drew near reluctantly. He had to be dead. No one could be so crumpled and be alive. One leg was bent under him and out from his body. The wrongness of the twist hurt to look at. The herdsman stared down at the body entranced. When Tillu touched him to move him aside, he looked at her as if she were an apparition. His wet lips trembled.

"They must have thought he meant harm to the calves. The vajor trampled him. Usually they jump over a fallen man, swerve aside from a standing one. I've never seen anything like this. What was he doing up here before dawn? Why did he come in here?"

Tillu didn't answer. The print of a cloven hoof was clear on Carp's face. His left eyelid was split open, and the eyeball dangled on his bloody cheek. He wore one of Joboam's fine tunics of bleached leather. Mud smeared it and blood seeped up through it. His hands were curled defensively over his chest. Two of the fingers twitched, and Tillu cried out softly. He heard her.

"Kerlew." Blood came out with the name. "A last word," he begged. She knelt in the churned mud and dung beside the old man. Something moved her to put one hand softly over his.

"Guilty hands. Say he has guilty hands." A grayish tongue moved briefly inside the bloody mouth. "I didn't touch it, but he did. I knew it would show." He stopped, struggled to draw a breath. Tillu heard a wet bubbling from his chest. She could not move. The herdsman was transfixed with horror. At the mouth of the pen, voices were raised, but no one came near.

"Fool to fear a woman. Only a woman. He say, kill her, kill the secret. I say, no. I laughed at him. Thinking he could kill a secret. Not when I knew. Fearing a woman. Weak man. Strong hands. When wolverines fight, one must die." His other eye opened, stared sightlessly up. "Take his drum. It's a good drum. Kerlew. My. Son."

His mouth sagged open, blood running thinly over his chin. Tillu bent closer to hear his last words. There was only a sigh.

"He's dead." She did not know how much time passed before she finally uttered the words. Time had paused as she knelt there. My son, my son. Her heart beat out the words. She could no longer hate the bones and flesh heaped before her. He was gone, and in his passing had stolen the hatred that had fueled her resolve. Like a mask cast aside, the najd was gone. An old man had died, an old man who had longed for a son. For a short time, he had had one. Could she begrudge him that?

She rose stiffly, not feeling the caked mud that clung to her legs and feet. She pushed through a crowd of herdfolk. They milled past, crowding about the body to exclaim over the horror of it. No one detained her. The ones that met her eyes faltered and looked away. Old Bror caught her arm, speaking words of concern, but she pulled free and walked on. She was nearly outside the pen when Joboam confronted her. She shook her head, not looking at him, and tried to step around him. He moved to block her. "What do you want?" she asked dully.

"Only to know what you saw, Healer." The contained glee in his voice lifted her eyes to his face. His mouth was solemn, but his eyes gleamed with a mocking challenge.

"Where is Kari?" she demanded suddenly.

For an instant his control slipped. She looked up into black anger, and felt suddenly small as the man towered over her. Then he smiled, slowly. The anger stayed bright in his eyes but he kept it from his voice.

"Why, Healer, I don't know. I looked all morning for her, but found no trace. When I went to tell Capiam I couldn't find his silly little daughter, he told me the najd had been killed. As he is too ill to move, he asked me to look into it. Pirtsi said the reindeer trampled the najd. Is that what you saw?''

The challenge was plain now. ''I saw an old man dying in the mud and filth,'' Tillu said carefully. Anger shook her body and voice. For an instant Joboam's confidence faltered.

''Pirtsi told me he was already dead,'' he said unevenly.

Tillu stood silent. Joboam lifted a hand to grip her, thought better of it and let his hand fall to his side. ''Don't toy with me, Healer.'' His voice was deadly soft. ''We both know how ill Capiam is. And his son. You see who has been chosen to take up the reins for him. Be wise. Please the next herdlord.''

''Have you buried him already?'' Tillu asked calmly. Some small part of her mind screamed for caution, but she could not find the control to be wise. Her eyes tracked the long, livid scratch down the side of his neck. ''You'd better beware of infection in that,'' she said coldly. ''Scratches from nails often infect.'' He twitched as if stung, but made no reply. She turned away from him, and he let her go. She walked on. Behind her, his voice lifted in command, calling for quiet and for one man to explain what had happened to the najd. The gabble behind her died. They would obey him. They would follow him, when the time came. She found she didn't care.

She walked back toward the tents, scarcely watching where her feet took her. Making plans. Heckram would bring Kerlew to her, and she would leave. She'd take her boy and leave these people, strike out across the tundra while the summer days were long. And Heckram? asked a small voice inside her. And Kari? And Ristin? And Lasse? the small voice nagged. ''I can't help them!'' Tillu heard herself declare aloud. ''Kerlew and myself. That is as much as I can take care of. Kerlew and myself.''

''Tillu?''

Lasse. She hadn't seen much of the boy lately. He was taller than she remembered him. Was he growing that fast?

After an instant, she realized he was silently staring at her. She tried to gather her mind. "What is it?"

"Are you all right?"

The question puzzled her until she glanced down at herself. Carp's blood was on her hands, and mud caked the front of her legs from her knees down. She couldn't know that it was the look in her eyes that most rattled Lasse.

"I think so. Were you looking for me?"

"Yes. Actually, no. I was looking for Kari, but no one knows where she is. I had heard she was missing. I wanted to talk to her, to tell her . . . there is a way to keep from joining Pirtsi. To join with . . . someone else, instead. I went by Capiam's hut, finally."

Tillu could guess the courage that must have taken.

"Ketla screamed at me to go away, but one of the women there came after me. She told me you had gone to look for Kari, and might know where she was hiding. Ketla thinks you told her to run away early this morning. She's very angry at you, but Capiam is too sick to do anything about it. I thought I should warn you . . . she's sent for Joboam. She's saying he'll bring you back to the tent and make you tell where her daughter is. Please, Tillu . . ." He looked desperate. "Do you know where Kari is?"

Tillu turned her worries carefully. She counted them out to herself. "Kerlew is missing. Heckram's gone to look for him. Carp is dead. Kari is gone, and I don't know where. But I know she's run away because she doesn't want to join with Pirtsi. And Joboam is coming to look for me." She looked into Lasse's stricken face. "Do you know the way to the Najd's Steps?"

He hesitated. "Yes. Yes, I do. Follow me."

She trailed after him as he led her swiftly through the village, slipping between the tents and threading their way past meat racks and hides stretched to dry in the sun. The effort of trotting brought order to her mind again.

"Heckram was going to climb the Najd's Steps," she explained to his back. "He thought he might find Kerlew there. He went seeking a najd's vision," she added in answer to Lasse's puzzled look. "I think I had better find Heckram. He'll know best what to do. And perhaps he has found Kerlew by now. Perhaps we could just slip away."

"Slip away?"

"Leave," Tillu said tersely. "Run away from the herdfolk and Joboam. Kerlew and I. Find a new life somewhere else. Again."

Lasse looked at her incredulously. "Alone?"

She didn't answer. Her eyes had gone ahead of them, up the gentle swell of grassy hill to where a group of young men and women gestured and exclaimed to one another, and beyond to where the wall of the Cataclysm rose, sudden as pain. It shone black against the blue sky, and Tillu's neck protested when she rolled her head back to see its top. It was a wall across the wide world, a buckled wedge of stone and earth pushed up to bar the herdfolk and their reindeer from further wandering. Some places were tumbled and rounded with weather, cupping small green pastures or pockets of blessed white snow where the stinging insects never ventured. Reindeer clustered on the white patches in refuge from the bugs. But at this place the Cataclysm rose, vertical and uncompromising. A slide of schist and shale at the base marked its only flaking concession to wind and rain.

She could not see what held the herders' attention but she thought she saw the Najd's Steps. They scarcely merited the name. A jutting scar crawled across the Cataclysm's face, up the expanse of sheer black stone, and ended abruptly far short of the peak. The ridge of stone looked as if it projected no wider than a foot path from the precipice, and in places seemed to have crumbled away entirely. Other cracks and juttings marred the surface of the Cataclysm, but only one could be the Najd's Steps. She was scanning the long narrow way for some sign of Heckram or Kerlew, when she heard Lasse give a low cry of despair. He gripped her arm suddenly, pinched bruisingly as he pointed up.

The figure materialized on a tiny outcropping of stone

beyond the end of the Najd's Steps. For a moment it hung
there. The wind billowed under its wings, spread the
pinions black and wide to the bright fresh day. The bird
rose, impossibly immense, lifting wide for flight.

And plummeted.

"Kari!" Lasse cried out, his voice cracking from boy to
man on the name. And in that utterance, Tillu saw her, the
wings becoming Kari's feathered cloak. Her small face
was pale, her black hair streamed behind her. She did not
scream. The Cataclysm thrust out a rocky spur to grip her.
She caught on it and tumbled, the wind roaring through
her cloak as she fell. Screams rose from the watching
herders. The instant was forever.

Lasse dragged Tillu with him as he ran, plunging through
the horrified herders. It was farther to the base of the
Cataclysm than it looked. Her breath caught painfully in
her ribs. Tufts of grass and low bushes scratched her
ankles and tore at her calves, but it could not distract her
from the crumpled black figure on the green sward.

They were there too soon. Lasse flung himself to his
knees beside her, reached to roll her over. Tillu didn't try
to stop him. He couldn't hurt her any more than she was
already hurt. But he pulled his hand back from the body
with a stifled cry. He turned a wide, white face up to
Tillu, horror and grief shaking his lips. Tillu dropped
stiffly to her knees, put a hand on Kari. And pulled it
back. Gelid. Beneath the black feathered cloak, the body
was sodden and still, pulped organs and bones inside a
sack of skin. Tillu swallowed dryly, her mind reeling. If
she had not stayed with Heckram last night . . . if she had
asked his advice earlier. If, if, and all useless.

"Get up," she croaked, rising on shaking legs. She
tugged at Lasse's sleeve, then gripped his collar and dragged
him to his feet. He did not resist her, but he didn't
cooperate as she pulled him back from the body. "Don't
look at her. Don't touch her. You can't help her now,
Lasse. Come away. Come away."

"What's happened?"

"Who was it?"

"Is he dead?"

The bright-cheeked girls and tousle-headed youths had caught up with them. Their urgent questions rattled around Tillu as she dragged Lasse back from the body. She didn't want to be here when they rolled her over. Two deaths in a day. She couldn't take anymore. "I have to see Capiam," she insisted, pushing her way past the young herders. "Let go of me. Let me through."

"It was the healer," she heard a young voice say behind her. "Why isn't she doing anything?" And then a sudden scream rose, piercing the bright morning. They had rolled Kari over. She kept her grip on Lasse's wrist, dragging him along.

The screams floated thin as splinters in the wind. Heckram flinched himself more tightly against the rock face. He wondered if someone had seen him. He doubted it. He considered leaning out, to look down the sheer rock face and see what the cry was about. He grinned harshly at the notion. He kept his hands and cheek pressed against the rock face and edged on another step.

He forced his thoughts away from the sheer fall behind him. He thought of Tillu, and how he had told her of his youthful venture up this same path. He wasn't sure if bravado or forgetfulness had made him speak so lightly. Now that he was up here, he remembered the ache of calf and back and shoulder. And fingers. He had taken the bandages from his injured hand to improve his grip. Every time he closed his hand now, the pain leaped up his arm. He refused to let himself focus on it. The path was substantially narrower than he remembered. He had been smaller then, he reminded himself. Narrower of shoulder and more sure of foot. Certainly more blithely unaware of death and pain. He pushed on, sliding his foot forward through the gritty rock dust that coated the trail. His toes felt raw. He had discarded his boots long ago, left them on the last wide piece of the Najd's Steps. His bare feet gripped the cold stone more surely, but felt every abrasion. Something light brushed against his foot. He looked down in the narrow space between his body and the cliff-face. A black feather. Another one. Odd. He had seen cliffs full of birds' nests before, but they weren't as windswept as this one. He wondered that the feather stayed on the narrow path at all. He pushed on.

The trickling sweat was from the warmth of fear and weariness. The sun on his back was still the thin warmth of morning. Its light touch reminded him of Tillu's hands on his body, of her hands spread against the small of his back as she lifted herself against him. A smile, almost foolish in its softness, came unbidden to his lips. Every time he thought he knew her, she surprised him. Her concern for Kari, her constant anxiety over Kerlew, her sober caring for Rolke had never prepared him for the woman she had shown him last night. She had cast her wariness aside, and revealed beneath it a deep hunger and an almost innocent joy in satisfying it. Like a child with a new toy, he thought, and blushed despite his isolation. No woman had ever so thoroughly explored his responses to her touch. The newness of it had made him a youth in her hands, ignited energies and curiosity he had thought outgrown. Even now, he wanted her again. This, he realized suddenly, is what Ristin meant. The feeling she had hoped he would have for Elsa, that no hardship was too great. Did Tillu feel it, he wondered? His face sobered an instant. Hadn't she trusted him to bring Kerlew safely home?

He wondered what he would do if he didn't find the boy up here. Look elsewhere, he told himself pragmatically, refusing to worry about time lost. He chuckled sourly at a sudden idea; how would it be to return to camp and find that Kerlew had already returned on his own? Good, he decided. It would feel good to find the boy safe anywhere. An image of his small, uncertain face rose in Heckram's mind. There were so few times when he had seen the boy's face unshadowed by fear or uncertainty. When they had carved spoons together. When he had given the boy the bone-knife for his own. The night his thin fingers had awkwardly plaited strips of leather for a new harke-harness. He understood suddenly a father's pride in his child's small accomplishments. A lost memory bobbed into his mind. He held a tablo board up for a tall man's inspection, and his heart swelled tight with pride at the grin that split the man's dark beard. "Well, and will you be the wolf now, son, and give your father a chance to win on your new board?" Heckram pressed flat to the cliff for a moment, feeling the light morning breeze finger his garments and hair. How had he lost a moment like that, forgotten it so completely? He had had so few moments like that. He stood very still. When he moved on again, he understood what drove him. It was time to close the circle. He wanted to look down into a boy's face and see that flush of accomplishment.

He edged on, occasionally finding a wider spot in the trail where he could crouch and ease his screaming muscles. At such times he glanced out over the tundra but never looked directly down at the tents below. In one such spot he found two small feathers and the clear outline of a small foot. Had Kerlew brought a dead bird with him? He shrugged and pressed on, step after careful step, his determination refueled by the footprint.

The afternoon heat found him at a wider spot in the trail. He crouched, stiff muscles screaming in the new position, and sipped water from his small pouch. He tried to relate today's climb to his boyhood one. Had it taken him this long that time? Had the boy Heckram moved faster, been more agile than the man? He poured water into his hand, washed the salty sweat from his eyes and lips. The end of the Najd's Steps could not be far. He was sure of it. He tried to see the end of the climb but the subtle rippling of the Cataclysm's wall and the climb of the path denied him. Kerlew might crouch at the end of this trail, or he might find only an empty spot and the sheer fall beyond it. Well, he would see. He started to rise, and then hunkered down in sudden consternation. With one thick finger he traced a peculiar imprint in the rock dust and fine gravel of the ledge. It was his imagination. Probably the boy had crouched here a moment, weight balanced on his toes. Yet he could have sworn the track was that of a wolf. He shook his head and pushed the fancy out of his mind. He slung his water skin over his shoulder, tugged it tight against his hip. On again.

The path narrowed drastically. Heckram hesitated. But Kerlew had gone this way. And so he must follow. Face to rock, damp hands suctioned against cold stone, he shuffled along. He peered ahead and down between his chest and the cliff. When he came to it, he stared at it for a long moment. Yes, he had grown. The mark he had scratched at eye level was now between his chest and the cliff. It seemed little weathered, the scratches gray against the cliff's black face. It was the same shape as the small flaps of skin he cut from his calves' ears. His mark, as individual as his face, never given to anyone before him, never to another after him. He shivered at touching hands with his childhood. He pushed his thoughts back to that day, leaned slightly out to have a better view of what came next.

It was as he remembered. A step or two more, and then nothing. Nothing. No path, no boy, just the narrow ridge of stone dwindling away to a crack in the stone's face. He felt the trembling start, suppressed it as he pushed himself tightly against the cliff face. He had seen the boy's footprint in the dust; he must have come this way. The next thought followed mercilessly. He must have gone that way. To the end of the trail and down, taking a false step in the darkness. Tears blinded him. Damn the old najd and his cursed vision. His wisdom had sent a confused boy to die. "Kerlew," he whispered agonizedly as the screams he had heard earlier took on a personal note.

The rustling of clothing, close at hand. The sound startled him, set his heart thumping. Awkwardly he turned his head, glancing forward and back along the ledge, but saw nothing. He edged another step along the dwindling ridge, felt the bare edge of stone press his sole. He looked again, and cried out in despair. "Kerlew!"

He had forgotten the najd's alcove. There it was, three steps beyond the end of the trail. He could barely glimpse inside. He thought of leaning back for a better view, but there was nothing to cling to. What little he could see was chilling enough. Kerlew stood within it, face suffused with gladness. His arm stretched out straight before him, hand pressed flat against the empty air at the cliff's edge. His eyes were bright but unfocused. Behind him the shriveled body of the mummified najd was exactly as he remembered it. Time had not touched it. "Wolf?" Kerlew questioned softly.

"Kerlew, it's me. I'm on the ledge. I've come to get you."

The boy jerked suddenly, then swayed and put a hand on the rough wall of the alcove for balance. The shallow cave in the stone was no more than two steps deep. Kerlew licked his cracked lips. "Wolf?" he asked again.

"I'm over here, Kerlew. Right here."

The boy's eyes moved in slow jerks until they came to Heckram. No recognition kindled in them, only curiosity. He stared at the man, and then stepped forward so that his bare toes curled over the lip of the cliff. Heckram's heart slammed in his throat. "Step back!" he cried.

The boy swayed. "Why?" he asked distantly.

Heckram's fingers found a tiny crack in the rock. He wriggled them into it. The sight of the boy standing so boldly on the edge of the fall rocked him with dizziness. "How did he get there?" he demanded of the inscrutable stone.

The question engaged the boy's mind. Kerlew's eyes suddenly met his and a faint smile touched his dry lips. "I saw the bone najd waiting for me. He had come here, so there was a way for me to come. So I stepped across."

Heckram tried to take deeper breaths. Fear had been an abstraction when he was climbing the Najd's Steps alone. Danger had been behind him, a thing he could cheat by clinging to the cliff face. But now that he saw the boy, fear boiled through his veins. Should Kerlew slip now, he could do nothing. But he knew he would reach for the falling boy, tumble alongside him, feeling his stomach lift into his throat, the wind past his eyes. He closed his eyes, squeezed the images away.

Slowly he opened them. He forced himself to look from

his ledge to the alcove. Yes, there were lips of stone, cracks, and knobs that an agile boy could use to get across. He doubted he could squeeze his toes onto those minute ledges or wedge his thick fingers into the narrow cracks. But Kerlew had. And Kerlew could.

He licked his dry lips, felt the wind snatch the moisture from them and crack the skin. He took a breath and steadied his voice. "Why don't you show me how you did it?" he suggested. "I'll move back out of your way, and you come across to me."

The boy stared at him. The wind blew long between them. "You want me to come down with you."

Heckram hesitated. If Kerlew came across, he would have to come of his own will. He could not seize the boy and drag him down the narrow path. It would be all both of them could do to get down safely. "Only if you want to."

"And if I don't?"

Heckram pressed his sweating forehead against the cold stone. "Then I'll wait for you until you're ready."

Kerlew smiled suddenly. "Did you think I would be afraid of you? You are already mine, for I've held you in the palm of my hand. I will come. Let me gather the things."

Heckram watched but saw little. Most of the tiny cave was out of reach of his eyes. He heard a rustling, and muttering. A shiver ran up Heckram's back and he edged himself down the trail. There. There was room for the boy now. In a few seconds he heard the rasp of his shirt against the stone, and Kerlew edged into view. His bundled shirt bumped against his back. His bared arms were thin and pale. He spidered over the rock until he was beside Heckram. His eyes were boyishly bright and alive as he said, "I see it is not the first time you have come this way."

Heckram grinned at the humanness of his words. He felt dizzy with relief, and warm with sudden comradeship. "Shall we make your mark beside it, to show you that you, too, have come this way?" he suggested.

Kerlew grinned with mischief. "Are you trying to trick me? Do you think I don't know we are of one and the same? One mark is enough for us both." He lifted his hand free of the wall, and pointed a thin finger. Blazoned slightly above Heckram's eye level, it glowed red against the black stone. The five spots of Wolf's track.

> chapter
thirteen

"WHERE IS KARI?"

Joboam's demand boomed across the distance between them. Tillu felt her body wince, but refused to let it cow her soul. She continued walking doggedly toward Capiam's tent. Busy folk paused, their eyes darting curiously from Joboam to the healer. She ignored them, her deep pain and anger driving her to the confrontation.

She had left Lasse sitting in Stina's hut. The boy was in shock, shaking and pale. But Stina had understood Tillu's brief explanation, and had immediately begun to warm tea for him and make up a soft bed. Tears had run down the old woman's seamed face. "If only she had come to me," she said once, brokenly, and then turned aside to her grandson. "To think that herdfolk could come to this. What is Capiam thinking of?" There was anger in her voice then, and it ignited the anger in Tillu's soul. She had left then, knowing Lasse would be all right again, given time and Stina's care. Tillu was not sure about herself. She wished she could slip into that distancing trance, could stare sightless until her soul had absorbed the impact of Kari's death. Instead her pain was a wound gushing blood, a thing she must cauterize. She went straight to Capiam's tent. She would be heard.

But Joboam guarded the tent, arms crossed on his chest. His flung question had drawn eyes. Folk were already beginning to gather. Tillu didn't care. She lifted her voice, careless of the shrill, hysterical note that rang through it.

"Kari is dead, Joboam! Dead at the base of the Cataclysm, as you have probably guessed. Didn't you find her this morning and chase her up the Najd's Steps? Aren't you the one who taught a little girl that death was preferable to the touch of a man?"

Joboam stood still. Women spilled from Capiam's tent and milled behind him, anxious to witness this confrontation but not to become part of it. Other folk, attracted by the raised voices, drew closer. Tillu ignored them. She saw only the fury in Joboam's eyes, and the careful way he cloaked it.

"Healer, you rave!" he observed calmly. "I have not seen Kari today. I have just come from Ketla's side. She weeps, for you have hidden her daughter away on what should be a joyous day for her whole family. She asks why you have done this, when the herdlord's family has shown you only kindness?"

Tillu knew that she should meet his calmness with cold composure. But her outrage gushed hot words, an unquellable flood of grief and anger. "NO! I did not take Kari away! She took herself away from a joining she did not want, and then took herself out of a life she could not face. She is dead, Joboam! She leaped from the Najd's Steps. Can you look shocked? How safe you must feel now, knowing she can never speak of the things you did to her when she was a little child trusted to your safekeeping!" Tillu's voice broke on a sob. She clutched at her throat, forced the weeping away.

Joboam turned calmly to the women behind him. "Telna and Kaarta. Please go to the base of the Najd's Steps and see if there is truth to this tale." He let his eyes roam over the assembled folk. "I fear it may be true. For since this 'healer' and her son joined our herdfolk, we have seen nothing but death and misfortune. Elsa died under her care, a death that so outraged the forest spirits that they sent a killing storm upon our new calves. The najd that sought to intervene for us lies trampled to death by our own reindeer. And the family of our herdlord is sickened to death, or driven to madness. It is no secret that Kerlew hated Rolke and was jealous of the najd's attention to Kari. Everyone has seen his strange tempers, felt his cold stares. There is no najd now to control him. Poor Kari. Her dreams of a joining poisoned by the wild words of a stranger. Ah, Capiam, Capiam! You were a good herdlord in your time, but too trusting. I wish you had listened to me. I marked her and her boy as demon spawn the first time I saw them.''

Tillu could not find words to reply. She saw the people drawn to his steady words and calm manner, listening to his solemn tale, and murmuring agreement. Surely, Capiam's folk were sorely afflicted with troubles and woes. For a herdfolk's najd to die was the worst of bad luck. And where was their najd's apprentice, this woman's strange child? Where had he been when his master died? Tillu took a deep breath.

''No healer can cure everything. We can but help the body find time and strength to heal itself. Elsa's body was too broken. Her head was . . . damaged. Inside. Do not blame me for her death, but blame the one who beat her. . . .''

''And where is Heckram?'' Joboam broke into her words. The deep timbre of his voice, his proud stance as the wind ruffled his soft hair drew the people to him. Tillu was the stranger, wild haired and dirty, blood upon her clothes. Joboam they had known since he was a boy, a sturdy, charming boy. Words were futile. They could only be turned against her.

''I asked you, where is Heckram?'' Joboam's voice had taken on a note of menace.

Tillu lifted her chin. She spoke softly, and the crowd hushed to hear her. ''I am the herdlord's healer, Joboam. I answer to him, not you. Or do you already claim his position?''

His silence was a moment too long. A subtle change of feeling washed through the gathered folk. ''I but speak for the herdlord, doing as he bids me!'' Joboam cried out too loudly.

Tillu laughed a short, ugly laugh. ''I came to speak to

Capiam, not to you," she said, and walked boldly forward. Herders edged away, making a wide path. Joboam alone blocked her way. "Do you dare to keep the herdlord's healer from his tent when his family is ill?" she asked in a deadly voice.

"Rolke!" The scream ripped the tense moment. Tillu dove for the tent-flap, but Joboam blocked her, thrusting her to the ground with his casual push. Ketla stumbled from the tent. Her black hair was wildly bedraggled, her eyes red and swollen in a face pale and sagging with illness. She took two steps before sinking into a shaking heap. "Rolke is dead!" she moaned. "Dead and stiff in his blankets. His skin was cold when I touched him. Cold! Ah! Rolke. My own little boy, my Rolke." Ketla's eyes suddenly found Tillu. "Where were you, Healer?" she demanded. "Why weren't you here to save him? And where is my Kari?"

"Oh, Ketla," Tillu began in shared grief, but Joboam's hand descended on her shoulder, gripping her with stony fingers.

"Do not listen to her, Ketla! She has just come with a wild tale that Kari is dead, fallen to her death from the Najd's Steps. What have you known but sickness and bad fortune since she came to your tent? Cast her out before she can do more harm to you! And throw away the herbs she has been feeding your family, lest you and Capiam be poisoned also!"

Joboam pushed her suddenly, contemptuously. "Relna! Keep this woman away from Capiam and Ketla. Do not let her add to their grief."

"Ketla!" Tillu cried out, but the woman was dazed. The deaths of her children were too great a shock. A sturdy woman seized Tillu's arm. Her eyes were full of disgust as she pulled Tillu away from the crowd. Tillu had a glimpse of Joboam kneeling by Ketla, talking to her gently while a sympathetic crowd murmured to itself. Tillu's mind reeled. For a short ways she stepped along blindly at the herdwoman's heels. Then she set her feet suddenly and jerked her arm free of the woman's grip.

"Where are you taking me?" she demanded.

Relna spun to face her, and then looked startled. "I don't know. I certainly don't want you in my tent. What would my own herdlord say to me if I brought upon us the same misfortune that Capiam's folk have found?"

"It was none of my doing!" Tillu hissed angrily. "It was Joboam, if it was anyone. He killed Elsa. If you do not believe me, ask Ristin. Ask Stina, or Elsa's parents what they suspect. And he drove Kari to kill herself with what he forced upon her. Do not tell me you remember Kari as a merry girl excited about her joining, for I shall know you lie! And Rolke and Ketla and Capiam suffer from an illness I do not know. But taking my herbs and care from them cannot make them better. Nor anyone else. Haven't you wondered about those with infected tick bites, those who have a fever this day, and are fine the next? Will you say I have brought this sickness on all of you?"

Sudden alarm wiped the anger from Relna's face. "My husband has a tick bite on his foot." She stepped hastily back from Tillu. She was not a member of a crowd now, to be swayed to Joboam's words. Alone, she had to listen to Tillu. And she feared what she heard. "I am not Joboam's to command," Relna suddenly exclaimed. "If he wants you kept away from Capiam and Ketla, let him see to it, or one of Capiam's herdfolk. Let Capiam's folk live under their own misfortune. If you are their bad luck, then let them cleanse themselves. Stay away from my folk!" The last was a low growl. Relna strode away from Tillu.

Tillu sighed in a mixture of relief and frustration as she watched her stomp away. She did not need to fear her or her folk anymore. But by sundown all of Relna's herdfolk would know that Capiam's healer was bad luck, a woman to be avoided. She would have no chance of leaving Capiam's folk by becoming healer to another herd. She would have to go alone.

Alone. She and Kerlew. Once that would not have meant "alone." Before Heckram. Her heart gave a sickening lurch. She had to gather her things now and go to find Heckram and Kerlew. She would leave with the boy now, while she had the chance. Joboam was too adept at stirring the herdfolk against her and her son. She had to leave now. Alone.

Most of what she owned and used day to day were in Capiam's tent. No chance of reclaiming them. Kerlew's things were in the fine new najd's tent, next to Joboam's. She dared not go there, either. The rest of what she had was at Heckram's tent, unloaded from the harkar he had led for her. She listed it to herself; the new tent, unused, that Capiam had given her when she had first joined the herdfolk, her cooking utensils, the extra skins and tools she had earned from her healing. She turned her steps that way, alert for any who might try to stop her. She would gather her things quietly and take them out of the camp. But when she pictured the burden that the tent and utensils would make, her step lagged. There would be no sturdy harke to carry them, no Kari to help her manage the beast. Did she imagine no one would notice a woman going laden as a harke? She would be stopped. It was not the first time she had fled from an angry and suspicious people. She must go lightly and travel fast. She could take only what would fit in a shoulder pouch or two. And she and Kerlew must recross the tundra alone, must get to the safety of the forest before the winter winds blew. Where would she get hides for a tent? What would they eat as she travelled? She pushed the questions from her mind. No use in asking them. She tried to find courage in reminding herself that she had taken care of herself and Kerlew all winter. They would survive again. She could not stay among these people. Joboam would stir them against her and her son, would agitate them until they turned on her. Better the wolves of the tundra and the rigors of privation than the unbridled fear and hatred of the herdfolk. Humans were the cruellest predators.

Heckram's tent was dark and cool inside. The sleeping hides were rumpled as they had left them. She stared at them without comprehension, wondering where the warmth and security of the night had fled. When she moved, she went stiffly, feeling as if she had plundered a stranger's tent.

She found her cooking pots hung alongside his. She selected the smaller, sturdier ones. It was harder to separate her sleeping skins from the tangled pile on the floor. She took up Heckram's one of fox-skins, reds and blacks sewn together in lustrous contrast. She held it against her face, smelling his smell on it. She wanted it. She hugged it tightly against her, fearing the tears that stung her eyes. It smelled of him and their brief time together. She lifted her eyes, suddenly saw an unspoken assumption in the way he had unloaded her possessions and mingled them with his. It touched her soul and stole her determination. All the other times, when she had run away from people who wished harm on her son, she had taken her world with her. This time she would be leaving a part of herself behind.

Slowly she folded the fox-skins into a careful bundle. She set it down atop the other crumpled bedskins. A dull ache numbed her body, while her temples pounded with the pain of grief and unshed tears. She did not move swiftly as she gathered the few possessions she and Kerlew could easily carry. She paused often, the effort of deciding which item to take overwhelming her. There came a time when both packs were filled and yet she did not have the will to leave the place. She sat down for a moment on the rumpled bedding and took the fox wrap into her lap. She stroked it, feeling its warm weight, cuddling it against her as if it were an infant. Slowly she lay down, her cheek pressed against the soft fur, thinking of all that would not be.

I am like Kerlew, she thought bitterly. Full of wild dreams and foolish fancies. What was I pretending last night? She thought of how she had taken him, in lust and laughter, finding a freedom she had never imagined a woman might know. And Heckram, delightedly encouraging her. Letting her be bold. And after, when she had been sated, on the verge of sleep in his arms. Then it had been his touch on her skin, his fingers trailing her thighs so softly that she shivered in their wake. "Lie still!" he had commanded her gruffly when she tried to capture his hand. And she had, while with fingers and lips he convinced her

that her satiation was an illusion, was only the first quench-
ing of a thirst he understood better than she did. His
fingertips had twined gently through the dense curls until
with a pleading moan she parted her thighs and pushed up
against his hand. He put his hand flat on her belly. "This
time," he reminded her, "it's my turn." She nodded
slowly, shivered as he knelt between her knees. Slowly, so
slowly he moved, watching her face as he touched her,
learning by experience what pleased her most. He was not
shy. He smiled as he teased her with his body, until in her
eagerness she gripped his buttocks and pulled him into her.
"I thought I was in charge," he reminded her. In reply she
had bucked beneath him, never releasing her grip, pulling
him into her frantic rhythm, thundering him into joining
her climax.

A sob shook her, and another. She wept into the furs,
mourning him as if dead, while every breath she took
brought his smell to her and reminded her of her body's
hungers. She wept with abandon, hiccuping sobs like a
small child, until she was exhausted. "I should never have
touched him," she told herself. She smoothed the fur
beneath her cheek. His hair was softer than this. She
wished she had never known that. "All the rest of my life
. . ." The enormity of the thought was too much for her.
"Heckram," she said. She hugged the furs tightly, unable
to let go of them, and let the quieter tears come.

She awoke to a touch on her face. A small fire burned in
the arran, and Heckram knelt over her, outlined by the
flames. On the other side of the fire Kerlew sprawled, his
deep eyes full of orange light. She sat up, slamming
herself against Heckram and clutched him tightly. He grunted
with the impact of her hug, and then held her, muttering
softly, "And I was about to complain that at least you
might have made food for us." For a moment he held her,
his breath soft against her hair. Then he moved to gently
disentangle himself. Tillu only clutched him more tightly.
"What is it?" he asked through her fierce hug.

"Everything. Everything that has happened. It is too
much to tell kindly and slowly. Carp is dead. He went to

the pens and the reindeer trampled him. Or so all others say. From his final words, I think Joboam had something to do with it. And Kari is dead, from a fall from the Najd's Steps. And Rolke has died, from the sickness, and Capiam now lies ill with it. And Joboam blames me for all of it, and has made the others believe him. I must leave and take Kerlew, I must run away tonight."

Heckram had gone stiff in her arms as she spoke. Kerlew sat up suddenly, his eyes gone huge. "NO!" he screamed, his cry sharp in the night. Tillu sprang clear of Heckram, seized the boy before he could flee from the tent. It took all her strength to drag him down and back. He struggled wildly, and only his long fast and the exhaustion of his day let her master him. He was all bones and muscles beneath her hands. For a long moment she struggled with him as Heckram looked on in anguish. Then the boy collapsed and began weeping noisily. "Carp! Carp!" His wails filled the tent. "You should have come back with me! Why did you fly away?"

The two adults exchanged puzzled glances. Then Heckram came to kneel beside them and put his arms around Kerlew. He didn't say anything to the boy, made no promises that all would be well tomorrow. He only held the gaunt young frame and let him cry out his anger and grief. Tillu withdrew, feeling strangely unneeded until Heckram looked over the boy's bent head at her and asked, "Can you fix him something to eat? Some soup or something?"

She nodded uncertainly, and then found her practicality again. She took down a cooking pot and went outside for meat from Heckram's supply. The familiar task calmed her. She moved efficiently, cooking enough for all three of them. When had she last eaten? Yesterday? They should all eat, and then they could talk. Cutting the meat into pieces and adding it to the heating water brought a strange relief to her. The simple routine of making soup pushed the day's tragedies back. Here, in the close circle of the firelight, she could pretend for this moment that they were a family, and that tomorrow would be another day for them. There was a strange comfort in how easily Kerlew accepted Heckram's touch. He wept himself out, and then sat, pale and hunched, leaning against Heckram's comforting arm. His pale eyes were deeper than Tillu had ever seen them, but his mouth had lost its slackness. Some childish determination set it, driving the foolishness from his face. He said nothing, only stared at the fire. Each shuddering breath lifted his narrow shoulders. As Tillu set a steaming bowl of food before him he fixed her accusingly with his amber eyes. "Where is Carp?" he demanded.

"Carp is dead." She said it gently but firmly. The boy would have to accept it.

He shook his head, impatient with her. "Where?" he demanded again, exhaustion now plain in his voice.

Tillu paused. The impact of the day's deaths settled on her again. "I don't know," she admitted. "I don't know what they did with any of them."

"I'm going to his tent," Kerlew announced, and began to rise. Heckram's hand on his shoulder pressed him down again. "Eat first," he ordered him gently. "And rest. You can do nothing for Carp, whether you go to him soon or later. And he is probably not in his tent. Probably the elders have taken him, to do what is correct for the body of a najd."

Kerlew subsided suddenly, the life gone out of him. He accepted the bowl of food Tillu pushed at him, and sat staring into the fire. "Eat something," Tillu urged him gently. Her words broke him free of his preoccupation, for he looked up at her. His face had a self-possession she had never seen in it before. "I know things." His same slow, hesitant diction, but there was a sureness to his words that made his pauses seem deliberate. He said the words quietly, daring her to challenge them. When she didn't, he took up the spoon in the bowl. He ate without interest or pause. When he was finished, he retreated from the firelight, to roll himself up in a sleeping hide.

Tillu and Heckram ate together in silence. She did not taste the food. She watched him, saw how weariness rode him, saw his silence absorbing the shock of her blunt news. She wanted to cling to the strength he represented, but she held herself tight and apart. She would not deepen the bond, would not make the parting any harder.

He set his bowl atop hers, and then pushed both aside with a sigh. She poured warm water into a bowl and took his hand in hers to soak his hand. The damaged fingers were puffy, the shale dust ingrained into his skin. He did not mention the pain, and she wondered if he was aware of it. He used his body as another man might use a tool, pushing it to its maximum without regard for tomorrow. She wanted to scold him for it, but could not find the heart. Could she say such words of caring, and then leave tomorrow? She put his hand into the water, massaged his fingers lightly. Her throat closed, nearly choking her. She bent her head over his hand so he couldn't see her face.

But with his free hand he lifted her chin and looked into her eyes. "Tell me everything," he said. She shook her head, but his eyes held hers. She had not realized the pressure the events had built up inside her until she released it as words. She told him the suspicions she had not been able to confide to anyone else: that Carp had been beaten before someone stampeded the reindeer over him; that Kari's leap from the Cataclysm had been the final step in her flight from Joboam; and her conviction that Joboam would take advantage of Capiam's illness to assume his position. She finished by saying, "He takes such a joy in Rolke's and Kari's deaths, and Ketla's and Capiam's illness. No. Not joy. Satisfaction. As if it were a task he had accomplished, a fine bit of carving, a tanned skin others would envy."

"You can't blame him for everything, Tillu." Heckram's voice indicated he would like to.

"I know things!" Kerlew's voice rang out clearly, startling them both. He sat bolt upright in his skins, staring at them.

"It's all right, Kerlew," Heckram said soothingly. "It was a dream. Go back to sleep."

"I know things," he repeated sullenly. "I know about the rabbit." He swayed slightly, his face going gray. Slowly he eased back into his bedding. The tent was long still again.

"It's hard on him." Heckram scarcely breathed the words. The deep timbre of his voice sometimes made him hard to hear. Tillu leaned closer to him. "He isn't going to accept it easily. His whole world, all his prospects have been taken from him, just when he succeeded in his task. Carp protected him more than I realized. Joboam is a danger to him now. And to you."

Tillu found herself nodding unwillingly. He was saying the things she had been putting off saying. These words could only lead to the same conclusion she had already reached.

"The herdfolk will be eager to find someone to blame. It is the way of folk, to want someone to be guilty when misfortune befalls them. You must leave the herdfolk."

Coming from him, the words held a chilling note of finality. Tillu bowed her head in agreement, both relieved and saddened that he accepted it so easily.

"It has to be tomorrow. So little time. I need to speak to Lasse; we have become close, close as brothers. I cannot leave him, grieving, without a word. And Ristin. Somehow I think she will be expecting it." He smiled, one of his wolf-grins. "The good part will be in the giving. There is so much I cannot take; it will be good to see Stina's eyes bright and angry, as she tries to refuse it and knows I will insist."

"I don't understand you." Tillu's words came out flatly.

"Three harkar, at most four. I don't think we shall want both tents, shall we? Kerlew may have to ride at first; the last few days have not been easy ones for him. But the rest of what I have shall go to those who will use it best. Lasse and Stina, Ristin. And Elsa's parents."

"You want to go with us?"

"I am not welcome?" He responded to her disbelief.

She let herself go to him, knocking him off balance with her embrace so that they fell and rolled on the hide-carpeted earth. His embrace held her tightly, but she felt freed by it. No words came to her mind. There was only holding onto the man who would not be left behind.

chapter fourteen

THERE WAS A disturbing pattern to the spread arc of items; a message that eluded Tillu, yet shrilled alarmingly at the edge of her awareness. Like a cry of warning in another tongue. She could recognize the urgency, but not the meaning. She reached a hand to touch them; drew it sharply back.

"What is that?" Sleep and bafflement in Heckram's voice. The dawn was young, and yesterday's weariness clung to him still. His hair was tousled boyishly, but the disarray exposed the gray scattered through it, making him look both older and younger in the thin light. It made her want to touch him, but she did not.

"Kerlew's things," she admitted, embarrassed. She dropped to her knees, feeling an urge to bundle them up, out of his sight. She couldn't touch them. She stared at them. Uneasiness ran over her with ants' feet. A red stone, a bit of amber, trinkets, and oddments that had caught the boy's fancy. Some bones, stained red and blue. It meant nothing to her. Nothing, she told herself. But she stood slowly, a terrible dread squeezing her heart. "He's gone to kill Joboam." The words came out so simply. Once she had uttered them, she could not disbelieve them. Yet she could find no source for her terrible knowledge.

Heckram said nothing. He glanced at the boy's empty blankets, then dressed in silence. He held his sprained fingers out from the rest of his hand, fastened his clothing awkwardly. He opened the travelling chest, rummaged inside it for a moment. He settled a knife in his belt, a knife she had never seen before. Bronze gleamed in the dim light. "How long has he been gone?" he asked in the awful stillness. Tillu shrugged helplessly.

"Then . . . where would he go?"

Tillu shrugged again, hating the gesture. "With Carp dead, he has nowhere to go."

Heckram considered what he knew of the boy. "I think he would still go to Carp first. Would death stop him?"

It took Tillu a moment to gather his meaning. "No. No, it wouldn't have stopped him last night. He'll go seeking Carp."

Heckram nodded. "But he won't have an easy time finding him. It's the worst kind of luck to look on a najd's grave. The Elders know that. They'd put Carp in a secret place, a place herdfolk never venture, not even by accident."

"There cannot be many such places." Tillu frowned to herself, trying to think of even one.

"You'd be surprised. It needn't be close by. And someone could be found to take him there. But Kerlew wouldn't know about that. He'd go to where he last saw Carp."

"His tent."

Heckram shook his head slowly. "Joboam's tent."

Tillu's breath caught. Her first premonition came back, gaining strength. "He'll kill him. Kerlew will challenge him and Joboam will kill him."

Heckram's face set suddenly. "Only after he kills me. I don't plan on that. Stay here. I'll be back," Heckram promised as he left the tent. She ignored his command, stretching her legs to keep up with his stride. He glanced at her and saw the uselessness of objecting. Together they hurried through the just-stirring village. For the first time, Tillu wondered why Joboam had pitched his tent so far from Capiam's, instead of claiming his usual place of honor beside it. And why had Carp, so conscious of status, been content to camp on the edge of the village instead of in its center?

Tillu's heart was thundering as they drew near the two

large tents, but Heckram didn't hesitate. He pushed his way boldly into Carp's tent. She followed more cautiously.

His wealth staggered her. The tent was not floored with bear or reindeer hides, but with soft lush pelts of fox and wolf. Not one, but two travelling chests stood casually open. Garments of wool and soft leather hung over their edges, draped with strings of amber and ivory beads. A tumble of garments and jewelry and tools surrounded the chests. She wondered what use Carp would have had for the large bronze cook pots that sprawled by the hearth. A fine bow and a quiver of black arrows were strewn across the furs. Many of the shafts had been snapped, the broken pieces flung wide. Her fingers stole out to run along one black arrow. A memory stirred. "Black arrow . . . like that one that hit Lasse that day . . ."

Heckram rounded on her. "I thought you had shot Lasse."

"Me?" Outrage touched her face. "I told you that day, there was another hunter on the hillside, shooting from the cover of a fallen tree."

For a long instant they stared at each other, remembering that day and the difficulty of speaking then. Heckram gave a snort of disgust. "Then add another stroke to the tally of what I owe Joboam. For that is his bow and his quiver. And these chests belonged to his parents. I remember his mother wearing those ivory beads when I was very small."

Panic squeezed Tillu's heart. "Are we in the wrong tent?"

"No. This was Carp's place. Though why Joboam would have given him all these things I do not know. There are things here I would have sworn he would never part with."

"Unless forced." Tillu finished the thought. "And he wouldn't long tolerate being forced to give up such things."

"Kerlew isn't here. But he's been here. I wonder what he was looking for?"

Tillu shook her head helplessly. "There is no sense to what Kerlew does. He has no reasons, no logic . . ."

Heckram shook his head in disagreement. "More and more, I believe he has reasons and logic of his own, ones we would find as strange as he finds ours. He is like a foreigner from a far land. Just because we cannot understand his words does not mean he speaks nonsense."

"Kerlew has been a foreigner to this world since he was born," Tillu said, between bitterness and pain.

"Come." Heckram drew her close for a minute and then took her hand. "We do no good lingering here. Let's find him."

"Joboam's tent," Tillu whispered.

Heckram nodded solemnly, and then flashed an incongruous grin, white teeth in his bronze beard. "Joboam's tent."

She followed him out of the tent, stepping softly. The morning was brighter, more and more folk emerging to greet the day. As they drew closer to Joboam's tent, her feet dragged. She could not forget the way the man towered over her, the coldness in his eyes. But Heckram stepped forward easily, not bothering to announce himself but pushing his way into Joboam's silent tent. Tillu seized her courage and followed him.

"Where's Kerlew?" Heckram demanded.

Joboam came to his feet in a frantic movement that spilled the pot of water before him. He was dressed only in a loin wrap and his hair was tousled from sleep. His hands were dripping and for an instant his eyes were empty. Then fury filled them. "What do you mean by entering my tent this way?" he roared.

"I'm looking for Kerlew. I believe he's been here." Heckram's voice was tight, demanding.

Joboam laughed. "The najd's little demon spawn isn't here. No one's seen him since the day before yesterday. Better luck to us!" he added challengingly.

"You're lying." Heckram spoke with certainty that Tillu didn't share.

Joboam shook the water from his hands, wincing as he did so. "I'm not. But it doesn't matter," he said quietly. "Even if the boy comes back, it doesn't matter. Things are changing. The healer and her son won't be tolerated any longer. Folks have been asking where all this bad luck comes from. They think they know. And Capiam's herdfolk are tired of a leader who doesn't keep them from harm. They look to me now. Even if I killed you, no one would say it was without cause. You are part of the ill luck that has befallen us. It was you who first met the healer and her demon son, you were joined to Elsa when she died. You found the najd and brought him to our village, you brought Kerlew back just when we were well rid of him. I could strike you down now and no one would mourn you."

"Try it," Heckram invited. He drew his knife.

"No!"" Tillu cried, but he stepped clear of her. Joboam wavered an instant before Heckram's rigid grin. Then he snatched up his own knife and came forward, hunched like a bear, snarling like a wolverine.

"Ketla wants you, Joboam. The healer's son, mad Kerlew, threatens Capiam!" The words tumbled from Pirtsi as he pushed in the door. Heckram and Joboam both turned to him while Tillu stood frozen. "You? Here?" He exclaimed in wonder as his eyes darted from Tillu to Heckram. In an instant more, his eyes had taken in the drawn blade, the attitudes of the two men. He backed hastily, his eyes darting from one to the other. In the entry he hesitated. "The boy holds a knife to Capiam's throat!" He flung the words as he fled.

"Good!" Joboam breathed recklessly.

Tillu ran from the hut. Heckram looked from her to the waiting Joboam. "Soon!" he promised him, and spun to follow her.

"Coward!" He heard Joboam's roar of frustration behind him, heard something flung to strike the tent's inner walls. The name burned, but he knew well that if Kerlew killed Capiam, Joboam would be pleased. Nothing could save the boy then. Or Tillu or himself. He stretched his long legs, caught up and passed Tillu, and then Pirtsi. Thin hysterical screams guided him to the herdlord's tent. He pushed through the folk that ringed it, ignored his name called out with distaste and anger. He burst into the tent, crashed against men who gripped him and held him back. He didn't struggle against them, but stared in disbelief.

Ketla crouched wailing. Her hair was tangled, her night garment wadded around her. Sickness and grief had wasted her, so that her skin hung in folds from her arms and cheeks. Her weakness was evident as she backed feebly against a travelling chest that blocked her escape. Her wailing was like a babe's thin cry.

Between her and the tent entry, straddling her husband's chest, was Kerlew. The change in the boy was startling. He wore only a twist of whitened leather around his loins and Carp's najd's pouch around his neck. His long fast had worn his body to bones and muscles. Thin as death he crouched over the herdlord, and his long bony hand held a white knife before Capiam's fever-sunken eyes. The boy's eyes burned.

"Kerlew!" Heckram cried, but the boy paid no heed. He let the bone knife droop until its point rested against the pulse in Capiam's throat. The gathered folk sighed fearfully. He looked up, his pale brown eyes roving across them.

"I said," he announced in a strangely calm voice, "that I want all the tent walls slashed, and the sides thrown open to the wind. I want all the herdfolk gathered." He tapped the point of the knife against Capiam's throat. "Can no one hear me?"

"Do it!" Capiam wheezed. His voice was hoarse with fear and sickness, but it still carried command. Heckram felt more than saw Tillu's barreling charge into the tent. She wormed in beside him, ignoring the clutching hands that would have held her back. "The healer!" someone gasped, and someone else filled in angrily, "She heals with death!" A rake of Kerlew's eyes silenced them, and men moved to the tent walls.

The long ripping sounds of knives against thick leather, and then the sides of the tent were peeled back, letting light into the dimness. Ketla blinked helplessly in the brightness, and then cried out in relief as someone helped her gently out of Kerlew's reach. He didn't care. He continued to crouch, straddling the herdlord and watching the people as they gathered in a great circle around the opened tent. He whispered something, and the muttering of the folk instantly died.

His hazel eyes scanned the crowd again; his head turning slowly, meeting every glance unflinchingly. He smiled a pleased smile. He spoke so softly that all strained to hear. "If you wish to live, you must listen."

"Kill him now!" It was Joboam, striding up to take command. He was dressed finely, a snug vest of bleached leather making him seem even huskier than he was. His hair was carefully smoothed and his eyes clear. His open confidence put him in charge and men turned to him.

"As you wish," Kerlew said sweetly, lifting the knife. "I kill him now, as Joboam so wisely commands."

"Not the herdlord!" Joboam bellowed. "The boy! Kill the boy!"

Men shifted uneasily, but no one dared obey. Kerlew lifted the knife swiftly, touched the tip to the hollow of his own throat, then to Capiam's, then his again, then to rest on Capiam's. He spoke only to Capiam, leaning forward to meet his eyes. "You see," he said, "It is as I told you. He wants us both dead. Speak to them, now, or they will make his wish true. Tell them."

"Stay back!" Capiam gasped. "Stay back. Hear what the boy has to say." Sweat dribbled down his face, and the look he gave Joboam was not a fond one.

"It is as I was telling you before Ketla awoke and made such a fuss." Kerlew spoke conversationally, his words still slow as they had ever been. "I have been to see the old najd up the cliffs. Long has he looked down upon the herdfolk, his own folk, and he is wise in many things. He has taught me when to speak, and when to keep silent. Now, he says, is the time to speak." The boy turned unforgiving eyes upon Joboam. "I know things."

"He lies!" Joboam declared. Too quickly.

"Your hands do not." Kerlew spoke softly, keeping the crowd gaping after his words. "You have carried sickness

to the herdfolk, Joboam. You planted the seeds, but it has
blossomed in your hands. Look at them."

He did not. He folded his arms slowly on his chest,
disdaining to obey. But his face paled.

Kerlew stared at him for a long moment. Then he
laughed, his high, ungraceful laugh, shattering the stillness. He stopped just as suddenly. "Capiam," he whee-
dled softly. "Listen to me. Joboam will not hear my
words. But you and your herdfolk will. You will hear me
and live and in days to come will call me one of your own.
I will be herdfolk," he promised, and paused. No one
breathed. Heckram stole a glance at Tillu. Her face was
sallow and she held herself stiff and tight. He wished he
could touch her for an instant. Then her eyes darted to his,
and they were together without touching. He felt her fear.

"I know much. Shall I tell you all? I think so." Kerlew
looked around, enjoying the audience. Then back to Capiam.
"Listen. Here are riddles for you. Find the answer and you
will be wiser. Who brought plague to the herdlord's family? Who traded a boy's life for a dead rabbit? Who would
trade your life for your position over the herdfolk?"

A puzzled silence followed his words. He had their
attention. The knife at Capiam's throat did not hold them
as tightly as a tale well begun. He let his eyes swing
slowly over them. Then he giggled, an incongruous sound.
"No one knows?" He suddenly flashed the knife aloft,
and then whisked it back to rest against Capiam's throat.
"The Knife knows," he said softly. He smiled slyly at
Joboam. "Doesn't it, Joboam?"

"He is mad!" Joboam exclaimed angrily. He turned to
leave.

"Don't go yet, Joboam. Or folk will think you are not
interested. They will think you already know the answer to
the riddles." Kerlew's voice was sweet, pitched to carry
well.

Joboam turned back, snarling. Kerlew smiled at him.
"Oh, you do wish to hear? Very well, then." For a long
moment he crouched silently over Capiam. The herdlord's
face was lined and gray; the merciless light of the clear

day illuminated the illness that devoured him. Kerlew ran his free thumb up and down the back of the knife. When he spoke, it was on a new topic. "Did I ever show you my knife? Heckram gave it to me, but he didn't make it. No. Elsa made it and gave it to him. The bone for it grew inside Elsa's reindeer. Elsa it was who took the bone from the reindeer, took it and shaped it and etched it with figures. Elsa's knife, when all is done, from Elsa's hands. And it knows who killed Elsa." The last words he whispered, leaning closer to Capiam. The herdlord's eyes were wide. In the back of the crowd a baby whimpered and was hushed.

He leaned closer. "Knife says it was . . ." and then he dipped his head down so that his long hair fell past his face and his mouth brushed the herdlord's ear. No one else heard what he uttered in that instant before he sat up again, his face gleaming with merriment. He looked down into Capiam's pasty face and dull eyes. "You don't believe me? Let me tell you what else Knife heard. Knife heard that that same one wanted to kill a boy. And the man who cared for the boy went to that same one, and said to him, 'Let the boy live on in peace, for he is harmless to you. And if you will do that, I will give you this rabbit.' But that one said to the man who cared for the boy, 'Why should I want your dead rabbit? Look, it has begun to stiffen already, and you have not even skinned it, nor taken its entrails from its body.' Then the old man said to that one, 'Why, this rabbit can be useful to you. For whoever eats of its raw flesh, blistered as it is, will sicken to death.' And that one thought long, and then told the old man that he would let the boy live on in peace, if he could have the rabbit. And so the trade was made." Kerlew looked out over the rapt people. "But the man who cared for the boy did not tell that one that whoever touched the rabbit's bare flesh would also sicken. That upon the hands that touched him, sores would open and run and swell. Did he, Joboam? Did he say you would die just as Rolke did?"

The big man came on, running in a flat charge, teeth bared wolverine white. Kerlew rose to meet him, stood

like a reed in a storm's path. The bone knife flashed before
Joboam's eyes, Kerlew snarling like a wolf, and then the
boy was falling backwards, stumbling over Capiam's body,
sprawling full length upon the hides. Knife in hand, Joboam
fell upon him, and a sharp scream rose above the yells of
the crowd. Men surged forward to drag their herdlord from
the melee, while women with babes in arms pushed their
way back, away from the danger. Heckram plowed a path
through them, seized the back of Joboam's collar and
dragged him up and off the boy. Blood ran from Joboam's
forearm, the only score the boy had made. Kerlew lay still
on the earth, red streaming down his chest. Screams rose.

The knife Joboam lifted to Heckram was bronze and
red.

Heckram howled his wrath, set free the killing frenzy he
had so long contained. He fell on Joboam without caution
or thought, his knife plunging in for Joboam's belly.
Joboam's hard forearm swept the wild blow aside, and
Heckram felt Joboam's blade skitter across his tunic and
then burn down his ribs. He roared with the pain and made
a grab for Joboam's wrist, but his swollen fingers failed
him. Joboam pulled free of his grip easily and drew back
for another stab, his blade snagging for a moment in
Heckram's shirt. Heckram seized the front of Joboam's
shirt, jerked him close. Hot pain and trickling warmth
down his side let Heckram know how well the blade had
scored him. He could not get a breath, but independent of
him, his knife fist thudded against Joboam's back. The
bronze blade, gift of his father, met the thick leather, sank
fractionally, met Joboam's shoulder blade. Joboam butted
him suddenly, his forehead smashing Heckram's lips and
nose and making the day sparkle blackly. His two-fingered
grip on Joboam's shirt weakened, while some cool part of
his mind noticed Joboam draw his knife back for a killing
blow. He twisted his body aside, felt a blow meant to sink
into his belly rip along his hip instead. His own blade
snapped as its ancient brittleness yielded to forces beyond
its tempering.

He staggered back from Joboam, saw a panorama of

folk spin past as the hot blood seared his leg. He should have known Joboam would be better at this game, more savage, more experienced. Better as he had always been better, stronger as he had always been stronger. Tillu's scream rose above the others, her hands reaching wildly toward her fallen son and the struggling men as Stina and Ristin clutched her and mingled their cries with hers. He glimpsed the broken haft in his own hand, oddly distant, and then felt the world explode against his jaw. He knew he was falling from the suddenly peculiar angle of Joboam's legs, from the traveling chest that leaped up against his forehead. It took forever to roll onto his back. The world spun around him, full of cries and searing pain. Joboam had felled him with his knife hilt and fist, was coming now with his knife's point. Heckram pushed against the skins that cushioned the earth, rose, but too slowly. Kerlew lay near him, blood leaking from his chest. With a sudden clarity Heckram knew he would not be the first person Joboam had killed with his hands. The thought brought with it a peculiar strength, and he surged full to his feet, crouched weaponless to grapple with him.

A small man suddenly leaped from the gaping, circled folk, screaming "No!" and flinging himself into Joboam's path. Joboam brushed him away, the small man tumbled back before the push of that muscled arm, struck one of the tent supports, and suddenly became Lasse sprawling at the edge of the circled folk. His eyes met Heckram's as he stood swaying stupidly and waiting for Joboam to kill him. "The bone knife!" Lasse screamed. "By your foot!"

He looked down dully to see Elsa's knife, his knife, Kerlew's knife lying on the hides where it had tumbled from the boy's lax hand. Joboam was coming, his bronze knife low, his mouth wide with teeth and madness. He stooped for it as Joboam collided with him, felt Joboam's knife momentarily stopped by his leather jerkin, then biting through into his flesh. Heckram cried out wordlessly at the new agony, felt the bronze knife within him, felt the bone knife under his hand. He gripped it as he fell. With a terrible wrench, he felt Joboam's bronze knife leave his body.

The blood that followed it was the river of his life; his thoughts seemed to flow out with it. "No!" he cried, as much to forbid the loss as from the pain. The world narrowed around him as blackness closed in from all sides. He felt the familiar hilt in his hand, felt Elsa's carving under his fingers. He was looking up at people spinning past him, their faces white, their mouths red and open in horror. The circle of his vision grew smaller and yellowed and Joboam suddenly filled it. He held a knife that dripped red, Kerlew's blood, his blood, Elsa's blood, and as the knife came down, Heckram saw only the yellowness around him. The light that surrounded Joboam was like the yellow glow of a wolf's eyes by night. Joboam was in the Wolf's eyes. Heckram cried out aloud at the sight and strove to surge up, to follow the bone knife that leaped suddenly in his grip. But there was too much pain, and his blood was ebbing out of him in pulses. Joboam's blade descended. All sound stopped.

Tillu screamed wordlessly, in pain and fury. She lunged forward, but Ristin and Stina gripped her with the force of hysteria, and she could not break their hold. Their screams mingled with hers, the cries of people who witness the unthinkable, men fighting like beasts and beloved blood spilling. The noise and the crowd around her had snared her, she could not escape their grip. She could only watch Joboam as he finished killing all she loved, all who loved her. She wanted to be unconscious, to be dead, but her eyes went on seeing.

She took a deep breath, willing it all to stop, to be a hideous dream, but it went on. She had to watch Joboam's knife leap in, saw Heckram twist his belly away from the danger only to take the blow along his hip. The blood, impossibly red, leaped out as if anxious to leave his body, and then Joboam's fist connected with the angle of his jaw with a terrible cracking sound. A small part of Tillu noted how Joboam used the butt of his knife to strike, and within her the healer was nodding, saying to herself, yes, even so was Elsa's jaw broken, only she was smaller, so it was torn loose entirely, and with just such a blow was her skull dented in.

Tillu stopped screaming, could make no sound at all. The pack noise of the herdfolk around her swelled up, filling her ears unbearably as she suddenly knew she must watch Heckram die as Kerlew had just died. Joboam was killing with savage efficiency now, with skill born of practice, and the shock was so great, the law broken so implacably, that no one could remember how to intervene. Joboam was an avalanche, a river in flood time, a killing force impossible to avert.

Heckram had fallen, the broken knife haft still gripped in his hand. "Oh, please, please, no!" Tillu cried out, her voice high and thin as a child's, and if in answer to that plea, Heckram scrabbled once more to his feet. He crouched, weaponless, looking more like a man getting ready to wrestle a calf down than a man facing a killer. Joboam, almost unscathed save for Kerlew's cut down his forearm, moved in. His lips were drawn back in a mirthless sneer. She was not the only one who saw the difference between the two men's attitudes. She heard someone call Heckram's name, in a voice deep with pain, and another cry out without words.

Then, impossibly, someone did act, someone leaped in as no one else had dared, small, unarmed, Lasse flung himself into the cleared area that had once been Capiam's home, to stand before Joboam. "No!" he roared, in a voice filled with fury and pain, and met Joboam's advance, only to be brushed aside with shocking ease. No one had ever suspected the true strength in Joboam's thick arms. Lasse went flying as if batted by an angry bear, struck on~ of the tent supports and slid down it to lie half-stunned on the floor.

Heckram was swaying. Blood dripping from his chin, running down his chest and leg in red swaths. His mouth moved, but no words came. His eyes were distant. Tillu wondered if he could see at all. Then, "The bone knife!" Lasse screamed. "By your foot!"

Tillu found she had fallen to her knees, that she could

no longer stand. Stina crouched beside her, her arms locked around Tillu's waist, and Ristin's grip bit into her shoulder. "Please," she begged, struggling to get free, but they were deaf to her, their eyes filled only with the horror of the spectacle of killing. "I have to go to him," Tillu whispered as she saw Heckram stoop slowly as an old man, to take up the bone knife. In the same long instant, Joboam was stepping in, his bronze knife was travelling down in a ripping arc. She heard the solid thud as it sank into Heckram, felt the impact of the blade as if in her own flesh.

"He's dead," she said softly, watching him fall, seeing Joboam's knife jerk clear of his body and the bright gout of blood that followed it. It was the way he fell, bonelessly, making no effort to catch himself, that told her he would not get up again. His heart might still beat, he might take a few more breaths, but there was nothing left in him to fight. He landed badly, his legs crumpled, his head turned to one side so that for an instant he seemed to be staring right into her eyes. His back was wide and exposed, and Joboam was moving in, coming swiftly, stooping like a hawk with talons of bronze, and all gasped, knowing he was as unstoppable as a falling tree.

"Heckram!" Tillu screamed, and still he did not stir.

And then he blinked, his eyes widening afterwards, his jaws opening in a snarl that displayed his teeth. An inhuman sound roared from his throat, and Tillu believed he finally saw his own death coming. She cried aloud, a sound that echoed his.

She knew that what happened next was not possible. Heckram flipped onto his back, and all saw the bone knife gripped in both his hands. He thrust it up before him, as if hoping Joboam might fall upon it, and then, incredibly, followed the knife up. It seemed to jerk him to his feet as if he gripped a lasso around a wild sarva instead of a knife carved from reindeer bone. Joboam's eyes went wide as Heckram rose to meet him. Perhaps for the first time in his life he experienced pure terror. His mouth gaped in disbelief as Heckram met his blow and stood before it. Joboam's knife skipped suddenly over Heckram's leather jerkin, finding no place to bite.

Terror still reigned on Joboam's face as he winced at the impact of Heckram's blow. All saw the thin blade slip sweetly into his chest, all felt the rush of red warmth that leaped out around it as it slid into his flesh. Joboam jerked spasmodically, his knife flung wide, and then his fists were hammering Heckram's back like the flapping of a desperate bird's wings. They fell together, embraced like lovers, to roll on the floor skins. From that tangle, Joboam pulled himself up, crawled a staggering reach of his arms, and fell again. His hands came up and curled around the bone handle that jutted from his chest. He looked down at it, swallowed convulsively, and died, his eyes open and full of disbelief. Heckram lay as he had fallen.

Pain opened his eyes again. No more than a moment could have passed. He rolled his head on the rich pelts that floored Capiam's tent. Joboam, he remembered suddenly, Joboam was coming to kill him. But Joboam was gone. Someone had stopped him. Someone had put an end to their fight. He blinked stupidly, wondering what had happened, why all was so silent. Folk still stood awe-stricken, frozen from watching the unimaginable: two herdfolk battling to the death. Horror transformed their faces, outlined skull bones, and aged them. Heckram lifted his head, feeling bloody fur cling stickily to his cheek. He tried to sit up, but found he could do no more than hold up his head. His head swayed on his neck as he gazed around the circle, trying to decide what had happened.

Joboam lay on his side, curled up, his hands clutching at the slender knife that had slipped so neatly between his ribs. He was still, and the puddling blood was still spreading. Heckram felt ill. Pain surged through him in waves, but could not distract him from the warm stickiness that coated his hand. It dirtied him. He lifted his head slowly, then gave it up, letting his cheek sink down on the bloodied furs. He wondered why the ring of people were so still, why the silence was so deafening. He had killed. Were they gathered to witness him dying of his wounds? Would they turn away now and walk off, leaving him to his punishment? "Tillu?" he asked softly, his lips moving painfully, and found her suddenly kneeling beside him, heard the mutter of folk begin.

"He lives!" a woman screamed suddenly. Heckram rolled his head toward the sound, saw the pointing finger that marked not him, but Kerlew. The boy staggered upright, his hand pressed tightly to his ribs and the sheen of blood across them. Tillu stiffened, her eyes going wide. Her hands, that had begun to touch his wounds, fell to her sides. "Go to the boy," Heckram croaked at her. But, "Stay as you are!" Kerlew commanded in a voice high with pain. "Stay, and see!"

Voices rose, but over them Capiam's panted shout, "Obey him!" Stillness followed, people shifting awkwardly but no one daring to step forward. Capiam, pale and sweating, staggered forward, seated himself atop a chest. He curled forward around the pain in his belly. "Listen to him," he gasped. He looked around the circle of gathered folk challengingly. "The herdlord commands it."

The boy staggered toward Joboam. He fell to his knees beside the body. With an effort that made the crowd groan he rolled the big man onto his back. "See this!" he panted, pointing to the protruding hilt. "Remember this. Heckram did not kill Joboam. Elsa's Knife did!" He lifted Joboam's hands from the knife-haft, held one palm out to the crowd. Two swollen abscesses dotted it. "The mark of treachery," Kerlew intoned, letting the hand fall, palm up, onto the skins. Boldly the boy seized the pale knife handle, jerked it from Joboam's chest. A last leap of bright blood followed it.

"Blade . . . calls to brother . . . blade." Kerlew panted out the words, his strength rapidly failing. Tillu tried to rise, but Heckram's frail grip on her wrist held her. The boy spoke on, his faltering words paced to his labored breathing. "This sign Elsa gives you. The mark . . . she left . . . Behold!" A woman cried out as he pressed the bone blade against the cut he had earlier scored in Joboam's forearm. "From this scar." He was gasping now, each word coming with an effort. Pain bobbed his head. "Elsa's Knife calls . . ." He pressed his cupped hand against the wound. "This!" He rose jerkily. In the hand he lifted, shining white and red, a fragment of worked bone. He lifted it high, hand shaking with the effort. "The broken edge of Elsa's blade, where she left it to tell on her killer. Where Pirtsi saw her put it, though he dared not tell." Pirtsi's head was nodding, his eyes wide, too fear-stricken to deny anything now. Kerlew was sinking, going back to his knees beside Joboam's body. "Because then Joboam would tell that Pirtsi had accidentally shot Lasse, with Joboam's bow. Shot him, and in his terror, ran away, instead of offering aid." Pirtsi whimpered his assent.

Kerlew's head fell forward onto his chest, his child's face twisting with pain. He slipped to the skins, panting suddenly from lack of breath. He turned his face to Heckram, and as their eyes met, Heckram heard him say, very softly, "And I am herdfolk, Wolf." The words followed him down as he slowly spun into a darkness filled with a pack's wise howling.

> chapter
fifteen

IT WAS DARK in the tent. She listened to them breathing, often holding her own breath to be sure she could hear them both. She was horribly tired, with a tiredness that was a pain in her back and head, but still she could not sleep. Whenever she closed her eyes, she saw blood. Blood on blades of bone and bronze, blood trickling down Kerlew's ribs, blood that flowed from Heckram's wounds as if spewed forth by small gaping mouths.

Yet again she held her breath, listening for his breathing close beside her. It was still there, hoarse and rasping, but steady. As was Kerlew's lighter breath an armspan away on the other side of her. They both still lived.

This, she thought, is what other women have felt, as I knelt over their men and put my hands in their blood. This helplessness.

She put a hand out in the darkness, rested it gently atop his chest. She felt the stiffness of her bandages, and through them the warmth of his life. His breath ebbed and flowed in him still. The wavering slash of Joboam's knife down his ribs had not been so bad; it had been the puncture wounds that had frightened her, the deep stabs in hip and back that looked so small on the outside, but had done damage within. What damage neither she nor any other healer would ever be able to tell. All one could do with such an injury was to bind it closed and hope against fever. As she did now.

If only he would open his eyes, she thought to herself.

As Kerlew had. He had been conscious, but silent as she bound up his chest. He had watched her, his eyes a stranger's, and made no sound as she washed and bound his wound. Stina, Lasse's old grandmother, had been right at her elbow, already waiting with a bowl of warm broth for "the young najd." In the darkness, Tillu shook her head suddenly. It was what he was, now. And ever would be. He was not her child anymore; that much she knew. But she also suspected that he was not what Carp had hoped he would be, either. From that, she took comfort. And from the steady beat that hammered in the wide chest under her hand.

"Tillu."

She stiffened, then sat upright. "I'm here," she assured him. She touched his bearded cheek lightly. He turned his face to her touch so that his mouth brushed her hand. His lips were dry and chapped. Immediately she rose, to bring cool water in a dripping cup. He could not help her lift his head and shoulders, but he drank thirstily from the cup she held to his mouth. She wanted to weep at how weak he was. Instead she eased him back onto the bed of hides. Then, even as she chided herself for making him talk, she asked, "How do you feel?"

He groaned in reply, then took in a stiff breath. "Kerlew?" he asked, and she realized he could not know.

"Kerlew will be fine. A knife score down his ribs, and some bones broken beneath them, but he will live. And will be up and around long before you are, I fear."

She heard him breathe again suddenly, and realized the depth of worry she had just relieved for him. She sat for some moments beside him in silence. Just as she thought he had dropped off to sleep again, he spoke. "He killed them all."

"Yes. He did." She went over the tally again in her mind. Elsa and Kari and Carp. Rolke, too. And he tried to kill Ketla and Capiam and Kerlew. The depth of revulsion that rose in her surprised her. As did her astonishment at Kerlew's solving of the puzzle. She had held the same pieces as he had; why had not she known what he had?

She spoke aloud, filling in for Heckram. "Back when the herdfolk were in the talvsit still, Joboam came to me. He had a festering wound in his forearm; I opened it and took out a piece of bone fragment. I thought he had been carving something that had broken, and sent a chip into his arm."

"Elsa's . . . knife." It took him two breaths to make the words, and she sensed the importance to him of what she had told him.

"Yes. Only I never knew it. I set the bone chip aside, and never saw it again. Kerlew must have picked it up, and somehow figured out what it was."

Heckram sighed his agreement. The silence stretched, and then, "Rabbit?" he asked.

"I don't know. Some kind of a disease, passed on to whoever ate the meat. Or touched it, as Joboam found out too late. What I do not understand is why others have it now, ones who never ate the meat nor touched it."

Heckram took a deep breath. Tillu waited. "I killed. I will be . . . set apart from herdfolk."

"No. Oh, no." She lay down carefully beside him, fitting her belly to his side. "Kerlew said it was not you; it was Elsa's knife and Wolf who killed Joboam. Not you. I heard the talk as I was bandaging you. Several came forward to speak for you. But Capiam said it was not necessary. That the najd had explained all."

He was silent then, and when she spidered her fingers lightly over his face, his eyes were closed. "Sleep, then," she told him, and lifted her face to kiss the tip of his ear. She thought briefly of Ketla. Tillu had insisted that she be moved to Carp's tent. It had given her great satisfaction to bed Ketla down in the lush furs, surrounded by the wealth that had paid for her misfortune. Capiam, too, probably slept there now. They would both live, or so Tillu believed, if they did not surrender to their grief. The unheard-of events in Capiam's tent had brought the other herdlords, eager to hear the tale, and had somehow increased his stature among them. He would live, she believed, to lead his people to the winter talvsit again, and for many winters beyond that.

She leaned her face against Heckram's shoulder, filling her nostrils with his scent. Now she could close her eyes and see, not blood, but reindeer, a vast herd of them spilling across the tundra, as many as the stars in the night sky. She would follow them, in the wake of this man at her side. She imagined the reindeer running, their heads up, their antlers thrown back, leading them on forever in an endless cycle. Heckram would always follow them. And she would follow him, she realized, wherever he chose to go.

Kerlew muttered in his sleep, then cried out suddenly, clearly. "If you would be Wolf's mate, learn to follow the herd."

Beneath her hand, Heckram murmured an assent. Tillu snuggled closer, and closed her eyes to sleep.

Kerlew:
The Najd

HE SAT IN the afternoon sun, feeling it touch his skin and shine redly through his closed eyelids. The bandages were still tight around his chest. Tillu said that the ribs beneath the scored flesh were broken, and had wrapped the bandages so tightly he could scarcely breathe. Then she had dared to scold him for standing up to Joboam. "You could have gotten both of you killed. You and Heckram both, and I would have had nothing in my life." Foolish talk. "The Wolverine could not have killed me," he tried to explain. "He could not stand against the Wolf and I." She had only leaned closer and whispered, "And don't think I don't know where that fragment of blade really came from." He had given up talking to her then. She could not glimpse the greater reality. Only the greater truth mattered. The blade had come from Joboam's arm; when was of no consequence. The herdfolk had needed to see it red still with his blood, so that they could accept the truth and be at peace with it. Pirtsi had needed to see it before he could admit the truth that was festering inside him. All had seen, and been convinced. All but Tillu. She alone still had no respect for him. She alone would not admit his powers. But he would teach her to. He grinned wickedly to himself.

"Najd?"

He opened his eyes slowly. It was a little girl child standing beside his bare feet. She was all big eyes and unruly black hair. She was very young, probably two years younger than himself. And very shy.

"What do you want?" he asked her gruffly. Her eyes grew bigger, her mouth smaller as she lifted a leaf cup into view. It held a red trove of early dewberries, probably the first ones she had found this year. She did not breathe as she offered it. He didn't reach for it. "You are Kelr's daughter, are you not?" he asked her. She nodded once, looking scared. He held out his hand slowly and she placed the leaf-cup of dewberries into it. He looked up at her through his lashes. He smiled at her slowly, watched her mouth widen with pleasure. Her own smile came cautious as a fox-kit peering from its den.

"My father, Kelr, sends me to tell you his eldest son breathes free now. He sat up this morning and ate."

"Good." Kerlew looked down at the cup of berries in his hand, and then measured half of them out onto his palm. He held the leaf-cup back to her. "Take these to your brother," he told her. "They'll do him good."

She stood transfixed. Then, "Thank you," she breathed, took the cup, and was gone. Kerlew sat up as he ate the berries. Then he picked up the piece of carving he had been working on, looked at it, then set it down again. He leaned back, closed his eyes, felt the sun against his face and the light of it red through his eyelids. Carp would have demanded a better gift than berries, Kerlew thought to himself. Carp would have called him a fool to take so little. He opened himself, let the sounds of the herdfolk wash against his senses. Children shouted at their play, men and women yelled to one another as they worked with the reindeer, mothers called after children. He smelled the cookfires, the meat and fish drying on the racks, the musty smell of hides stretched to the sun to dry, the wild smell of the reindeer. The herdfolk were all around him. He felt them like a spider in its web feels the vibration of every strand. Another block of awareness tumbled into place. This was what Carp had been missing, why he had not cared when he set the sickness loose among them. Carp had not been herdfolk. Kerlew was.

Tillu's voice was leaking out of the tent. He could hear her nattering at Heckram, fussing at him because he had only risen from his bed yesterday, and today he was working at something. Kerlew smiled to himself, knowing. Heckram was stretching leather from a wolf's hide carefully over the old drum's frame. First he had marvelled at the workmanship in the old drum. Then he had shook his head over the old wood and said it would not take the strain. But Kerlew knew it would, and he had insisted. So Heckram worked on it now, fastening the leather down so carefully, stretching it as tight as might be, damping it, and stretching it again. Kerlew had grown weary of watching him, and had come outside to work on his own carving and to nap on the soft fox-skins that Capiam had given him. But again Tillu's voice broke in on his dreaming. She was annoyed.

"Willow bark. That was all it was, no matter how long he chanted over it. Willow bark and salt. And to each one that came, he gave a portion of willow bark, to be taken for the fever, and salt, to make a poultice for the sores. The same things I had been telling them. Salt to draw the poisons from the abscesses, willow bark to keep the fever down. But now they noise it about as 'The Najd's magic,' and loudly tell me how much better they are."

"And you are jealous." Heckram's deep voice, the amusement in it even deeper.

"I am not. I only think, why cannot it be seen as it is? Why can't the folk see . . ."

"Maybe it isn't that simple. Does it matter?"

Kerlew could sense her sigh of resignation. "I suppose not. As long as they get better. Capiam was better, yesterday. Ketla tends him well."

"She has no one else now," Heckram pointed out.

There was silence. Broken by Tillu's muttered, "I suppose not." She changed the subject suddenly. "What are you doing?"

"Taking this to Kerlew. It's finished, I think."

"Sit down. I'll take it to him."

"No. I'm tired of sitting still. A glimpse of the sky will do me good." He heard the sounds of shuffling, could imagine Tillu scowling over him as he stood. Kerlew turned his eyes inward a moment, grinned to himself, then wiped the smile from his face as the tent-flap was lifted.

"You walk like an old man," he observed as Heckram crabbed out of the entry.

"Kerlew!" Tillu rebuked, and was ignored.

"I feel like an old man," Heckram admitted. "Here. What do you think?"

Kerlew accepted the small drum. He turned it over in his hands, looking at the creamy new leather stretched across the old frame, already seeing the figures he would paint on it, red and blue, reindeer and men and wolves. "From Wolf," he said to himself, and "Yes, wolf hide," Heckram agreed, not understanding at all.

"It will do. Luckily, you are better at this than you were at fighting." He looked up at Heckram slyly, through his lashes as he asked, "Did you learn anything from your fight with Joboam?"

"Kerlew!" Tillu, in angry rebuke. But Heckram only knelt slowly, and then sat beside him. "Was I supposed to?" he asked in a voice breathless with pain. A sincere question, from a man who glimpsed his powers. No need to teach Heckram respect.

"Of course."

Heckram's eyes were turned inward, unaware of the angry look Tillu was giving her son. "I'd never fought a man before. Not like that. I'd never realized what it would be like to fight hoping to kill." He looked at Kerlew with a strange respect. "Joboam was better at it than I. I don't know why I'm alive."

"Because of the magic. Because you are more herdfolk than you know. You thought you might be a man-killer. You aren't. You fought Joboam like you were wrestling a pregnant vaja. But for my magic, he'd have killed you. There is no murder in you."

"I'd come to suspect that," Heckram admitted grudgingly. He fingered his still swollen mouth. "So I'm not a fighter. But you like the drum."

"Yes." Kerlew laughed his cracked laugh. "You learn from me now. But I have learned from you, too. See?" He lifted his work into view. Already Heckram knew not to touch it, but only to look with his eyes.

"It looks like a wolf's paw," Heckram said. Kerlew smiled at the uneasiness that tinged his words. "Yes," he agreed. He leaned suddenly, touched the carved wand to his mother's belly. "The baby will be a girl-child. Name her Willow, for luck."

Silence.

Then, from Heckram, "What baby?"

Tillu fled, whirling away from them both and back into the tent. Heckram looked at Kerlew incredulously. He stood up much faster than he had eased himself down and limped after her, struggling with the tent-flap, and then demanding again, "What baby?" Kerlew heard Tillu's muttered reply, and then Heckram's deep voice going high on incredulous words. He didn't bother to listen.

He drew Wolf from his najd's pouch, set him atop the new drum head. "Now, she will respect me," he told him. Black eyes bright, red tongue lolling, Wolf stood and laughed with him. With the wolf's paw Kerlew tapped the taut drum-skin, and Wolf began to dance for him in the warm afternoon sunlight.

NOTES

THE REINDEER FLY is an insect that afflicts reindeer by laying eggs on their hide that develop into larvae. The larvae burrow into the animal's back. Boils develop around them, and the larvae live off the pus within the boil until the following spring. Sometimes the fly will hover near the reindeer's muzzle, to inject minute larvae in a glutinous liquid into the muzzle. When this happens, the larvae are inhaled and a stream of larvae make their way on the nasal mucous to the throat. Animals thus afflicted often die of a cough, cold, or asphyxiation. This is the condition referred to in the story as the Great Plague. Reindeer usually escape the flies by seeking the ice fields that remain intact on the tundra even in summer.

Tularemia is an acute, plaguelike infectious disease, caused by the Francissella tularensis. It can be transmitted to man by the bite of an infected tick or other bloodsucking insect, or by direct contact with infected animals, or by consuming inadequately cooked meat or drinking water that contains the organism. Symptoms appear one to three days afterwards. Symptoms include headaches, chills, vomiting, fever, and aching pains. The site of infection may develop into an ulcer, and the glands at the elbow and armpit may become enlarged and painful. Later, it may develop into an abscess. Sweating, loss of weight, and general weakness follow. The fever may come and go over a period of several weeks. If the bacteria enters through the skin, local sores occur at the site, usually on the hands and fingers. The most common complication is pneumonia. Wet saline dressings are generally soothing to the lesions, and analgesics relieve the headaches.

—MEGAN LINDHOLM